HOLLOW

TITLES BY KARINA HALLE

Dark Fantasy, Gothic & Horror Romance

Contemporary Romance

Love, in English/Love, in Spanish

Where Sea Meets Sky

Racing the Sun

Bright Midnight

The Pact

The Offer

The Play

Winter Wishes

The Lie

The Debt

Smut

Heat Wave

Before I Ever Met You

After All

Rocked Up

Wild Card (North Ridge #1)

Maverick (North Ridge #2)

Hot Shot (North Ridge #3)

Bad at Love

The Swedish Prince
   (Nordic Royals #1)

The Wild Heir (Nordic Royals #2)

A Nordic King (Nordic Royals #3)

The Royal Rogue
   (Nordic Royals #4)

Nothing Personal

My Life in Shambles

The Forbidden Man

The One That Got Away

Lovewrecked

One Hot Italian Summer

All the Love in the World
   (Anthology)

The Royals Next Door

The Royals Upstairs

Romantic Suspense

Sins and Needles
   (The Artists Trilogy #1)

On Every Street (An Artists
   Trilogy Novella #0.5)

Shooting Scars
   (The Artists Trilogy #2)

Bold Tricks
   (The Artists Trilogy #3)

Dirty Angels (Dirty Angels #1)

Dirty Deeds (Dirty Angels #2)

Dirty Promises
   (Dirty Angels #3)

Black Hearts (Sins Duet #1)

Dirty Souls (Sins Duet #2)

Discretion (Dumonts #1)

Disarm (Dumonts #2)

Disavow (Dumonts #3)

Karina Halle

HOLLOW

ACE

NEW YORK

ACE

Published by Berkley

An imprint of Penguin Random House LLC

1745 Broadway, New York, NY 10019

penguinrandomhouse.com

Copyright © 2023 by Karina Halle

Excerpt from *Legend* copyright © 2023 by Karina Halle

Book design by Katy Riegel

Map by AS Designs

Library of Congress Cataloging-in-Publication Data

Names: Halle, Karina, author.

Title: Hollow / Karina Halle.

Description: First Ace edition. | New York: Ace, 2025. |

Series: A gothic shade of romance; 1

Identifiers: LCCN 2024061292 (print) | LCCN 2024061293 (ebook) |

ISBN 9780593952344 (trade paperback) | ISBN 9780593952351 (ebook)

Subjects: LCGFT: Romance fiction. | Fantasy fiction. | Gothic fiction.

Classification: LCC PR9199.4.H356239 H65 2025 (print) |

LCC PR9199.4.H356239 (ebook) | DDC 813/.6—dc23/eng/20250108

LC record available at https://lccn.loc.gov/2024061292

LC ebook record available at https://lccn.loc.gov/2024061293

Hollow and the excerpt from *Legend* were originally self-published, in different form, in 2023.

First Ace Edition: October 2025

Printed in the United States of America

1st Printing

The authorized representative in the EU for product safety and compliance is Penguin Random House Ireland, Morrison Chambers, 32 Nassau Street, Dublin D02 YH68, Ireland, https://eu-contact.penguin.ie.

For the readers

who wait all year for spooky season:

This one's for you.

Certain it is, the place still continues under the sway of some witching power, that holds a spell over the minds of the good people, causing them to walk in a continual reverie. They are given to all kinds of marvelous beliefs, are subject to trances and visions, and frequently see strange sights, and hear music and voices in the air. The whole neighborhood abounds with local tales, haunted spots, and twilight superstitions; stars shoot and meteors glare oftener across the valley than in any other part of the country, and the nightmare, with her whole ninefold, seems to make it the favorite scene of her gambols.

WASHINGTON IRVING—

"The Legend of Sleepy Hollow"

Important Notes

Hollow and *Legend* are a duology based on "The Legend of Sleepy Hollow" by Washington Irving. *Hollow* is a multi-POV why-choose/poly dark academia gothic romance and contains graphic sexual scenes of M/M and M/F. *Legend* will contain M/M/F.

I would hesitate to call this "dark," as it is nowhere near as extreme as a lot of dark romance books, but it still worth mentioning that it contains: drug use, attempted sexual assault, violence, domestic violence, dub con, praise and degradation kinks, spit play, soft BDSM elements, dom/sub/switch vibes, and mental health struggles including suicide (off page), student/teacher relationships, and pastor/congregate child abuse (off page).

Hollow takes place in 1875, so the dialogue is more reflective of that time while I've also modernized it a little. I tried to be as historically accurate as possible to the era, but I am sure some transgressions were made. (And just FYI, the majority of white horses are technically called gray.)

While terms for autism and ADHD were not around during the Victorian era and thus are not included in the book, Crane (like myself) has autism and ADHD, while Brom has ADHD and depression (also like myself LOL/sob).

And a final note, I have a Pinterest page for *Hollow*, so if you want to give that a look, you can find it here: bit.ly/HOLLOWPIN).

Welcome to Sleepy Hollow. May you never leave.

Playlist

"Invisible Hand"—+++ (Crosses)

"Corrupt"—Depeche Mode

"Feral Love"—Chelsea Wolfe

"Daffodil"—Florence + The Machine

"Built on Bones"—Emily Scott Robinson

"Werewolf Heart"—Dead Man's Bones

"Me and the Devil"—Soap&Skin

"Burn the Witch"—Queens of the Stone Age

"Bitches Brew"—+++ (Crosses)

"Phantom Bride"—Deftones

"Stripped" (single version)—Depeche Mode

"Ghost Ride"—+++ (Crosses)

"House of Metal"—Chelsea Wolfe

"Halo"—Depeche Mode

"Total Depravity"—The Veils

"The Sinner in Me"—Depeche Mode

"Dusk"—Chelsea Wolfe

"In Chains"—Depeche Mode

"Bones"—Finnegan Tui

"Flatlands"—Chelsea Wolfe

"Seven Devils"—Florence + The Machine

"Crawl Home"—Desert Sessions

"Anhedonia"—Chelsea Wolfe featuring Emma Ruth Rundle

"Snake Song"—Isobel Campbell and Mark Lanegan

"Mercy in You"—Depeche Mode

"Light as a Feather"—+++ (Crosses)

Classroom

Stables

Classroom

Student Dorms

Cathedral

Classroom

Library

Classroom

Student Dorms

Faculty Dorms

Pocantico Lake

Trail to Sleepy Hollow

SLEEPY HOLLOW INSTITUTE
Where Learning Goes Beyond

Prologue

1862

Baltus Van Buren sat in front of the roaring fire with a stiff shot of bourbon in his hand, pretending he wasn't waiting for his wife, Sarah, to leave. She took her time as she always did when she went to the school, puttering around the house as if she were perpetually about to forget something. Over the years, Baltus realized it wasn't absent-mindedness, though that sometimes came into play, rather it was her reluctance to leave him and Katrina on their own. Sarah went to the school only on the nights before, after, and during a full moon, but one would think she had to go to the other side of the country, not a forty-minute horse ride into the dark woods of Sleepy Hollow.

She's afraid, Baltus thought absently as he swirled the amber liquid in his glass. *But of what?*

Though he always asked the question, he had his suspicions. That was why he was waiting for Sarah to leave that night, because he wanted a moment with Katrina alone.

She was nine years old, and it was time for his daughter to finally know the truth.

"Goodbye, dear Baltus," Sarah said, leaning in to kiss him on the cheek. She smelled of cloves and something earthy, like the hard, dark soil that lay under the thin layer of evening frost, rich with decaying leaves.

Baltus forced a smile and eyed her. She was looking worn, her face like parchment, the wrinkles deepening around her eyes and mouth. But she always looked this way before she left for the school. She'd look much better upon her return.

She would have said goodbye to her daughter, but Katrina was already in her bed, fast asleep. At least that's what Sarah thought. Baltus knew otherwise.

The door opened and closed, and Sarah was gone, a blast of frigid air blowing in and tickling the fire. The flames leaped and danced and then settled, and the entire house seemed to relax as if letting out a sigh.

Baltus waited a moment, had another swig of his drink, and listened to the branches of the bare trees tapping the narrow windows of the sitting room, wanting to come in. They sounded like a ticking clock.

Then he said in his loud, fatherly voice, "Katrina?"

He waited a beat, and the door to her bedroom opened a crack, and her pale face peeked through.

"I know you're not sleeping," he continued, and gestured to the velvet chair beside him. "Why don't you come here so we can have a chat."

She paused in the doorway, large blue eyes, pale skin, and hair like cornsilk. "Am I in trouble?" she asked in a small voice.

"Not even a little," he said, his smile raising up the corner of his mustache. "Come here, my child."

Katrina walked toward him, her bare feet smacking the floor loudly, which made her father smile to himself. His daughter was never the most graceful little girl, always loud and brash and clumsy, as if her feet were too big for her body, and she had no sense of the space around her. He wondered if one day her mother would make her attend a finishing school or if Sarah would use her own magic to help Katrina be more "refined." He prayed Sarah would leave Katrina as she was.

Baltus was a kind and loving man, beloved all over town for his thoughtful and genial ways, but he was a coward when it came to his wife, and he knew it. Sarah Van Tassel's roots in Sleepy Hollow were so deep that sometimes he worried he could be uprooted at any moment and tossed away with one defiant look from his wife. After all, when they married it was she who decided to keep her maiden name—Van Tassel—because of tradition on her maternal side, and pass that name on to Katrina. And though Baltus was a witch too, his magic paled in comparison to Sarah's.

When it came to Katrina, however, her magic was yet to be seen.

"What is it, Papa?" she asked, climbing into the chair beside him, her legs swinging back and forth. If she had been sleepy before, she was fully awake now, her bright blue eyes looking him over curiously, eagerly, for it wasn't often she was encouraged to stay up late. "Did something happen to Mama?"

He glanced at her, bushy brows furrowed like dueling caterpillars. "What makes you say that?"

She shrugged. "I don't know."

"Your mother is fine," he said. He shouldn't be surprised at how observant she was. That was the whole point of this talk. "She left to go to the school."

"I know. I heard her say goodbye. It's just that the house feels different."

"How so?"

"Like it was holding its breath, and now it's not."

Very astute, he thought. He cleared his throat. "Well, dear Kat, that feeling you have, what you're noticing, that's energy. And not many children your age would be able to put that feeling into words like you have, but that's what makes you special."

She stared at him, a tiny smile on the corner of her lips. He knew she liked being called special.

"You know what else makes you special?" he asked.

She shook her head.

"I think you do." He gestured to the fire with a nod. "The fire listens to you, doesn't it? You can make the fire dance with your fingers."

Her eyes went wider, like fancy blue-and-white porcelain saucers Sarah brought out when they had company.

"It's your secret, I know," he said gently. "But I am your father, and there is no hiding things from me. I also know that you talk to birds and animals and that they understand you. That when you're really upset, a gust of wind will flow through the house, slamming all the doors. And I know you've made yourself disappear on more than a few occasions, something that has always given me such a fright."

Katrina swallowed hard, her legs no longer swinging. She chewed on the inside of her cheek, and Baltus felt bad for bringing it up.

"I'm not telling you all of this to punish you, my dear," he said. "For I know it is not your fault. If anything, it's because of your mother and I. Because we are also special in similar ways."

She nodded slowly. "I know."

He chuckled. "Of course you do. Do you know what that's called? The name we have?"

She shook her head.

"A witch," he said.

She stuck out her lower lip and pouted for a moment. "No. That can't be. Witches are bad. You're not bad. And men can't be witches."

He straightened up in his seat. "Men can very much be witches, and witches aren't bad either."

Except for a few, he thought.

"Witches are special," he went on. "But the world doesn't know that. They think what you have been told. That they are bad and wicked and up to no good. That is not the case, but the world doesn't understand. Sleepy Hollow is the last safe haven for us, and even then, not everyone is . . . as special as we are. As *you* are."

She seemed to think that over. "So I'm a witch?"

"You are. A beautiful, wonderfully good witch. But because you are a witch, you have a responsibility you must adhere to. It will keep you safe. It is so important to keep yourself safe, Katrina."

"You keep me safe," she said with a smile.

His heart pinched at that. "I won't always be there to keep you safe, my dear."

"Then Mama will keep me safe."

"Of course she will," he said, feeling the pinch in his heart grow tighter. "But one day, your mother might not be able to protect you. One day, you'll be on your own."

"I won't be on my own. I'll be married to Brom Van Brunt," she said proudly. "You always tell us that we are to marry each other when we're older."

Baltus tried to keep a smile plastered on his face, but it faltered. "Yes. Your mother has seen to that."

"Brom is my best friend, so that's okay," she said. "And he'll protect me."

Brom was a couple of years older than Katrina and a good kid, if not a bit wild. His parents were spineless though, and Baltus always thought it odd how much Sarah pushed for the two children to be together. Brom's mother, Emilie, was a witch, but his father was not, and Brom himself showed no signs of magic at all. But when Sarah set her mind to something, she'd keep going until the whole town agreed with her. She was persuasive like that.

"Be that as it may," he continued gruffly, "one day, you might be alone, and you'll need to keep safe. So in order to stay safe, I need you to promise me something. Are you ready to promise your father something very, very important?"

"What?" she asked.

"I want you to never tell anyone that you're a witch. Even your own mother. I want you to keep it a secret from the world, even from yourself. We don't show our magic and powers, and you won't show yours either. You must hide all of that deep down until you've forgotten it."

"Why?"

"Because the world is cruel. You know what happened to the witches of the past."

"But they were bad," she said, her nose scrunching up.

He quirked a brow. "Were they? Or is that what people were told? They might have been as innocent as you are. The world isn't ready for people like us. Even this town."

"Are there other witches in Sleepy Hollow?"

He wasn't sure how to answer that. The truth would come out soon, once Katrina learned what her mother was doing at the institute and what the school was doing with their students. Who the students really were.

"There are other witches," he said carefully. "But they hide it too."

"So we can't all be friends?" she asked.

He shook his head. He knew it was safest for Katrina to seem like a magical dud, to appear uninteresting, to appear to have no powers or interest in the occult at all, whether that was among other witches or normal people.

Because if she let her magic keep developing, they would discover her. And they would take her for every ounce of her soul.

Panicked by the thought, Baltus reached out and grabbed Katrina's hand, squeezing hard. "Promise me this, Katrina. Promise me that when you feel the call to magic, to the strange and the unusual, to power, that you ignore it. That you bury it deep inside you. That you will do all in your power to not be a witch. That you will never show it or tell anyone about it. Including Brom, including your mother, including me. Please."

Katrina blinked at him in shock, then studied his face. He knew there was nothing but anguish on it, a desperate plea for her to understand and obey.

Finally, she nodded. "Okay," she said. "I can do that."

"Do you promise, dear daughter?"

"I promise," she said.

And God, he hoped she meant it. He hoped that this would stick and that it would keep her safe in the end.

It was as if he knew he didn't have much time left with her.

1

Kat

There's something at my window.

I hold my breath, my eyes darting across the dark room. I had been in a deep sleep, and the noise brought me out of the depths.

A tapping sound.

At first, I think it's a tree branch at the window, moving in the wind, but the elm outside doesn't reach this far.

Then I hear it again.

Something small strikes the pane.

A stone or pebble.

Brom, I think, getting to my feet. I look around for my dressing gown. When I was younger and he came visiting, I would have just gone to the window, but now that I'm eighteen, my mother has drilled a sense of modesty into me.

I slip on my dressing gown and hurry to the window, looking out onto the yard. Brom is lurking in the shadows beneath the elm, its leaves shadowing his face from the half-moon. Beyond him and the fields is the Hudson River, which laps softly at the edge of our property, reflecting the moonlight.

I push up the window, a chill sweeping into the room, bringing with it the first smells of autumn, fallen leaves and damp earth, and the fading smolder of a bonfire. And something else. Something dark and strange that puts a shiver down my neck.

"Brom? What are you doing?" I whisper harshly, sticking my head out the window. I hadn't seen Brom for a few days, which wasn't unusual lately. This past year, he's been around less and less. Where he goes and what he does and who he does it with is a mystery to me, despite there being less than a thousand people here in the town of Sleepy Hollow.

"I wanted to talk to you," he says, his voice low and gruff.

A tiny thrill runs through me that I do my best to ignore. We were the best of friends when we were younger—spending every moment playing together, sharing secrets, creating dreams— and to have this distance now as we've gotten older has felt a lot like rejection. I know that we've been betrothed to each other by our parents since I was born, but I often wonder if Brom really has any intention of marrying me when I turn eighteen or if he'll rebel against his parents and choose someone else.

For the first time in my life, that thought strikes a pang of jealousy in me.

"It's the middle of the night," I point out.

He gives the faintest of shrugs, but his silhouette is tense, like an animal ready to run.

Or to strike.

"Can we go somewhere private?"

I nod. "Let me grab my shoes."

I pull out of the window, tying my dressing gown tighter around me, then swipe my slippers out from under the bed, hoping he doesn't plan on going far. I put them on and go back to the window, sliding the rest of it up. I'm not the thinnest nor the most graceful person, so getting through the window is a bit of a struggle, but luckily, Brom comes forward just in time to help me down.

My skin tingles where his strong, warm hands wrap around my waist, my dressing gown feeling too bare and thin under his grip. I want to apologize for weighing so much more than I used to—I can't remember the last time he helped me sneak out through the window like this—but I don't want to bring it to his attention. My body has gone through so many changes these past few years, and it's now more apparent than ever that we are no longer the children we used to be. The more I think about it, the more it overwhelms me, like I'm barreling toward adulthood faster than I can breathe.

But despite my weight, he easily places me down on the ground, my slippers sinking slightly into the dew-damp earth. We're so close here that I suck in my breath, suddenly feeling too shy to meet his gaze. How odd it is that someone can go from feeling like your friend to feeling like a stranger, and so quickly.

"The barn?" he murmurs, and I finally meet his eyes. They've always been dark, the deepest shade of brown, but in the shadows, they are coal black and brimming with an intensity that I can't read.

I nod, and he grabs my hand, taking it in his, leading me silently along the side of the house and across the back meadow, the grass now short and stiff from a dry August. We don't have a working farm anymore, not since my father passed, so we lease out the fields to neighboring farmers to use. The red barn that sits among leafy oaks remains neglected, though the two of us used to use it all the time as a secret clubhouse of sorts, a place where we could escape our families.

"Is everything all right?" I ask him quietly as we approach the barn. I don't think I've ever come here in the middle of the night, and the half-opened doors remind me of a jaw about to shut. I suppress a shudder, not liking where my thoughts are going.

He doesn't say anything, but he gives my hand a squeeze, his skin damp now and not as warm as it first was.

Brom has always been a moody boy. I think that's why we've gotten along so well. I'm prone to similar tempers, so I know when he needs space and time to work through things. Often, we'll just sit together in silence, enjoying each other's company but letting each other be lost in our own thoughts.

Tonight feels different though. There's something unsettled and tense about him, more so than normal, and the early September air feels thick and electric.

Change is coming.

For a moment, I close my eyes, my body wanting to become one with the cool breeze, to join with the natural world and uncover its secrets, but I remember what I had promised my father. My inner witch is to stay buried.

But I'd already broken that promise years ago.

Brom walks to the barn, his strides long, and pauses at the door, poking his head in. With his near-black hair, he disappears into the dark chasm of the building. Then he nudges one door open with his shoulder, making it creak like rattling bones.

He pulls me inside. It's pitch-black for a moment until my eyes adjust. There are several holes in the roof, gaping wounds that show the night sky, and moonlight filters through, illuminating old bales of hay and rusted tools piled in corners. The smell of hay brings me back to when I used to help trample it down for my father, and tears threaten the corners of my eyes. I blink them away in surprise. How sneaky grief can be.

Brom leads me over to the hayloft ladder. "Think this will still hold me?" he asks over his shoulder as he drops my hand and places both of his on the sides of the ladder, one boot bouncing lightly on the bottom rung, testing it.

"I'm fairly certain the last time we were up there, we were both half the size," I point out.

Brom was a stocky kid growing up, and now that he's eighteen, an adult, he's tall and broad-shouldered, equipped with muscle that wasn't there before, suiting his nickname of Brom Bones. I've been trying hard not to notice these manly changes in him, but perhaps I haven't been trying hard enough.

"I'll go first," he says, seemingly satisfied with the condition of the ladder, and goes up slowly. The wood groans under his weight but doesn't break.

He reaches the top and pulls himself up onto the loft, then turns around and offers his hand, beckoning me to come. "Come on, Daffy," he says, using the nickname he had given me when I was young. Daffodil.

I take in a deep breath and follow him. My dressing gown is long, and I have to bunch it in my hand, and my slippers feel thin against the rungs, but I manage to climb just like I once did.

He grabs my hand and pulls me the rest of the way until the

scattered hay is digging into my knees and I'm flipping over onto my seat. I give the loft a cursory glance. The hole in the roof above is large and ragged, and the moon illuminates what we used to call our secret meeting place: the bales we used to sit on, an apple crate stacked with molding books, a chipped tea set that is probably home to creepy crawlies. Somewhere in these ruins of our childhood is a deck of tarot cards from when I used to practice on Brom. That was the promise I had broken to my father. I don't show my meager magic around my mother or anyone else in town, but I have shown it to Brom. I can't keep anything from him, even though it often feels like he's keeping everything from me.

We sit in silence for a few moments, the both of us looking around and taking it all in. It feels like our past and present have melded, but the future is more unknown than ever.

"What did you want to talk to me about?" I ask him after a couple of minutes pass by. Somewhere in the depths of the barn below, I hear a flutter of wings.

He doesn't say anything to that. I know he's heard me, so I just let him wait and decide.

Finally, he says, "I've done a bad thing."

His voice is so low and strained I can barely hear it, but that doesn't stop my pulse from quickening.

"What do you mean?" I ask. Even with the moonlight, his face remains shadowy and hard to read.

"I can't explain," he says.

"You can't, or you don't want to?"

Silence.

"You can tell me anything, you know that, Brom," I tell him. I want to reach out for his hand, but I'm afraid to. Not until I know what the bad thing is. "Did you kill someone?" I whisper.

He gives me a sharp look, his thick brows arching. "No," he says defensively. "Why was that your first thought?"

To be honest, I don't know. I've never thought of Brom as someone murderous or cruel, but he is quick-tempered and hotheaded, prone to impulses and flights of fancy, and I suppose if he accidentally killed someone because he overreacted or couldn't get a handle on his emotions, I wouldn't be too shocked.

"I've just never seen you so upset," I admit.

He swallows, the sound audible in the barn. "I didn't kill anyone."

"Then what did you do?" I inch close to him, the hay sticking to my gown as I move. "Tell me, Brom."

"I . . . ," he begins, his voice hoarse.

He stares at his splayed hands for a moment, then looks at me, and now I can read him. Now I see the change that's come over his face.

He's tormented and torn, and inside of all that, there's desire. Red-hot, potent desire that I've never seen him wear before, never seen on anyone in my sheltered little life.

It makes my breath hitch in my throat, excitement flutter in my chest.

"I don't know how to deal with my feelings for you," he finally says.

Oh. Oh!

"Feelings?" I repeat, so scared to let that flutter in my chest turn into full-blown wings and fly away toward hope. Even though I have tried to ignore the changes between us and I've pretended that I still see him as just a friend, it turns out I've secretly hoped that one day we could be more, become what we were always promised to each other.

I don't know what else to say, and it doesn't matter.

Because Brom leans over and grabs my face in his hands, and he kisses me.

He's kissed me before, a shy peck on the lips when we were young and sitting under Hollow Creek Bridge, but this is completely different. This is warm and soft and strong all at once, the press of his lips, the wetness of his tongue. It shocks me, lightning that jolts down my spine, this sudden intimacy and intrusion. I don't know what to do—I don't know how to kiss him back, but it doesn't seem to matter.

He's taken the lead, and I'm following.

His kiss deepens, coaxing me, and he slides his tongue against mine, showing me what he wants. I oblige, already feeling like I'm being swept away, taken to places I've never been before, and drowning in him. I kiss him the best I can until I feel my entire body grow warm and tense, like I'm hungry for the first time.

But there's no hiding his hunger for me.

He moves so that I'm falling back into the hay and his body is on top of mine, and it's all such a blur. His mouth goes to my neck, kissing and licking and sucking along my skin, the weight of him taking my breath away. I don't know where this is going, but even though it scares me, I'm willing to go along because this is our destiny, isn't it? The two of us together, married, until death do us part—that's what we were always supposed to be. The act of our bodies coming together is inevitable.

We don't talk as this is happening, as his hands go to my

dressing gown and touch my breasts until they ache, as another hand slips up between my legs. I'm nervous, and I know I could say no, but this is Brom, and I trust him more than anything. Even though I'm worried I won't be good enough for him, even though I'm afraid of how much it will hurt, I want him.

I want him.

And all I've wanted is for him to want me.

He fumbles for his pants, undoing them, and then I feel him on my thigh, and I'm shocked at how warm he is, how he's both solid and soft against my skin. My cheeks flush at the intimacy of it all, at this new side of him, my body heating up from the inside.

"Daffodil," he whispers to me, his voice thick with want.

Then he's kissing me again, parting my legs farther, and we both take in a sharp breath as he pushes himself inside me. Hot, sharp pain bursts between my thighs, white sparks exploding behind my eyes as I pinch them shut and try to breathe. I don't dare cry out because I don't want him to stop. I know he would if he knew I was in pain, and I want him to keep going.

But I'm able to ignore it. Brom continues to push himself into me, soft grunts filling the air, the loft creaking under our movement, the hay sticking to my hair, and I'm enraptured by the look on his face. The moon still casts his gaze in shadow, black sockets under black brows, yet from the set of his firm jaw, the grit of his teeth, the glint in his eyes, I can see pure wildness radiate from him. Like he's both hunting for something and being pursued. Predator and prey.

Where are you running to?

What are you running from?

But those thoughts are taken from me when he slips his hand

between my legs again and touches me with slippery fingers, and it's as if all my pain melts away. A strange ache throbs, and my body coils as tight as twine, and suddenly, my world explodes. It's all bright lights and colors behind my eyes, and I'm gasping loudly while he lets out a low moan that fills the hayloft.

I'm barely aware of his body stiffening above me, the sound of his heavy breathing. I still feel like I'm floating, higher and higher, through the roof and all the way to the moon.

It's the most delicious feeling in the world, a whirlwind of energy unlike any I've felt before, and I never want it to end. I feel powerful, so powerful, as if I could crush the world like rose petals in my palm and take anything and everything I've ever wanted.

But eventually, my heart slows, and I feel back in my body again.

I'm smiling. Feeling stunned and stupid.

Until Brom removes himself, and I gasp. I'm going to be in so much pain tomorrow.

"I didn't . . . ," I begin, trying to look down as he makes himself decent. "Is my nightgown all right?"

Despite what we just did, I feel too bashful to ask if I had gotten blood on my clothes.

He seems to understand though. He looks down and shakes his head. "You're fine," he says, still sounding breathless. "Come on, we should get you back in your room before your mother notices you've been gone."

I nod, feeling a little shaken. I don't want to go back to the house and be apart from Brom. I want to stay with him. Talk to him. Talk about what just happened. Perhaps even do it again.

But there isn't time.

We get to our knees, and he starts down the ladder, with me following. With each step I take, I feel sore, but I keep on going.

Brom grabs my hand once I reach the ground, and then he leads me out of the barn and into the field.

The world looks different now. The white paint of the house glows in the moonlight, the windows like dark eyes. The field itself looks silver, the Hudson River a sparkling ribbon, and the sky above is a velvet cape dotted with stars. The moon is so bright that it hurts my eyes to look at it. All around us are crickets and rustling in the grass and other sounds of the night. Everything is so alive.

I feel so alive.

Just like before, we don't talk, but perhaps we don't need to. Perhaps we've grown so close now that we don't need to say a word.

When we get to my window, he helps me up inside. I had left it open by mistake, but the chill in the air feels good on my overheated body.

"Good night," I say to him, feeling awkward as I stand at the window. "I suppose I'll see you tomorrow?"

"Good night, Kat," he says, clearing his throat. He opens his mouth to say something else but then closes it.

Then he turns and walks off.

And I'm left wondering if all of that was a dream.

The next morning, I sleep in later than normal, my mother waking me up as she pushes the door open without knocking.

There's a hard line between her brows as she bustles into my room before I can even say good morning.

"Have you seen Brom?" she asks, an accusatory edge to her tone.

I freeze, my fingers curling around the edge of my blanket. "Brom? No. Why?"

She knows. She must know. Do I already look different to her? Had I turned into a woman overnight?

"Because he never came home last night. Emilie said he was supposed to let out the cows first thing, and he never did. His room is empty, bed made." She pauses. "His satchel is missing, and . . . there's a general sense that he's gone."

The way she says those last words, the weight on them, makes me realize that the energy around us has shifted in some way, like the world feels incomplete, as if a piece of a complete puzzle has been taken away.

"Gone . . . ," I say uneasily, my heart a thunderous sound in my head.

"That he's left Sleepy Hollow."

And even though she doesn't add anything to that, I can almost hear it in her head.

He's left Sleepy Hollow for good.

At first, I think it's me. My fault. That I scared him or that perhaps he took my innocence and ran, that I was used and discarded, or that he discovered he didn't like me in that way after all, despite how he made it seem last night. But not only does that not seem like Brom, there's still the thing he said to me at the start of the night:

"I've done a bad thing."

2

Kat

1875

Y ou're so lucky, Kat," Mary says to me with a sigh, leaning against the fence post as she stares up at me, a wistful look on her freckled face.

My mare, Snowdrop, shifts her weight from under me, probably wondering why I'm not dismounting and tying her up to the post as I usually do when I visit with Mary. Little does my horse know that I'm not staying. Today is the first day of classes at Sleepy Hollow Institute, and I have to stop by Mary's house so that her younger brother, Mathias, can escort me to the college.

The whole thing is ridiculous. I know the way, and I've been riding off into town whenever I want with nary an escort for years. But my mother was insistent that I not ride alone. I have no idea why since it's not an especially long ride, and the weather today is warm and pleasant, like summer has bled over into autumn. And it's not like I'm a child anymore—I just turned nineteen a month ago and am capable of taking care of myself.

But my mother isn't someone you'll win against when it comes to a battle of wills.

"Do you want to trade places?" I ask Mary, sounding hopeful despite knowing the futility.

Mary wanted more than anything to attend the institute. The tuition is free, they accept women in all areas of education, and many students are said to go on to do stupendous things with their degrees. Mary has always had a dream of becoming a bota-nist, and the institute has a biology and botany department.

But the school isn't open to just anyone.

Mary scrunches up her nose. "I think they'd notice," she says with a deeper sigh. "Just promise me that you'll teach me every-thing you learn. I don't care what it is."

"Even Shakespeare?"

She laughs, a light ringing sound. "Even that."

While Mary yearns for education, that school is the last place I want to be. I'd grown up believing I wouldn't have to fulfill the family tradition of attending. For so long, my future had been set out for me by my parents: become Brom Van Brunt's wife and start a family. But ever since he disappeared four years ago, my mother changed trajectory. I thought the moment I became eighteen that she'd try to marry me off to someone else—a dif-ferent kind of trap—but instead, she told me I'd be off to Sleepy Hollow Institute to earn a liberal arts degree like all the Van Tas-sel women before.

What I really want is to leave Sleepy Hollow for good. Part of me wants to try to find my childhood friend and onetime lover, see where Brom could have gone and ask him why he could so easily leave me behind. Another part of me wants to head west, discover the new lands, places I've only read about, and see my country through new eyes. Yet another part wants to go to Manhattan and write a book and eat at cafés and get lost in the people and sounds and life of the big city that beckons just thirty miles south of here.

But my mother had other plans for me. Sometimes I lie awake at night and think about slipping out the window, much like I did on that last night with Brom, and disappearing into the night, never to return.

Then I remember my father's dying words.

"Watch your mother," he said, pulling my ear to his mouth as he took his last breath. "Watch her."

With endless tears in my eyes, I promised him I would, and since I'd already broken one promise to him, I knew I'd carry this one to the grave.

I would watch over my mother.

I would stay in Sleepy Hollow.

And because it means so much to her and that side of the family, I would go to the institute and try to become the very person I'd hoped to find if I ran away.

"Good morning, Ms. Van Tassel," Mathias says as he walks out from the corner of the stable, pulling his horse along, a strawberry roan that matches his hair. He sticks a toothpick in his mouth and nods at me, like he's pretending to be an adult for the day. Mathias is about twelve but still stuck in that phase between being a kid and a gangly-legged teenager.

"Good morning, Mathias," I say to him with a jaunty tip of my head. "Are you ready to escort me through the dangerous woods of Sleepy Hollow?"

His brows go up at the mention of danger, his toothpick going slack in his mouth. "Do you think I should bring a gun?"

Mary rolls her eyes. "Go get on your horse, boy," she says to him. "And when you stop by McClellan's orchard, see if you can get me a few apples."

He groans. "If McClellan sees me stealing again, he's going to have my head."

"Wimp," Mary says, smacking the fence. "And here you are supposed to be Kat's protector."

He looks steadily at me, ruddiness on his cheeks. "I won't let you down," he says.

Now it's my turn to roll my eyes. "Come on, I don't want to be late."

He gets on his horse, and we say goodbye to Mary and start on our way toward the school. The village of Sleepy Hollow is located north of Tarrytown and situated between the wide expanse of the Hudson River and low, wooded hills to the east. My house and Mary's house are at the northern end of Sleepy Hollow, where the town streets and houses turn to farmland and forest.

"So what really goes on at that school?" Mathias asks me after we've ridden in silence for a bit, just enjoying the morning chirp of finches and sparrows, waving hello to farmers in the fields and a couple of carriages riding past. The hot breath from the horses rises in the cool air, but it's growing warmer by the minute, and I wish I had gotten dressed in a more breathable gown instead of the one I'm wearing now. It's yellow and ruffled, my favorite, and I obviously hoped to make a good impression on my first day.

"What do you mean?" I ask him.

"They're so secretive," he says, flicking the toothpick around in his mouth. "That's what Mary says anyway. Maybe because she doesn't know why they didn't let her in."

"I believe all private institutions are secretive. That's what makes them so prestigious."

He squints at me. "It's your family that runs it. I'm sure it's not so secretive to you."

I shrug with one shoulder. Every year at this time, strangers filter into the town to attend the school, coming from all over America and sometimes even Europe. They live on campus while earning their degrees, from botany and astronomy to liberal arts, philosophy, and ancient civilizations. They rarely venture into town during that time, and when they do, they come in groups and keep to themselves. That alone creates an air of mystery. What really happens at Sleepy Hollow Institute, and why are the students so strange?

Of course, by now I know the truth about the school. My mother sat me down and explained it to me a few days after my father died. A lot of people in town also know the truth and accept it, while others put blinders on and refuse to believe the rumors. I always thought that was ignorant, considering the magic that runs in Sleepy Hollow's veins.

Brom believed it. His mother was a witch, after all, and he'd seen the few things I could do. But Mary and her family moved to Sleepy Hollow only a couple of years ago.

Since the Wilsons were the closest neighbors to us and Mary was only two years younger than me, we became good friends. She filled a void that Brom left behind, even if she came from a pragmatic family, focused on science and having zero interest in the occult. I assume any talk of witchcraft would go over Math-ias's head too. Besides, I've been sworn to keep it a secret.

Sometimes it feels like my life has amounted to little more than keeping one secret after another.

"I guess I'm about to find out," I tell him. "I'll be sharing a lot of my studies with your sister, so if you ever want to glean some knowledge from me, all you have to do is ask."

Granted, I won't be sharing everything, but that's enough for Mathias to make a face.

"No, thank you. I learn enough at school. I'm just grateful my ma asked me to give you a ride to your classes so that I can miss the start of mine."

We ride in the sun along rambling fences and pink hollyhocks that tower over us, reaching for the clear blue sky beside the sun-flowers, their yellow heads nodding as if paying their respects. Then we cross the old wooden bridge over Hollow Creek, hoof-beats echoing on the wood, a comforting sound. The creek that flows underneath is a soft murmur of water, waiting patiently for the autumn rains to replenish it. We then emerge to where the road forks, with one road skirting off toward the river and settle-ments farther north, while the other becomes a narrow trail that goes through the woods and up a slight hill toward Pocantico Lake, where the school resides.

The minute we enter the woods, a hush comes over us. Par-ents always warn their children never to go beyond Hollow Creek Bridge, that the woods hold dangers and wild animals, that you could easily get lost and never come out. I always thought it silly, since my mother would ride here in the dark alone every month for a meeting with her sisters. Still, even when I used to play here with Brom, we never ventured too far.

"So how come you're not living at the school like everyone else?" Mathias asks me. His voice trembles slightly, and I can tell he's getting more anxious the farther we ride into the forest, passing by the stagnant water of Wiley's Swamp.

"My mother said it made more sense to stay at home since I live in town," I say. I know the school represents an escape from Sleepy Hollow in its own way, but it didn't feel right leaving my mother alone. Even aside from the promise I made to my father, she hasn't been the same since his death, her health steadily falling ever since.

We ride for another twenty minutes, the trail getting so narrow in parts that the branches are reaching for us, and if there hadn't been fresh wheel ruts in the ground, I'd have a hard time believing that anyone could have come through here on a carriage.

Finally, the morning light reaches through the gaps in the canopy. I see the slick surface of the lake through the trees, and the trail opens up to reveal the school in all its dark glory. In front of us are large iron gates flanked by a high stone wall crawling with ivy. A brass placard reads *Sleepy Hollow Institute: Where Learning Goes Beyond*.

Looking past the gates, I can make out the shapes of the buildings, most old and castle-like, though there are two more modern and squat. The modern ones are made of brick, but the rest are this dark stone that looks perpetually wet, flanked by gargoyles. All of them are surrounded by a thick fog that seems to hang over the entire complex.

As we get to the gate, it becomes apparent just how far back the school extends, disappearing into the woods. There are several large buildings sprawled around a central courtyard that looks like it could have been taken straight out of a fairy tale, with its cobblestone paths lined with statues and lanterns that cast light onto small patches of groomed grass and gardens of orange dahlias.

But despite how impressive the school looks, a strange feeling of fear kicks up inside me like a wild horse, a tightness in my chest. Perhaps this is because, even in broad daylight, all the windows are shuttered tightly. As if it's trying to keep something out.

Or something else in.

3

Kat

"This is where I leave you," Mathias squeaks fearfully, pulling his roan to a stop.

I stare at the gates to the school for a moment, expecting them to open toward me as if operated by phantoms, but they remain closed. And from the looks of the snake-and-key emblem in the center, they're locked shut.

I glance over my shoulder at Mathias. His face has paled, and his horse is snorting impatiently, either picking up on his fright or the energy of the school. "You know you don't have to escort me back later," I tell him. "I won't tell. I'll be fine."

He swallows, looking torn as he mulls that over, chewing on his bottom lip. Then he shakes his head. "You can count on me, Ms. Van Tassel. I'll be back here at four." His horse raises its head and paws at the damp earth. "I should go now," he adds quietly.

He turns the horse around, and they take off at a gallop, disappearing into the woods in a ruddy blur.

I look back to the school. I don't blame Mathias for leaving. I doubt they would let him past the gates anyway—seems like I'm not even able to go through. I bring Snowdrop closer to investigate, and she, too, begins to protest. She's always been a good mare when it comes to magic, but my magic is small compared to what is taught behind these stone walls.

The more that I stare at the school, the more it seems like a sentient beast and the more the gates look like a cage. I came here with my parents when I was a child, and I remember it being this large, endless kingdom in the middle of the woods, flanked by the darkest lake, a lake that seemed to hold monsters in its depths, but all the other details from that visit are blurred, like memories from childhood often are.

And yet, my visit this July seems blurred too. I came up here with my mother to meet with my aunts, and complete an interview and a test that was required for admission. I remember standing outside the gates with my mother, staring in awe at the fog that was still present even in the height of summer; the black, inky surface of the lake; the foreboding feeling of power behind the stone walls; and then . . . that's it. I don't remember anything from inside. I don't remember who I met or what we discussed or what anything looked like.

A shiver rolls through me, passing down onto Snowdrop, who snorts anxiously, her skin quivering. I lean down and give her a pat.

"Easy there," I coo to her, stroking her silky soft neck. "Nothing to be afraid of. It—"

"Katrina Van Tassel?"

I jolt in my saddle, and Snowdrop rears back with a whinny. I manage to stay on, holding her reins in place, staring down beside us, where a woman in a hooded cloak has appeared from out of nowhere.

"I'm sorry!" I exclaim as Snowdrop spins around. "You gave us a fright."

"That's quite all right," she says in an even voice. "I've been waiting for you."

Snowdrop lets out another loud snort and a shake of her head, but she's calming down. I can't help but stare at the woman, wondering who she is. I've never seen her before, and I thought that was impossible in this town.

"I'm Margaret Jansen," she says. "I know you don't remember me."

I blink at her. It's the strangest thing. When I was first looking at her, I couldn't make sense of her face, like her features were arranged backward, and now they're finally coming together to create something I recognize. She's fairly tall and angular, her thin frame visible despite the thickness of her black cloak. Under her hood is a long, brittle-looking neck and, perched on top, a small face with a sharp chin, reminding me of a heron. Her cheekbones are hollowed out, as are the circles under her eyes, her lips thin and dry, her brown hair streaked with white and gray. Only her eyes remain bright and shining and very, very dark. The more I stare at them, the darker they seem to grow, making me feel dizzy.

"Of course I do," I say dumbly. "I met you when I was last here. You showed me around."

It's like remembering a dream. None of it is clear—it's as if the fog that surrounds the campus is doing the same thing to my brain. But I remember this woman now, sitting with her and my mother in a cold, drafty office, sipping tea with mugwort leaves and talking about my "gifts." She looked different then, younger somehow, her energy warmer.

She gives me a thin, patient smile as if she can hear my thoughts. Maybe she can. Telepathy is a gift that I may not possess, but perhaps others do.

"I'm sorry we don't have a welcome committee," she says, pressing her bony hands together. "First day of school is always a bit chaotic."

I glance over her head at the school, noticing for the first time how empty it is. Silent. Even the birds are quiet, the air completely still.

"Am I late?" I ask, a thread of panic around my chest. Is this even the right day? My mother had woken me up this morning, talking so fast about my first day at the institute that I couldn't focus on anything else. Did she get the dates wrong? Should I have been here earlier? Later? All she had said was when Mathias was to meet me and pick me up.

"Not at all," the woman says. "You will go at your own pace here. There is no punishment for being late nor a prize for being early. All that matters is at the end of each semester, you're able to demonstrate yourself in your tests." She pauses, casting a shrewd eye over me. "Perhaps we should have a little demonstration now."

She points at the gate with her thin white hand. "Are you able to open the gate from where you are?"

I stare at her blankly. "What do you mean?"

"Can you open the gate using your mind?"

"My mind? No. Sorry, I'm a little confused." Where did she get the idea I was able to do that?

She stops at the gate and looks at me over her shoulder. "We've had this discussion before, Katrina."

"It's Kat," I say absently. Another memory comes flooding back. I was sitting in a tall wooden chair in a cathedral-like room with stained glass windows. The windows were covered in red and blue flowers, and when the light came through, it made the stone floor look bruised. I was holding a cup of tea in my hands, steam meeting my face as I sipped it, and there were four cloaked women standing in front of me, their eyes closed and chanting under their breath. Two of them were my aunts, Leona and Ana; the others were Margaret and someone else. Her sister Sophie, I think.

"Kat it is," the woman says. "So as long as you call me Sister Margaret. We are a family here, yes, and the sisters run the show." She tilts her head, reading the confusion on my face. "You were tested, Kat, before you were admitted. You proved yourself worthy of the institute. I apologize that we only came to a decision to admit you last week. There had been some . . . shuffling around."

That explains why none of this seemed real until a week ago.

"And when you were tested, you showed great promise," she goes on. "All students carry potential deep inside them. It's up to us to bring it out. You showed promise in the realms of telekinesis, as well as elemental magic, shadow control, and mimicry."

"Mimicry?" I repeat. I'm not even sure what that is. "Why don't I remember any of this? When did you do all this testing?"

"You know when, my dear," she says. "All the memories will

come back once you step through the gates. Slowly, and over time, but they will. Come along now. We'll go inside, settle your horse in the stable, and get you to your first class. I must admit, you'll be the first student we've had in a long time who hasn't stayed on campus."

With a flourish of her hand, the gate unlocks itself with a loud click and opens out toward us.

I marvel at the open display of magic, my jaw dropping slightly. My father had made me promise to keep my magic buried, even around my mother. It made sense at first, especially as my mother didn't show any magic around me. These past few years, however, she's become more curious about what I can and can't do, yet she's kept her own magic to a minimum.

To see it here so boldly gives me a thrill. For the first time, I'm a little excited about attending this school. Maybe it won't be so bad. Maybe this place will provide me with all that I've been searching for.

With the gates fully wide, I cluck softly to Snowdrop, encouraging her to follow Sister Margaret into the campus. Snowdrop stops midway through, throwing up her head, and I have to nudge her sides to get her to keep walking.

Please do this, I say to her inside my head. *You will be safe, I promise.*

As usual, when I speak to her in my mind, she listens. She walks through, and the moment she does, I feel something ice-cold slide over me, like submerging in a river. This must be the wards. Both of us shiver in unison but keep on moving through until suddenly, the world seems to shrink and expand, the pressure in my ears building and building until they pop.

And then all is still. I hear birdsong. Faint laughter coming from the buildings. A breeze blows back my hair, smelling of bonfire and roses.

Sister Margaret stares up at me. "Welcome to the institute."

I wait, expecting to be inundated by forgotten memories of my admission and testing, but I don't remember any of it. Not yet anyway.

But as she walks down the cobblestone path that cuts down the middle of the school, tall stone buildings on either side, I have a strong sense of having walked here before. Snowdrop seems content to follow her, so I sit back in the saddle and marvel at the architecture. From far away, the gargoyles on the stone buildings seemed faceless, but up close, they all have very distinct humanish facades. The statues that line the path are the same, men and women who are frozen in white marble and mossy stone. The gardens are more vibrant than they looked from outside the gates, not just dahlias but blue poppies and black-eyed Susans that dazzle in shades of yellow.

Even the windows that looked shuttered earlier are clearly open, and voices come and go as we pass them, classes already in session. I can feel their energy and excitement seeping out, swirling in the air around me. Only the perpetual fog remains the same, resting among the buildings like a white cape that won't stir, even with the lake breeze.

Sister Margaret takes us over to the stables that line the back of the campus, giving me a closer look at all the buildings. They all seem to form a circle, with the path and gardens cutting through and between like a wheel and spokes, with the newest buildings in the back by the stables. There are more trees here, oak and elm and a few maples, the color of their leaves blazing despite the gloom, shrouding the two brick buildings as if they were built into the forest like an afterthought.

I dismount just as a stable boy appears. He can't be more than ten, with dark blond hair, and he watches Sister Margaret with full attention, his body tense and fidgeting.

"Simon," she says to him. "This is Leona and Ana's niece, Kat. Do take excellent care of her horse, Snowdrop, while she's here. Have her saddled and ready to go by three forty-five."

"Yes, Sister," Simon says, glancing at me ever so briefly with a fearful nod before he reaches for Snowdrop.

For a moment, I wonder how Sister Margaret knew my horse's name, but then I realize she likely knows a lot of things.

Thankfully, Snowdrop lets out a soft nicker the moment Simon clasps his hands over the reins and dutifully follows him inside the stables.

"Now," Sister Margaret says to me, "while your horse is in good hands, I think it's best we get you to class." Then she frowns as she looks at me. "Did you not bring any pencils or paper? Not even chalk or a slate?"

I shake my head, feeling foolish. "My mother told me all would be provided." Actually, my mother barely told me anything at all. Every time I asked her about what my classes would be (since I never had a chance to pick any) or what to expect, she would give me a small smile and say, "You'll see."

This information seems to bother Sister Margaret though. Her eyes narrow a little. "Is that so? All students were given their textbooks and supplies, but because you're the only one who lives off campus, you must have been overlooked. Luckily, your first class is energy manipulation, and I've heard it's very hands-on. Or should be. The teacher is new, you see."

Energy manipulation? She walks off toward the closest stone building, and I follow, careful not to let my dress drag on the path. They aren't starting me out with philosophy or Shakespeare? Not even reading tea leaves?

"We don't believe in starting slow," Sister Margaret explains as she opens the large wooden door and ushers me inside. "We prefer to dive headfirst into our studies. But don't be alarmed. You'll take to it much like an eaglet does when the mother kicks it out of the nest, forcing it to fly for the first time."

I make a face. I don't think I like that analogy much.

"Besides," she says, giving me a sidelong glance, "all your classes were chosen based on your aptitude tests. I'm surprised your mother didn't give you the schedule."

"She didn't give me anything," I admit. "Just told me to show up before nine a.m."

"Typical Sarah," she says with a dry laugh, though there is a bitter undertone to her words, an animosity toward my mother that I don't think I'm imagining.

She takes me down the hall, a long stretch of stone walls adorned with paintings of animals in gold frames, just a single animal in each one—a horse, a frog, a butterfly, a cat—all done in the same vivid brushstrokes. Their eyes seem to watch me as I pass, making me feel unsettled.

Then she stops in front of a door with the name Ichabod Crane typed on a nameplate and raps on it with her knuckles.

Ichabod, I think to myself. *What an unusual woman's name.*

And then the door opens with a blast of warm air, and on the other side stands an especially tall man who is staring at us quizzically. An especially tall and handsome man with smooth pale skin, floppy black hair, and dark gray eyes that remind me of the deepest thunderclouds.

"You're a man," I blurt out in surprise. I had been expecting a woman. I knew the school was progressive in every way, but I'd never had a male teacher before.

The man frowns at me. "That I am," he says. "And you are terribly late."

4

Crane

Three weeks ago

I'm being followed. I'm sure of it.

The moment I stepped out of the building, a shadow moved off the brick wall on Mott Street, lurching toward me out of the corner of my eye. I turned around to face my attacker, thinking it was a thief preying on those coming out of the opium joints, seeing an easy target to rob.

But there was no one there except a lone carriage rolling down the street and the sound of garbage bins rattling in a nearby alleyway. The rest of the city was sleeping.

I kept walking, the drug starting to leave my system. The August air was sticky even at night, but it felt fresh in my lungs, and I was taking gulps of it as I went, as if I hadn't taken a breath in weeks. I knew it was a matter of time before the opium wore off completely and I would have to face the ruins of my life again, but for now, I was fine. I was an anonymous man with no future and no past, just footsteps echoing down the empty streets of Manhattan at three in the morning.

But then my footsteps were joined by another.

Coming closer, closer.

I whirled around and saw nothing there.

Nothing except the movement of a puddle, as if something had just splashed through it.

I walk faster, breaking a sweat, and I feel nearly sober now. I'm just a minute from my hotel room, and though I have this nasty tingling at the back of my neck like I'm being watched, I feel I might be safe once I'm inside. My room is just a dirty hole-in-the-wall, but at least I'm surrounded by other dirty holes-in-the-wall.

"Ichabod," a female voice whispers from behind me. It's like it reaches into my chest and grabs my heart, stopping me dead. It sounds so much like Marie . . .

"Ichabod Crane," the voice says again, but now it sounds rough and low and vaguely sinister.

I slowly turn my head.

There's a cloaked woman standing behind me.

She doesn't have a face.

No eyes. No nose. Just a thin line for a mouth.

Lord Almighty.

"Ahh!" I cry out, trying to bury my scream and failing, raising my arm as if to shelter myself from the sight of her.

But with the pass of my arm, I see her again, and now she does have a face.

Of course she does. For heaven's sake, I think I smoked too much tonight.

"Ichabod Crane," she says once more, and now her voice

changes yet again. It's lighter, softer, and when she takes a step into the light of the gas lamp, I can see her more clearly. She's old but of an indeterminate age, with smooth, even white skin with deep lines framing her eyes and mouth. Her lips are red and wet, like she just bit her lip, and her eyes are a bright green flecked with gold that seems to dance under the light. It's her eyes that make her seem younger than she is.

She also has an aura about her that I can't place. It's constantly shifting in color, disappearing completely at times.

Witch, I think to myself. *She's some sort of witch.*

"You'd be right about that, Mr. Crane," she says.

My eyes widen.

"But you shouldn't look so scared," she goes on. "After all, you're a witch too."

I dare to take my eyes off her for a moment and glance worriedly around me. The street is empty and bare, save for a rat scampering near a drain, and my hotel is just at the end of the block. I wonder if I can get there before she can stop me. I don't know how she would—I'm at least a foot taller than her, but witches aren't to be trusted.

"I won't stop you," she says. "But you might want to listen to what I have to say, Mr. Crane. I'm afraid it involves your future and an opportunity I hope you're not too daft to refuse."

I'm tempted to push her away. To walk to the hotel and slam the door in her face. Or, hell, perhaps turn around and head right back to the opium joint. Lie down on the mat with a pipe and let all this dissolve into a dream.

"What sort of opportunity?" I find myself asking, my tone wary.

"A financial one," she says. "A rewarding one. You see, I'm a recruiter for a prestigious college, and we're looking for a teacher with your background."

I choke on a laugh. "My background?"

"Yes," she says simply. "We know you went to medical school in Chicago and that you were all set to graduate with flying colors until you abruptly quit. We know you went on to teach at an academy in San Francisco, where you met your wife. And we know of the tragic circumstances, of which I'm sure you need no reminding, that led you here to New York . . . and what your life has become since."

I stare at her, absolutely befuddled. "You got a hold of the police records?"

"You couldn't blame me for learning all I can about a potential employee, could you?" she says. "But no, there is no record to speak of. You're not the only witch who can see someone's past. I know what your hands can do when you put your mind to it. All that *I* need to do to see someone's past is hold something they've touched."

The woman reaches into her cloak and pulls out a blue handkerchief that looks like the one I had earlier. I quickly pat my coat pocket but am not surprised to find it gone.

"Mage," I manage to say.

"Pardon me?"

"I'm a mage, not a witch." I scowl, narrowing my eyes at her.

"Semantics," she says, holding out the handkerchief. "Take it. You left it at the opium den."

"You were there with me too?" I ask bitterly, swiping my

handkerchief from her. I've never met anyone with these sorts of powers. It's practically grotesque.

"Shadow magic," she says, a self-assured smile on her lips. "Renders one invisible in the dark. It's one of my many gifts. Gifts that you will soon have if you come join me."

I shake my head, raising my hand dismissively as I take a step backward. "Look, Madame Witch, you seem like a nice person, but I think we're going to have to part ways. You see, I'm quite happy here." I gesture to the city. "I like New York. I don't want to leave. And I'm definitely not doing so for some handkerchief-stealing woman I met on the street."

She remains unfazed. "This college is only thirty miles north of here. In the state."

"It's not the state I love," I say, stepping backward. "It's the city. And as I said, I am quite happy. So very happy. Now, if you'll excuse me, it's late, and I need to sleep for several days."

I turn around, hoping she will let it be and go find some other hapless professor to teach at her school. I walk a few feet, look behind my shoulder, and see her standing there under the street-light. The farther away I walk, the more her features start to meld into nothing again.

No nose, no eyes. Nothing but a thin-lipped smile.

I swallow and turn around, my skin feeling both hot and cold. A bath would be good. A hot bath. A cold bath. Something, anything.

By the time I get into the hotel though, lurching past the old man asleep at the front desk, and to my floor, the communal bathroom is occupied, a bath already running, so I keep going.

I fish out my keys to my room, hands shaking slightly as I turn the lock, then fling the door open and stumble inside. I slam it shut and quickly lock it behind me.

Then I lean back against it, my arms splayed as if to hold it closed, and shut my eyes, trying to take a deep breath.

What the hell was that? Who was that woman? Did she really know all that information about me through my handkerchief, or had she been following me for years?

How much did she *really* know?

I exhale, trying to urge my heart to calm down. I open my eyes. Even in the dark, my room is a disaster. Clothes on the floor, my bed unmade, and a plate of half-eaten roast chicken that I had gotten down the street sits on the windowsill.

For a moment, I see my life through her eyes. For a moment, I see where I started and see how far I've fallen. For a moment, I wonder if I've made a mistake in walking away.

Then, a shadow moves away from the wall.

I open my mouth, and a scream dies in my throat. It's not just that I couldn't find the strength to scream but that my voice was taken from me. Stolen from my throat.

"Quiet," the woman hisses. "Do you want to wake up your neighbors? Do you want them to know what you are? A trouble-maker and a drug addict is something this lurid city will accept. A witch is not."

She steps away from the wall, and the lamps around us flicker to life, casting the room in moving shadows. I swear I see eyes in those shadows, watching me. Black snakes that writhe in and out of my vision.

"What do you want from me?" I manage to say.

"I want you at Sleepy Hollow Institute," she says, pressing her thin hands together in a motion of prayer. "Your background plus your magic makes you a top contender as a schoolmaster."

I frown. "Sleepy Hollow Institute?"

"I don't blame you for not knowing what it is."

"Oh, I know what it is," I say, letting out a deep breath. My shoulders drop slightly now that she's mentioned a place that actually exists, not a mystical hut in the woods. "A lot of brilliant minds have come from there . . . or so your school's propaganda wants people to think."

She gives me a grin that isn't exactly kind. "Because it's true. We do brilliant things with brilliant people."

I stare at her for a moment, trying to think. Despite the fright I've had, the opium is still in my veins. "What do these brilliant people have to do with magic and witchcraft?"

Her grin widens. For a moment, her teeth look razor-sharp, but again, it's just a trick of the light, just as the snakes in the shadows are. Just as they have to be, or I will lose my mind.

"The students are brilliant because they are disposed to magic. Don't fret, Mr. Crane. Everyone who passes the curriculum ends up with a degree. They go on and do great things in the world. They were all such misfits, misanthropes, miscreants at the beginning, you see. Kicked around by the world because they felt different, were different."

She gives a sympathetic cluck of her tongue. "But at our school, they are transformed into the best versions of themselves. The students there are allowed to shine. To discover who they really are and unleash their true potential. And the longer you're there, the more the same will happen for you. We're offering you a salary, plus room and board, and you only need to commit to one year. After a year, you are free to leave if you wish. But I'll warn you. You'll never want to leave Sleepy Hollow. Once you are one with us, you'll want to stay for life."

It all sounds too good to be true. Well, I suppose it also sounds a little extreme. If I've learned anything about myself, it's that I don't stay in one place for too long. She should know that about me too, considering.

"How much is the salary?" I ask warily. I hate that this is starting to appeal to me. The idea of being a teacher again, having students worship your every word. I've missed that feeling of control and power, akin to feeling like a god. A poor man's god, but a god nonetheless.

"Fifteen dollars a week," she says. "Sixteen for the second year."

I chew on that, my heart leaping with temptation. That's over twice the rate across the country. "And the housing?"

"You'd be in the men's faculty dorm. Your own accommodations. Room with a view of the lake. Your own private bathroom and toilet. Delightful meals served daily." She says this while eyeing my half-eaten chicken meal with disdain. Then she looks back to me, her eyes glimmering. "You were a disciplined teacher who brought out the best from his students because you demanded the best from them. You made them rise above once, and you will make them rise above again. This doesn't have to be your life, Mr. Crane. You don't have to live like this. You can choose to live anew. You can choose magic above all else."

"Magic," I scoff. I gesture to my messy deck of tarot cards by my bedside. "That's my magic. Not much else."

"You can bestow energy," she says. When I look at her in surprise, she nods and goes on. "Yes, I know what's happened to you, but I can also see what's in you that no one else can. That, most importantly, *you* can't see. But I see your potential. I know that you can give someone else energy at no expense to yourself. We call that bestowal. It's very rare and so important as a teacher."

Bestowal. I finally have a word for it.

A flashback of me touching Marie slams into my head, the look of shock and betrayal on her face, and then the scene fades.

"And what about your divination?" she goes on, smiling still. "You deride your tarot cards, but you can see futures, especially the futures of others. They're vague, but they're there. And what if there's more locked inside you? What if there is so much more just waiting to come out, simmering below the surface? Enough with the drugs, trying to dim that light inside you. I know this world doesn't want to accept you as you are, and I know you use opium and alcohol to hide it, to escape from it, to try to make your brain blend in. But you weren't put on this earth by Goruun to blend in. You were put here to shine. You were put here to help others."

"Goruun?" I ask. I've never heard that word before.

A solemn look comes over her eyes. "You will find out more once you agree to the job."

I rub my hand over my jaw, suddenly feeling the weight of the world on me. I'm crashing, whether this witch woman is here or not. My eyelids flutter, feeling heavy.

"I will be back," she says, stepping forward. She reaches out and places her hand against my cheek, and I flinch at the feeling.

Her skin isn't cold nor hot, but it stings like a paper cut. "You need to rest before you can make such a life-changing decision. Because, believe me, it will change your life. Forever."

She removes her hand, and I stumble away from the door as she opens it, the locks magically coming undone.

There will be no keeping this woman out, I think wearily.

"My name is Leona Van Tassel," she says with a nod. "It's been a pleasure to meet you, Mr. Ichabod Crane."

Then she steps out into the dark hall and disappears, the shadows swallowing her whole.

5

Kat

Did this schoolteacher just say that I was late for class?

"Late?" I repeat, tearing my eyes away from Professor Crane in the doorway and facing Sister Margaret. "You told me there was no such thing as being late here," I say to her.

Sister Margaret doesn't look at me, instead just gives the professor a thin smile. "This is Katrina Van Tassel," she says to him with emphasis. "I told her she can go at her own pace."

His dark brows raise. "Van Tassel?" he repeats. His voice is low and rich. He glances at me briefly before looking back to her, bowing his head slightly. "My apologies. I had no idea."

Sister Margaret raises her chin and gives an even thinner smile to him before patting me on the shoulder. "I'll be back after your class to finish giving you a tour."

She walks off, her cloak flowing behind her like ink, and I feel my cheeks flush with embarrassment as I look at my teacher. I didn't think I'd be getting special treatment, and I can tell Professor Crane is already annoyed with me.

"Katrina Van Tassel," he says, clearing his throat and stepping aside to let me in the room. "After you."

"It's Kat," I tell him, a vague smell of fire and spice lingering in the air as I brush past him.

The classroom is nothing like I expected, other than the fact that every student is staring at me as I walk in. The teacher's desk is at the center of the room with a small, low platform in front that resembles a stage, and the desks are arranged in a horseshoe shape around it, probably a dozen or more students in total. Along one wall is a row of windows that look out onto the trees, and at the back of the room is a collection of empty cages and jars half hidden by a dark curtain.

"And it's Professor Crane to you," he says stiffly, flicking his hand to an empty desk directly in front of his.

I suppose no one wanted to sit in the line of fire.

"And despite your relationship with the headmasters of the school, this is where you'll be sitting. Sorry you didn't get first pick."

A few students lean in and whisper to each other, eyeing me up and down. None of them are dressed as fancy as I am; in fact, the girls' dresses are plain, high-collared, and threadbare at times, the boys' shirts wrinkled, suit jackets ill-fitting. My skin flames even hotter. I immediately feel like I don't belong here.

I quickly take my seat.

"And, Ms. Van Tassel," the professor continues, his gaze piercing, "you'll be expected to be here every morning when class starts, not twenty minutes later. I don't care who you are and what Sister Margaret told you, but how she operates isn't the same way I operate, and I am the god in this classroom."

My eyes widen as he rounds the back of his desk, his hands clasped at his back as he stares at the floor. But when he turns his head to meet my gaze, I keep mine steady, lifting my chin to let him know I won't consider him to be any god at all. It's by some sort of miracle that I bite my lip and refrain from telling him so. I'm not sure my so-called status would prevent me from getting kicked out of his class.

"Now," he says, his charcoal eyes still on me, "let me get back to the lesson at hand."

He circles his desk, snapping up a textbook, and steps onto the platform right in front of me. His trousers are a little on the tight side, framed by the long length of his black jacket, and I immediately look down at the desk, not wanting to get any inappropriate thoughts. Someone had scribbled something in pencil at the corner of the desk, the words faded: *Welcome to Sleepy Hollow. May you never leave!*

"As I was saying before I was interrupted," Professor Crane goes on, his voice louder as he addresses the class, "energy manipulation is all about giving rather than receiving. You're all in this class because you've shown potential to the sisters, and they've deemed that worthy of being explored. Many of you might not even be aware that you have this specific magic, that it's been lying dormant inside you all this time. Some may have an inkling of this talent. Others yet may practice energy manipulation on the daily . . . away from prying eyes, of course. Perhaps trying it out on your dog or cat. Or a bothersome little sibling."

A few chuckles and appreciative murmurs sound.

"But the first step to figuring out what to give is figuring out what kind of manipulation you can do. What kind of energy." He clears his throat. "I want you to take out your pad and pencil and jot down the first five things you think about when you think about energy."

Everyone rustles around me while they reach into their book bags and satchels, and I'm just sitting there, feeling Professor Crane's eyes on me.

"Ms. Van Tassel?" he says in a low voice, an edge to it.

I dare to meet his eyes. "I'm afraid I don't have anything to write on or with." I open my mouth to explain that my mother never told me to bring supplies, but it would just sound like an excuse, so I shut it. "Perhaps you can lend me some."

"Perhaps *I* can?" he repeats, his forehead wrinkling beneath a strand of floppy hair. "The school should have provided you with all you need." He sighs and looks to the students. "Does anyone here have an extra pencil and paper they can lend her for now?"

The Black boy next to me rummages through his bag and pulls out another pencil. He rips out a few pages from his ledger and hands it to me.

I give him an appreciative look, knowing how expensive paper is. "Thank you," I say softly. Like everyone in this classroom, his face is unfamiliar, a stranger to Sleepy Hollow.

He just nods, his attention rapt on the professor, as if afraid to look away again.

"Well, go on," the professor prods. "Five things."

I twirl the pencil in my hand, trying to think. It's hard. My eyes keep being drawn to my teacher as he paces around his desk, looking deep in thought and then occasionally casting a glance around the room. He meets my eyes, and they flash with frustration, probably because I'm staring at him and not writing anything.

I look down at my paper and scribble down the numbers one to five on the margin, hoping that my brain will start working in the meantime. What do I think of when I think about energy? I should be learning Plato or reading a guide to runes or something. Not something that sounds like science.

Professor Crane's fingers appear in the frame of my vision, pressed against the top of my desk. I stare at them for a moment, his long, slender fingers tapping the wood. *He has beautiful hands*, I think absently, struck by the sudden impulse to reach out and touch them.

Thankfully, I pull my own hands toward me and look up at him.

His gaze holds me in place, like there's no one else in the room. *What a peculiar man, so singularly focused on me.*

I have to remind myself I'm also focused on him.

You don't have to be here if you don't want to be, he says in such a low voice that I barely hear it. In fact, he's not even moving his lips.

Is he playing tricks on me somehow? Is *my* mind playing tricks on me?

It's like you don't even want to be a witch, he goes on, that voice still so low, as if it's seeping into my brain like mist. His lips are moving now, but barely, and I twist in my seat to glance to see if anyone else is listening, but they're all focused on their writing. *How strange, coming from a family like yours.*

His fingers still on the desk, he leans in closer. *I am talking to you, Ms. Van Tassel. No one else. I can tell that you don't want to be here. Perhaps it's what your family wants, and so you must. But I won't force you to stay here. You are free to leave.*

"I'm not leaving," I say, and now my classmates stir, shifting in their seats, looking up from their papers at us.

"Then perhaps you'd like to participate," he says in his normal low voice, smooth as silk.

I can't help but glare at him. Doesn't seem fair that he's able to throw his voice around like that and speak to me so privately when he chooses but I can't do the same to him.

I close my eyes and breathe in deeply through my nose until I feel his presence leave my desk. I exhale, like I can finally breathe, and try to think about the task at hand. When I think of energy, I think of the bright, blinding sun on a summer day. Of the creek flowing under the bridge, of the wind bending the tops of the pines in winter. I think of Snowdrop galloping across the pasture, kicking up the grass with her hooves. I think of my heart beating, steady and strong, drawing its own energy from some mysterious place inside of me. I think of love. The love I have for my father still that flows through me in a constant stream with nowhere else to go.

I write down these five things. But then I lift my pencil, tempted to write down one more.

Because there's energy that I've been forgetting. The energy I both created and expended with Brom that night in the barn, the last night that I saw him. There is no energy like love, but there's also no energy like sex.

It wasn't just with Brom either. I was intimate with Joshua Meeks last summer, a farmhand who was new in town. He was a true gentleman, kind and soft, and though my heart didn't flutter like it had for Brom, he did teach me a thing or two. He taught me the power one can derive from sex and in more ways than one. Through him I learned what I wanted from the act, something with a little roughness, with a hint of danger.

The memory of it makes my skin grow hot, and I shift in my seat, immediately pushing those memories and feelings away. I open my eyes and see that I've written down the word *sex*.

I gasp and quickly scribble it out so it's unreadable, wishing I had a rubber eraser. The last thing I want to do is have the professor see what I'm really thinking about.

"Very good," Professor Crane says. He's suddenly beside me, peering over my shoulder. I suck in my breath, automatically sitting straighter. I quickly glance up at him, and he's frowning at where I had scribbled out the word *sex*. He cocks a brow and gives me just a hint of a smile before walking on to the next student.

Oh goodness. He couldn't tell what I wrote, could he? I peer closer at the mess of charcoal, and I can't make out the word at all. Must be my imagination that he can read it. I pray it's my imagination.

Twisting in my seat, I watch as the professor looks over everyone in the class. I take the opportunity to nod at the boy across from me. "Thank you for the pencil and paper," I tell him. He's cute, maybe a few years older than me, his skin dark and luminous. "I'm Kat, by the way."

"I know," he says before giving me a quick bashful smile. Then he sits up as the professor comes walking back between our desks. "I'm Paul."

"There will be time for everyone to get to know each other

later," Professor Crane says as he passes by us. "We'll know each other very, very well by the end of the school year." He steps onto the platform and claps his hands together. "And let's start by doing a little practice. I will need a volunteer."

No one puts up their hand. I'm not surprised. I keep my head down and avoid eye contact, hoping I won't attract his attention.

"Ms. Van Tassel," he says with a hint of triumph in his voice.

I sigh. Boy, did I ever get off on the wrong foot with this man. I look up. "Yes?"

He gestures beside him. "Would you care to join me?"

"I'd rather not," I say.

A few classmates snicker while another gasps. I suppose talking back to the teacher is rather uncouth.

But the professor only chuckles. "That's plain to see. So let's see how energy works with an *unwilling* participant."

I exchange a glance with Paul, who gives me an encouraging nod. I get out of my seat and walk around the desk, one hand gathering my dress, wishing I wasn't wearing such a fancy outfit, wishing the class wasn't staring at me.

The professor sticks out his hand to help me up on the platform. It's only a couple of inches off the ground, but with my dress and my clumsy luck, I'll probably fall. Reluctantly, I place my hand in his.

And the world goes black.

6

Crane

I've always been a curious man. I suppose that's why I decided to become a teacher. Well, I suppose that's why I wanted to become a doctor first, so I could uncover the mysteries of the human body. Unfortunately, when I started to have a nasty habit of communicating with the cadavers in medical school, I decided becoming a doctor wasn't for me. I preferred the dead when they didn't talk.

But being a teacher has always felt natural. My curiosity rubs off on the students. Makes them study harder, the yearning for knowledge like a drug. And it wasn't until a few weeks ago, when Leona Van Tassel stopped me on the streets of Manhattan and offered me a position at Sleepy Hollow Institute, that I fully understood how that came to be. It's not that I'm particularly interesting or commanding, though I like to think those things are true. It's that I can bestow my curiosity onto others, even without either of us knowing it. That I can literally make others *want* to learn.

Granted, I can't get them to *do* anything. My powers of persuasion work best when combined with equal parts passion and discipline, but their free will always remains their own. I'm merely influencing them. Nudging them in the right direction.

When I accepted the job and was brought here to the institute, a whole world that was previously buried inside me was unearthed like a grave, a monster of potential crawling out. I went through their aptitude tests, tests I'll admit I don't remember much of, aside from sitting in a cathedral and drinking wine while the four cloaked sisters of the institute chanted spell after spell after spell. I don't know what they did to me, but I remember the feeling of opening up, like they were cutting me open and taking a look inside me. It went beyond the telepathy and mind reading that Leona Van Tassel had done in Manhattan. They were sifting through me for parts I didn't even know existed.

But after that initiation, things began to change. I became more aware of the magic I already had, especially with bestowal. I started spending time in the school's library, another expansive cathedral filled with books on the occult and peppered with arcane artifacts, nothing like my father's church back in Kansas. I read; I learned; I filled the well. I started to feel like, perhaps for once in my thirty years, I had found a place that truly accepted me for what I was. Well, most of me, anyway.

And now, here, in my first class of the school year, I find myself presented with a young, pretty woman who seems able to resist my gift of curiosity. This shouldn't be a surprise—after all, there's always some pupil in my classes who doesn't take to my methods as well as I want them to. But because this woman is a Van Tassel, related in some way to Leona and Ana, it surprises me. It's as if she doesn't want to be here at all. I didn't even see her on my class attendance list, like she was some last-minute addition.

Perhaps she was. But she's here now, and I'm determined to get through to her. I'm nothing if not stubborn when it comes to teaching.

So I asked for her to be a volunteer in my demonstration. The animosity on her face was worth it. Her blue eyes went wide before turning to an icy glare that made my pulse skip a beat, a snarl on her soft pink lips.

She refused at first but then succumbed. From the wary way she's been looking at her classmates, I can tell she doesn't want them to think she's getting any special treatment by being a Van Tassel, and I suppose that's why I'm singling her out like this as well.

She gathered up her dress in her one hand, and I held out my hand for her other and braced myself for what was about to happen. There are ethical issues, I suppose, to doing this, but I've never been one to stake my life on ethics when it comes to magic.

The moment her hand touches mine, a cacophony of feelings floods through me. They don't come in images as they usually do when I try to read someone, but instead, I'm quickly overwhelmed with grief. Grief and love and . . . loss. So much loss that I'm not even sure this girl knows it's deep inside her, rooted there like a tree.

And there are other feelings here too, like yearning, longing, the need to fit in and belong, the urge to be elsewhere, to find a life worth living. A need to escape.

Then there's something else. Something that surprises me

that comes in hot and dark. Lust. Desire. Arousal. But it's not that she has these feelings in general that catches me off guard—I know witches tend to be very in tune with their sexuality—but that the way she feels them is the same way I once felt them. Almost as if I'm looking into a version of myself from the past. Almost as if . . .

I can't quite grasp it, and the longer I hold her hand, the faster her feelings drain from me, like they're being poured through a sieve. It's through this transaction, her memories and feelings flowing into me, that I can usually bestow things unto her. We give so we receive. We receive so that we must give.

But I can't bestow anything onto her. There's a blockage here, and it's only then that I finally notice she's been staring at me with her big azure eyes, the color San Francisco Bay would get on a cloudless day.

She rips her hand out of mine and holds my gaze steadily, her eyes narrowing, and I know she knows what I was trying to do. I can't help but feel bad about it, like I've violated her somehow.

I'm sorry, I whisper to her, using what I call *voice* to say it so that no one else can hear it. Another thing I picked up while perusing the library for spells.

She opens her mouth to say something but then averts her eyes, rubbing her lips together. She knows that whatever she says back won't be hidden from her classmates' ears.

Instead, she puts her hands on her hips and throws her head back. As she does so, her chest comes forward. She's in a pretty yellow gown with a V-neck lined with ruffles that's a little too low-cut for school or even daytime, her full breasts on display. All the other women in the class are wearing dresses with high necks, though they also probably cost half the price. Katrina Van Tassel in all her pretty, blond, defiant glory, stands out like a sore thumb here.

"Will that be all?" she asks, giving me a way out. I won't get any further with her today. I'll have to demonstrate bestowal on someone else.

"That will be all," I concede.

"*Katrina, may I* have a word with you?" I ask as the class ends and she's about to leave the room. A few of the students make a low "oooh" noise under their breath as they go.

"It's Kat," she corrects me like I knew she would. She punctuates that with a heavy sigh as she walks over to my desk, her gown rustling, the paper and pen she borrowed from her classmate Paul clutched in her hand.

I rest against the edge of my desk and wait until the last student leaves the room before I say, "I just wanted it to be clear that just because you're a Van Tassel, that doesn't mean you'll get any preferential treatment from me."

"I think you've made that *very* clear," she says with an indignant scoff.

"Have I?" I ask, leaning forward to stare at her intently. "Because in all the classrooms I've taught in, it's punishable to talk back to a teacher the way that you do."

For a moment I imagine having my ruler in my hand, giving her a hard paddling for being so obstinate. I have to push the image away before I get aroused.

"That's only because you refer to yourself as a god," she says, thoroughly unrepentant. "And you think yourself one too. Why else would you try to read my memories without my consent?"

I stiffen. "How did you know I was doing that?" I thought I'd learned how to hide it, how to look through memories and slip them into my own consciousness without the person ever finding out, like a street thief in the night.

She shrugs. "I don't know. I could tell, that's all."

"So then you figured out how to block me from your memories," I muse. "I couldn't see any of the images like I usually can. I could only feel them." That had happened just once before where someone's memories were off-limits, leaving only their emotions behind. Naturally it just left me wanting to find out more about him.

Now I feel the same pull of curiosity toward her.

She tilts her head at me, a strand of curled straw-blond hair falling across her delicate face. The girl may look like a complete lady, but she reminds me more of a princess, the kind that's accustomed to getting what she wants. "I suppose I did," she says thoughtfully.

"That in itself is worth studying," I say, feeling excitement well up inside of me, the prospect of heading into the unknown. "We may be here to learn about energy manipulation, but being able to stop unwanted energy is a gift in its own right."

"Perhaps," she says, woefully unimpressed. "What was it that you were trying to glean from me?"

"I was curious as to why you act like you don't want to be here. I thought it was tradition for the Van Tassel witches to attend this school. At least, that's what I learned from your aunts."

Her jaw tightens a little. "Perhaps I wanted to make my own decisions. It had never been my destiny to attend this school."

"What changed?"

She swallows and look down as her fingers fiddle with a ruffle in her skirt. "It became important to my mother. So it became important to me."

"I haven't met your mother, I don't think. It's hard to say when so much of my time has been a blur here so far."

She frowns at that. "For you as well? I feel like I can't quite get my head on straight. I don't even remember the last time I was here, when I came and took the tests. They say my memories should return, but they haven't yet."

"I've been here nearly a month, and I still don't remember much of the tests," I admit.

"Oh," she says, looking crestfallen, her full lower lip jutting out. "Anyway, I don't think you would have met my mother. She doesn't have much to do with the school."

I have to wonder why, given the history of the Van Tassels.

I hold out my hand. "You didn't seem to know you were blocking my attempts to read you. Care to try again, this time with purpose?"

She stares at my hand suspiciously. "You're just going to try harder, aren't you?"

"Maybe," I tell her with a smirk. "Are you up to the challenge?"

Her chin lifts. Of course she is. I knew that would convince her.

She places her hand in mine, and I clasp it. Her eyes flutter, but they don't close. Instead, they stare into mine with fierce determination while I try to push my energy through my hand, up her arm, then her neck, to her brain. But now there is a locked door that I'm up against. She's figured out how to keep me out entirely.

Still, I'm not giving up that easily. I push, taking the energy that is growing red and hot inside me, bubbling up like molten rock, and try to knock down that door. It works for a moment, enough to get another glance at something I don't understand. It's like looking into my own past. I've never met this woman before, and it's as if we share something in common, something intimate and wild and forbidden.

What is it?

Then I feel a blast of cold air rush through my palm, like ice cracking up my arm, and I immediately withdraw my hand, trying to shake out the pins and needles.

"How did you do that?" I gasp, my hand still feeling numb and hot at the same time as I cradle it against my chest.

She stares at her palm, her eyes big. It's clear it was a surprise to her too.

"I don't know," she says slowly, turning her hand around. "I just took the energy you were giving me, and I gave it back to you."

"Were you thinking of anything at the time?" I ask, opening my desk drawer with my other hand and fishing out a pad of paper and a pencil.

"Just that it felt hot, so I imagined ice. Like I wanted to freeze you out."

I give my hand a final shake, flexing my fingers, then excitedly write down the findings on the paper. "That is very interesting," I tell her.

"Is that not normal?"

I glance up at her. "Normal? No. Most can't tell when I'm trying to sift through them. The fact that you not only could but that you were also able to combat me means you're a lot more in tune with your energy than most." I give her a wry smile. "In time, I think you might be at the top of your class."

She doesn't look too convinced. But I am determined to convince her now. She may not want to be here, but it's undeniable that the power her aunts have runs in her blood. Who knows what kind of powerful witch this girl might become.

And then there's the fact that we share something, something in our pasts that we've both experienced, something indulgent and raw that's on the tip of my tongue, and yet I can't quite wrap my head around it. What on earth could possibly link the two of us together?

"Is this the only class you teach?" she asks.

"Not at all. I also teach divination and manifestation through tarot and crystals, mimicry, and psionic skills." I pause. "Are you in those classes too?"

She exhales. "I don't know what my classes are. I feel so utterly ill-prepared to be here. No books, no pencils or paper, no class schedule. My mother just put me on my horse, and away I went."

"You rode here?" I repeat. "No chariot to take you?"

"You may be from New York City, Mr. Crane, but I live on a farm," she says with a bemused twinkle in her eye. "I've been riding horses my whole life. No point in taking a carriage if you don't have to."

"But I'm sure your family is quite wealthy."

"We are," she says, then shakes her head, her eyes turning melancholy. "We were. My mother was born into wealth, of course, but my father died when I was young. Without him working, we don't have as much money as we did. But we live in a great house on a lovely old farm, and we aren't lacking for anything."

"Certainly not your wardrobe," I note, still avoiding her chest like the plague.

She glances down at her ample décolletage. "Yes, well, that was all my fault. I thought people dressed up for school. I overestimated the types of students who would be coming here."

"Lower class, you mean," I say. "Tell me, Kat, are you a bit of a snob?"

"No," she says adamantly, her cheeks flushing. "I just meant—"

"I know what you meant," I say, raising my hand. "I'm only teasing you. From what I gather, you're an outlier. Most men and women with any sort of magic tend to exist on the fringes of society. It's their otherness that puts them there, whether they like it or not."

She folds her hands in front of her and studies me. "And is that where you came from? The fringes?" She looks me up and down. "I see a smart suit, a nice watch. I see a man with intelligence and manners. And magic."

"I have lived a life of many beginnings," I admit. "Along the way, I discovered that's the best way to live."

"So what was your last beginning?"

"Knock knock," a voice says, and I turn to see Sister Margaret at the door, her cloak over her head, casting shadows over her face. Her features seem to dance and sway for a moment, as if rearranging themselves, something I noticed that's consistent among Leona and Ana Van Tassel, as well as Margaret and Sophie Jansen. I know it's some sort of spell they must have going on, a glamour of sorts, but I can't figure out the point of it.

"It's time for your tour," Sister Margaret says to Kat. "If you're still interested, of course. We have an hour before your next class with Ms. Peters."

"Of course," Kat says. Her hand flexes over the ripped sheets of paper in her hand.

"Here," I say, going into my desk drawer and pulling out a notepad. I hold it out to her. "You'll need this for your next class."

"Thank you," she says, taking it from me, and I notice she's careful not to touch my fingers again. "I guess I'll see you tomorrow," she says.

"You'll be seeing him this afternoon," Sister Margaret announces. "For your mimicry class." She then shoots me a knowing look. "Crane, I'll make sure you get your updated class list by tomorrow. There have already been some changes. One student has been sent home early. It always starts this way, when people realize they're not strong enough for the curriculum. But I'm sure that won't be the case with either of you."

She places her hand on Kat's arm and leads her out the door. Kat looks back at me over her shoulder as she goes, and our eyes meet. I manage to give her an encouraging smile, but her eyes are hard to read.

It's only when the door closes and she's gone that I realize what that look was.

It was fear.

7

Kat

"A re you sure you're doing all right?" Mathias asks me as he looks me up and down yet again as we ride side by side through the trail back home. "You're looking paler than an egg white."

"I'm fine," I tell him. "Just hungry, that's all."

"They don't feed you in that school?"

"I didn't have much of an appetite at the time," I tell him. It's true. After my herbs and tinctures class with Ms. Peters, who was a plain and quiet spinster, I went to the dining hall. I think I was most excited about this concept because we didn't have one at the schoolhouse I went to, where we all had to bring our lunch to school in tins and drink out of the pump, sharing one metal cup.

But my excitement was quickly dashed. It was odd walking into a place where everyone already seemed to know one another. Even though it was only the first day of school, I had to remind myself that the students all lived on campus and had been there for at least a week, whereas I was the odd one out who lived at home and got to leave every day when class was over.

Needless to say, I didn't eat. Growing up in Sleepy Hollow, I never had trouble making friends. It's just that when I found my good friends—such as Brom or Mary—I stuck to them like glue and tended to forget everyone else. So while I knew that I could make friends if I tried, Professor Crane's words hung in my head. He asked if I was a snob, which meant that's probably what the other kids think of me. I can't blame them. I'm a Van Tassel; I showed up late and without any supplies, as if I thought I was better than everyone, not to mention what I was wearing. There's no way anyone at this school would want to be friends with me, and I was too wary to test that theory.

So instead I spent my lunch hour walking around the grounds, going over all the places that Sister Margaret took me on the tour, plus a quick stop at the stables to check on Snowdrop. Despite the sprawl of the campus and the buildings that extend back into the forest, it really isn't that hard to navigate.

Maybe it has something to do with memory loss, because the farther we get away from the campus, the less that I remember. By the time we ride past Wiley's Swamp, all I remember clearly are my interactions with Professor Crane.

"So what did you learn today?" Mathias asks. "Normal stuff or something more . . . titillating?" He bursts into giggles at that, as if he was waiting a long time to use that word in an appropriate sentence.

I give him a placating smile. "You don't learn much on your first day of college, Mathias. What did *you* learn today?"

While Mathias starts complaining about Roman numerals and why he, as an American, has no business learning them, I try to think about what I did learn. I know in Ms. Peters's class, we went outside to talk about the plants grown in the class herb garden situated right outside the windows, but the details are fuzzy. The tour I took with Sister Margaret seems to be fading by the minute. All history of the school is forgotten. I don't know why my sessions with Crane remain clear. Perhaps when I'm with him, I'm really paying attention. Perhaps he's bestowing it on me.

When we eventually reach Mathias's farm, the sun low and golden above the trees, Mary runs out to greet me, and I feel bad that I don't have a lot of information to share with her. Not that I would be allowed to talk about what I learned even if I could remember, but I make a promise that by the weekend, we can have a real talk about my first week at college.

By the time I get home, untack Snowdrop, give her some mash, and turn her out for the evening, I'm more exhausted than I've ever been before.

"There she is," my mother says as I stagger into the house. The warm and comforting smell of chicken soup on the stove, courtesy of our Dutch housekeeper, Famke, instantly makes me feel relaxed. "Supper is almost ready."

"I'm going to put on my tea gown and freshen up," I tell her, tired of this dress already.

I can tell she wants to ask me questions, but I bustle past her to the bathroom and let out a deep breath as I lean over the basin. It feels good to be home, though I have a feeling this journey twice a day, five days a week, is going to wear on me.

I splash water on my face and stare at myself in the mirror. I look different somehow, older and more mature. My cheeks have thinned out just a bit, my eyes deeper and brighter, my lips more lush, like I lost all remnants of girlhood this morning, as if the school and the magic helped usher me into the future. Until recently, I had been wearing my blond hair down like girls do, but now that I'm considered of age, my hair is half up, adding to my maturity. I don't necessarily look bad, but it's a noticeable change. I look like a woman.

I wonder what Crane thought of me, I think. *Did he think I was attractive?* I had noticed him staring at my chest a few times. I have to say I liked his eyes on me as much as I liked the feeling of his hand around mine.

I just didn't like what he was trying to do while holding my hand. Trying to read my memories? I can't think of anything more invasive than that. Luckily, my body knew what was happening. I'm not sure if I was born with some sort of defensive mechanism against magic like that, but when his hand first touched mine, it was like the world went completely black, and I could see him in a large, black, empty space, just him standing in the void with me.

So I turned and ran. I put my back to him and ran through the darkness, and somehow, that prevented him from seeing who I really was.

Though perhaps that wouldn't have been a bad thing. Maybe it wouldn't hurt for someone else to have a look inside your mind. They might end up knowing you better than you know yourself.

I'm starting to think I don't know myself at all.

I splash a little more water on my face from the basin and

blink. Just thinking about what happened has me feeling off-kilter, but at least I still remember it, unlike the rest of the day.

Will my memories ever come back? I go to my bedroom and change into my tea dress, my fingers quickly working through the laces of my corset, stretching out my lungs in a long exhale. Then I unpin my hair and run my fingers through my curls before heading to the dining room.

My mother is already sitting there, staring at me expectantly, the food dished out on the table. She smiles as if a little unsure of how to act. I can't help but notice she's looking worse today, her skin more pallid and waxy, her eyes downturned at the corners, her graying hair straight and dry.

"How are you, Mama?" I ask her as I sit down at my place, gathering my napkin in my lap.

"Me?" she asks, folding her hands in front of her. They look thin and veiny, speckled with liver spots, the hands of a woman much older than forty-five. "I'm fine. Just tired. You know how it is, running the house."

I glance at Famke as she comes back into the room carrying a bottle of wine.

"Well, that's why we have lovely Famke, isn't it?" I point out.

"She needs to rest more," Famke says with a *tsk* as she pours us the red wine. "I keep telling her so, but you know, she is stubborn."

"Mama," I scold her as Famke leaves the room. "You must do as Famke says. Running this house is her job, not yours. You're supposed to be a well-kept woman."

She snorts at that and has a sip of her wine.

"Perhaps another trip to Dr. Fielding?" I venture, though the town doctor doesn't seem to help anyone. He loves to label every issue a woman has as "hysteria."

"No, no," she says dismissively before putting down her glass and fixing her eyes on me. "I am fine. Enough about me. Tell me all about your day."

My stomach growls loudly in protest, and she seems to hear that.

"No, wait. Eat first. Eat. Then tell me."

I oblige, drinking some wine and having some of my soup and bread. When I've taken the edge off my hunger, I begin. "My day, well, it's honestly very hard to describe."

I wanted to launch into a diatribe about how she sent me ill-prepared with no supplies and no class schedule, but now that I'm sitting here with her and she seems especially frail today, I decide to hold off. Besides, Sister Margaret gave me my schedule earlier, and when I had my mimicry class in the afternoon with Professor Crane, he presented me with a notebook bound with black ribbon, a couple of pencils, a writing slate, and some chalk. I didn't have a satchel to carry it back with me, so he said he'd hold on to it until my class with him tomorrow. Which was rather nice of him. I think he feels bad about the attempt at mind reading.

"The first day is always overwhelming," my mother says with a nod.

That's putting it mildly. "Can I ask you something?"

She dabs her napkin at her mouth. "Of course."

"Is there something . . . strange about the school itself? Is there some sort of magic or spell that protects the campus? I can barely remember the tests I took when we went this summer, nor anything else from that visit. Even right now, I'm having a hard time recalling what happened today. I feel like I'm forgetting almost everything."

"It's normal, dear," she says with a swallow of wine.

"In what way is that normal?" I question.

She picks up her spoon and gives me a steady look. "It's normal for *that* school. There are a lot of things you're going to experience there that are going to seem strange and unusual. You just need to trust the program. Trust the process. I wouldn't send you to that school if I didn't think it was necessary."

"But you waited so long," I say.

"We know why we waited," she says stiffly. "I always thought Brom would be brought back."

My heart sinks at the mention of his name. I feel like no one really talks about him anymore. Sometimes it's like he only ever existed in my head. But my body remembers, and so does my heart.

"Besides," she goes on, dipping her bread into her soup, "the school is for students of all ages. There is no getting a head start. It's not a competition."

She is right about that. Some of the students I saw were my age or younger, but all were at least eighteen. Some looked to even be in their thirties.

"But if I can't remember what I was taught when I leave the grounds . . . ," I begin, "how can I learn anything?"

"Katrina," she says, her voice lacking patience. She never calls me Kat. "Think about that for a moment. Where are you doing your tests? At the school, the same school you'll go to tomorrow, and all the information will come flooding back." She fiddles with the napkin in her nap. "There are spells, wards in place, put there by your aunts many years ago. There had been a few accidents where students had left the school and started talking about what they were learning. Cast a shroud of suspicion on us from the state. Took a very long time to convince the government that our school was fairly run and we were paying taxes."

"What happened to the students who blabbed?" I ask.

"They were punished," she says in a clipped voice, enough that it makes me wonder how they were punished. "So your aunts took action. It's much easier this way."

"Surely the students know that they are studying magic, though, when they leave," I point out. "How do they replicate their magic out there in the real world if they can't remember how to conjure it?"

"That's not for you to worry about."

"But it doesn't make sense."

"Look, by the time they graduate and move on, the magic will be so innate, so ingrained, they won't have to remember it. You'll understand all of it when you get there." Though she sounds wistful at that last part. I guess because it means I'll be leaving her, probably for good.

We both eat in silence for a bit before my curiosity gets the better of me. "What was your favorite class?"

She gives me a crooked smile. "I wouldn't know. I don't remember."

"I only remember one of mine," I admit. "Well, two."

Her eyes go wide, her spoon clattering against the bowl. "You remember two of your classes?"

"Yes. Both of them with Professor Crane."

Her eyes blink fast, trying to process. "I don't know who that is at all. What does he look like?"

"Tall, dark, and handsome," I say, trying not to smile. "Strict, invasive, and infuriating. Thinks of himself like a god. But actually quite nice, when he wants to be."

"And you remember the actual lessons?"

"Yes. We did energy manipulation and mimicry."

"Hmmm," she says, her brow furrowed. "I'm not sure I like that."

I frown. "Why not?"

Silence. I hear the tick of the clock in the living room, Famke puttering around in the kitchen, and somewhere, far off in the distance, a faint rumble of the season's first thunderstorm.

"It's dangerous to carry that knowledge outside of the school," she finally says.

"Why?"

"Because you're a witch," she hisses, leaning in. "And any chance of you practicing here and getting stronger means you're more of a target for the outside world. I'm not losing you like I lost your father."

"But he died of heart failure, not because he was a witch," I say, feeling my hands go clammy at the memory.

"I know." She clears her throat. "I'm just afraid of losing you, period. I suppose there isn't much you can do about what you remember. Perhaps it's the professor who's doing this with his own magic. What did you say his name was again? Maybe I'll bring this up with Leona."

"I don't want to get him in trouble," I say quickly. "But if you're so worried about other people finding out I'm a witch, even in

Sleepy Hollow, where I think half the population is magically in-clined, then I have a solution."

"What?" she asks warily.

"Let me live on campus. That would solve everything. I would remember and—"

"No!" she suddenly yells at me, slamming her fist down on the table, the soup and wine sloshing over the edges. "No, you are not going to live there! I will not share you with them! They have no claim to you!"

I stare at her wide-eyed, and she puts her hand on her chest, her wild gaze dropping to the mess she made on the table.

"No," she adds quietly, calming down. "They always get what they want, and I'm tired of it. And I don't want to be alone. I can't be alone, Katrina."

"All right," I tell her reluctantly, just as Famke hurries into the room. "I won't go. I'll stay."

"Oh dear," Famke says, eyeing the mess and wiping her hands on her apron. "I'll get something to clean that up."

After that, I don't dare say anything more about the school, and my mother doesn't ask me any more questions. We finish our meals and separate for the rest of the evening. But as I lie in bed later, I hear thunder rumbling in the distance. The storm never quite made it here tonight, but I know it's only a matter of time before one does. I can't help but think about what I learned with Crane in my mimicry class. That I could take something, like lightning, and harness it for myself. The next time there's a storm, I could practice. I could try to use it.

I could do the very thing the school doesn't want me to do.

8

Crane

I awake with a start. Heart pounding, ears ringing. I sit up in my bed and look around, and for a moment, I can't remember where I am. I can't even remember who I am. I feel like I've been stripped of all my flesh and guts and I'm just a bag of bones floating through nebulous space.

Then it comes back to me. Where I am, who I am, and what I'm doing here. I've been waking up like this every single night since I arrived at the institute. In a cold sweat, covered in confusion, sitting up in my bed in a very dark and unfamiliar room.

I let out a shuddering breath, surprised to see my breath cloud over. It's not that cold in here, and I can hear the occasional tick of the radiator pipes.

I also hear something else.

A soft wail.

A woman in tears.

I hold my breath, straining to hear it better. In the men's faculty wing of the dormitories, there are only a couple of men: Professor

Daniels, a verified mage who teaches the non-magic curriculum; Aman Desi, the linguistics teacher from India; plus Gale Winslow, the custodian; and myself. I'm unsure if Winslow has any magic or not, but if he doesn't, he doesn't seem all that bothered having to live among it.

But there are no women in this wing, and most of the rooms here are empty. However, that doesn't mean Daniels or Desi doesn't have a woman over. Same goes for Winslow, though he's in his sixties and doesn't talk much. I can't imagine him ever making someone cry.

"Ichabod," the woman says through a sob.

My heart comes to a standstill. It wouldn't be the first time I've imagined hearing Marie's voice in the night, but tonight it feels different. It feels painfully real.

"Ichabod," the voice says again. Very clearly Marie.

"No," I say, my fingers gripping the edge of the blanket. "No, you're not here. You're dead."

"Ichabod," she teases now, her voice changing. Getting mean. Getting more vibrant. "You think you can outrun your past, but you can't. You certainly can't outrun me. Not here. Not here, of all places. They will eat your soul, and I will only watch. I've led them to you!"

"Shut up!" I cry out, getting out of bed, my blankets tangled around my legs. Once I'm on my feet, the solidness of the rug under me, I feel a little more grounded. I wait and I listen, and her voice doesn't come back.

Thank God.

But there is something else now. An unusual solid yet wet sound.

Coming from outside my door.

Thump.

Thump.

Thump.

Followed by a soft scraping noise, as if something heavy is being dragged.

I swallow hard, a cold wash prickling down my neck.

What on earth is that?

I reach for my lantern and fumble for the matches on my desk. Luckily, there's enough light from the moon coming in through the window for me to light the lantern's candle quickly.

It flames up with a soft glow, my room cast in light and shadows. There's not much to the rooms here, but they are a lot nicer than the ones I had been staying in before. I have a wardrobe, my bed, a desk, plus my own private toilet, basin, and tub. All of it overlooks the lake, which tonight is just a black oil slick beneath stagnant fog, the moon barely reaching through.

Slowly, I creep toward my door and stop once I reach it, listening once more.

Thump.

Thump.

Thump.

What the hell is that? I steady myself and put my hand on the knob and turn, curiosity getting the better of me as it always does, my lantern shaking, causing the light to dance.

Slowly, I open the door, the hinges creaking, terribly loud, and look out into the darkness of the hallway.

My breath hitches. There is a long trail of what looks like blood leading down the hall, a slick path that dances dark red in the lantern light, and at the very end is a figure, an adult body on the floor, dragging themselves around the corner.

Jesus Christ.

I stand there, and I stare, and the fear is so overwhelming that I can't even take a breath.

What if this isn't in your head? I think. *What if this isn't a ghost? What if this is real? What if they need help?*

I set my jaw and steady myself and step out into the hall, my lantern held like a shield against the dark. Ghosts exist, but so do horrible accidents that involve humans. What if this person was involved in one?

The person on the floor has disappeared around the corner now, leaving only the trail of blood. I take a moment and crouch down, my fingers brushing lightly over it. It's thick like blood, and when I bring my hand to my nose, it smells like it too, sharp and metallic. All my senses are saying this is real, that this isn't some transmission from the afterlife.

I straighten up and carefully make my way down the hallway. I want to call out after them, but I stop myself time and time again, as if there's some hidden part of me that's making me stay quiet. I suppose if the person is so grievously injured, whomever committed the crime could still be on the floor, and I don't want their attention. At least, that's what I keep telling myself.

The building that houses the staff is an old stone one closest to the lake, shaped like two *L*s that come together in a grand circular staircase. The bottom floors are full of classrooms while the upper floor of one of the *L*s houses the women while the other *L* houses the men. My room is at the end of the men's *L*, so when I come around the corner, I expected the person to be gone for some reason, as if they wouldn't dare venture into the other wing.

Instead, the trail of blood continues past the staircase mezzanine and across to the women's quarters, rounding the corner.

My stomach twists. There is no possible instance that the body moving at the speed it is could have made it to the women's quarters so fast.

The blood is wet, smells real, I tell myself, trying to keep myself in stride. *The way it catches the lantern's glow, like red oil, that's real. But the speed in which it moved, that couldn't be real, couldn't be . . . human.*

I'm not usually a cowardly man. I've seen and done things in my life that would land people in jail, that would make others run. But here, with the lantern swinging in my hand, on a quiet night in this old building, I feel fear like I've never felt it before.

Something is strange here. Strange in a way that could be very, very dangerous if I'm not careful.

Taking in a deep breath, I manage to find my courage. And I keep walking.

I go quietly, sneaking past the staircase and into the women's wing. I try to keep that bravery with me as I turn the corner, expecting to see the body down the other hall.

But there's nothing. There's no blood either. I look down at my feet and see the floor is just faded wood. The house feels like it's sleeping.

I let out a long exhale, running my hand down my face for a moment. None of it was real. Not the blood, not the body. It was all in my head. All the pressures of the job and this need to create a new life are building up inside me. Not to mention the last time I had any drugs or alcohol in me.

I stand there for a moment, then realize a teacher could come out of her room and see me loitering in the halls. So I get my wits together and walk back the way I came, marveling at how dry the floor is as I go. I know I touched blood, I smelled it, but what if it was all an illusion? What if none of this is real, like a dream?

That's it, I think to myself. I'm overstimulated and exhausted and dreaming. Once I get back to my bed, it will all be over. I'll wake up, and the day will start again, and all of this will fade away into memory.

I round the corner to my hallway.

I see the body.

Right outside my open door, long arms in a pale, bloodstained nightgown pulling themselves inside my room.

There is no blood this time, but the body is there, slender gray feet disappearing through my door until the hall is empty again.

I feel sick, the lantern shaking in my hand again, bad enough that the flame of the candle flickers, threatening to go out.

"Fuck," I swear, managing to keep the lantern away from my breath.

This isn't real, I tell myself. *Remember, there's no blood this time. This doesn't follow the laws of physics, the laws of science.*

Yes, but neither does magic, and that's very much a tangible thing. It governs my life. How can I be so bold as to assume all of this is in my head?

And yet I find myself walking down the hall back to my bedroom as if being compelled by the thing that's waiting for me there. One step in front of another, the lights wavering on the stone walls, the building so quiet that my heartbeat is the only thing I hear. Even the thump of the woman is gone; the dragging sound of her soiled nightgown has vanished. It's just me.

It's just me.

There's only me.

I get to my door, and for one second, I fear the horror will kill me. The idea of what's waiting for me inside.

They will eat your soul, Marie had said earlier.

Joke's on them. I might not even have one.

I step inside my room, my lantern held out in front, casting the darkness into light.

There's no one here.

Nothing except a row of candles all along the windowsill, the flames dancing as if there's a breeze. What in God's name? I didn't light those. I know I didn't.

I quickly walk in all the way and look around, including my bathroom and closet, making sure there's no place for this thing to hide. Satisfied, I march over to my desk and the candles on the sill above it.

I suck in my breath.

On the desk is a black snake with several sewing needles stabbed through it, in the eye, the middle, and the end of the tail. Dead, except for a faint twitch of the tail.

And below it, there's something written on a scrap of paper in very fine handwriting.

Written in blood.

Welcome to Sleepy Hollow. May you never leave.

9

Crane

Suffice it to say, I barely slept a wink last night. After I found the message, I quickly disposed of the snake in the forest. Mercifully, the creature was fully dead—it must have been a reflex that caused it to move. It was only then that I realized I needed to hold on to the sewing needles and the piece of paper. Sure, the blood I had seen in the hallway wasn't real, and the woman I saw dragging herself on the floor disappeared, but this was evidence that I had. The only problem is I don't know what it is evidence *of.*

By the time the sun came up, casting pale gold on the surface of the black lake between the patches of fog, I was already in the dining hall getting breakfast, a tray of eggs and salted pork, before anyone else was up, including the students. I'm amazed I have an appetite at all, and it's only when I finish my meal and get a cup of coffee from the cook that other teachers and students start coming in.

There are the two girls who walk in wearing matching outfits.

They must be sisters, their faces similar, their braids coiled on their heads matching. They exude a quiet energy, a shy one, and even though it's been only a week since classes started and I'm still getting to know everyone, I recognize them from my mimicry class. They're from Oklahoma, and they both seem fascinated by astrology. One of them, in particular, I know has prophetic dreams.

There's a man, Doug Smith, who is probably a few years older than me, his beard peppered with gray, who shows promise in psychometry, which is what Leona has—the ability to gain foresight by touching objects. He showed this off in my psionic class yesterday.

Then there are the teachers, who don't always eat in the dining hall at the set times. This morning, I recognize the shy and quiet Ms. Peters with her sad eyes and ruddy complexion, sitting alone with a slice of bread and syrup, but there's no one else to be found. I at least wanted to see Daniels or Desi to inquire if they had heard any peculiar noises last night. I know I might sound a bit daft by asking, but I have to know it wasn't all in my head.

I reach over to my coat pocket and slide my fingers inside, finding the paper. As long as I have this, I know it wasn't a dream.

I finish the rest of my coffee and get up to procure another cup when I bump into Sister Sophie in line.

"Professor Crane," she says to me, her face brighter with her head free of her hood. Sister Sophie is the twin of Sister Margaret, both looking exactly the same except for a small mole above Sister Sophie's lip. But while Sister Margaret is rather cold and stiff, Sophie's personality is a little more pliable, and she's easier to talk to.

"How are we this morning?" she asks, adjusting the copper pin at the throat of her cloak.

My jaw tenses while I think of what I should say to her. Would the truth make me look weak? I take a chance.

"Tired, actually," I say as the iron-eyed cook refills my coffee cup. I nod my thanks and walk with her slowly across the hall. "I didn't get much sleep last night."

"I know what that's like," she says, blowing on her coffee. "Too many thoughts in your brain rattling around."

"You're not wrong," I tell her. "That's usually the case."

That's why opium was such a godsend for me. I'd been clean ever since I came to Sleepy Hollow—Leona forbade it—but boy did it ever help in making me feel at peace for once. It made me feel normal for a change, as if my brain was orderly instead of absolute chaos.

"It was different this time," I go on. I come to a stop and fix her with a pertinent gaze. "I woke up because I had heard something out in the hall."

"Oh?" she asks, her thin brows knitting together.

"I heard crying, and then . . . it was enough for me to get my lantern." I go on and tell her the rest of what happened, ending the story by bringing out the piece of paper from my coat pocket, careful not to spill my coffee on it. "This is what they wrote."

I wave the folded paper until it snaps open and show it to her.

Her lips purse as she looks it over. "I see," she says in a low voice. She glances up at me. "Not a very funny prank, is it?"

"A prank?" I gape at her. "You think this is a prank?"

She gives me a wry look, like I'm a complete dunce. "The students' dorm is in the building across from yours. Do you really think that a little harmless ribbing isn't in the repertoire for them? It's part of the hazing, Professor Crane. Surely you've been through that before."

"A hazing is a thumbtack left on the teacher's seat or a student hiding all the chalk," I say indignantly, though I'm careful to keep my voice down. "It is not someone killing a snake and putting it in a teacher's room and writing a warning in blood!"

She chuckles, smoothing her hair back before pulling up her hood, enveloping her face in shadow. "Oh, you are fretting over nothing. First of all, that is not a warning. That is a saying that we have here. *Welcome to Sleepy Hollow. May you never leave.* Because you'll love it here so much. And the dead snake, which I'm sure they found in the garden, probably died from natural causes. No harm, no foul. Let me ask you, when you went to explore the halls, did you lock the door behind you?"

I shake my head. "No, I . . ." I didn't even close it.

"There you go," she says with a satisfied smile, though it looks eerie with her eyes in shadow. "Anyone could have snuck in, and it sounded like you were gone for long enough. As for the blood, probably a trick of the eye. You know you see what you want to see. And don't forget, you are at a school for magic. Don't underestimate some of these students. More than a few of them showed an inclination toward the power of illusion."

"I know what I saw," I say firmly, my molars grinding together. "That was no prank."

"Perhaps a student dressed in a nightgown or, as I said, an illusion," she says. "The students here will continuously surprise you. Keeps you on your toes, doesn't it?"

Then with a flick of her hand, she waves goodbye and turns,

gliding out of the dining hall like a ghost in black, sipping her coffee as she goes.

I watch her go, absolutely befuddled. Could she be right? Could it have been a prank by the students? I look around the room, trying to see if any one of them is looking my way and laughing, but no one is paying any attention to me.

I let out a low breath before taking a large gulp of my coffee, which has already gone lukewarm from talking so much. Probably for the best that I don't have too much—I don't want to add to the anxiety that I already have.

I go back to my table where I left my textbook on crystals in ancient Rome, surprised to see Ms. Peters flipping through the pages.

"Good morning?" I ask as I approach.

She looks up, and her face reddens even more. "Oh, I'm sorry," she says in a breathless, dainty voice. "I was looking for this at the library. Didn't realize you had taken it out."

"You're free to borrow it if you want," I tell her. "Or I can return it to the library, and you can officially borrow it if you like playing by the rules."

"No, that's quite all right. Take your time," she says. She sticks out her hand. "We haven't been formally introduced. I'm Clara Peters."

I shake her hand. It's cold but sticky, like she just put on oil. "Professor Ichabod Crane," I tell her. "You're the kitchen witch."

He'd heard nice things about her. Good with herbs and plants and food. Tinctures. Medicine of sorts. Not unlike a forest or hedge witch.

She nodded.

"How long have you been teaching here for?"

"Four years," she says.

"Ah. So not quite a beginner like myself but not someone with tenure either."

"Actually," she says with a faint, disbelieving smile, "I've been here the longest out of everyone. Most teachers don't last more than a year or two. Vivienne Henry, the woman you're replacing, she was here the longest. Seven years. I thought she would never leave."

Welcome to Sleepy Hollow. May you never leave.

"Why did she leave?" Of course, I know nothing about the teacher whose position I had taken over. I hadn't even thought to ask. "Work get too much for her? The isolation?"

Did students leave dead snakes in her room?

Clara shakes her head, pressing her lips together until they go white. "No. She liked it here. And she was a good witch too. Very powerful. Put on fantastic shows for us. Really believed in the students."

I cross my arms, intrigued. "So what happened?"

She looks a bit nervous. Perhaps I'm pressing too hard.

"She . . . she had a bit of a breakdown. Mentally. Hysteria, they said. One day, she just snapped and said some things about the school that just weren't true. She was acting all paranoid, and then . . ."

"Then?" I prod.

"She was found in the lake. Dead. Everyone said it was suicide."

I was not expecting that. "I'm sorry," I say quickly, feeling bad for asking so much. I should have noticed the signs. "I didn't know."

"No one knew it was coming," she says softly, looking down at her hands. "Until her episodes, she was always so happy. Everyone loved her."

"Sounds like I have some big shoes to fill," I admit, rubbing the tense spot at the back of my neck.

"She was kind, and you seem kind too," she says with a placating smile. "I'm sure you'll do just fine."

I try not to laugh at that. I've been called many things by my students, but *kind* hasn't been one of them.

"Anyway, I better get going," she says, stepping away from the table. "It was nice having this chat. I'll see you later."

"Of course," I say. But as she turns her back to me, I call out softly, "Clara?"

She pauses to look at me, a fretful look on her face, like an animal close to escaping. "Yes?"

I walk over to her, lowering my voice. "You say that she was saying things about the school that were untrue. What sorts of things?"

A dark look comes across her face, her body tensing. "I don't really remember. None of it made much sense." She looks around her, eyes darting as if someone else is listening in.

"Can you give me an example? I'm just curious," I add, smiling at her as if that will help her lower her defenses.

"Just strange things like the school was a trap. That's it, really—the school was a trap, and we were all just flies in a web. She sounded out of her mind, to be honest with you."

"Sounds like it," I say carefully. "Thank you very much, Clara."

She just gives me a quick nod and hurries along her way before I can ask her anything else.

I wonder what else I can find out about Vivienne Henry.

10

Kat

Looks like it's going to rain," Paul says, his focus out the library's ornate windows and not on our textbook at hand. We have only an hour to study up on the Major Arcana before our test with Professor Crane, and we've barely quizzed each other on the card's meanings.

I glance up just in time to hear thunder rumble and see a mass of dark clouds above the row of maples outside, their quivering orange leaves a blazing contrast to the gloom. "It better not," I say. "I have to ride back home later."

Paul gives me a quizzical look. It was only two weeks ago he lent me that pencil and paper on the first day of class, and it already feels like a different lifetime.

"You ride to school?" he asks incredulously. He looks down at my dress, which is maroon and high-necked and better suited for the institute. "I would have thought you'd be carted around in your own private coach."

"Nope. We have a buggy, and I suppose we'll have to pull it

out once the weather really turns sour, but I ride here. Astride too, none of that sidesaddle business." I kick out the layers of my dress, showing how voluminous it is. The fashion these days tends to lean toward a more narrow silhouette, but I never feel as connected to Snowdrop when I ride sidesaddle. I don't care how unladylike it is that I ride astride. That's for women in the cities to worry about.

"All alone in those woods," he comments with a shake of his head, flipping a page in the textbook over and scanning the words.

"Actually, I have an escort," I tell him. "A neighbor's kid."

"Then the kid has to ride all the way back alone in the woods."

I chuckle. "That's true. But the woods aren't scary at all. They're actually beautiful this time of year with the leaves all turning and the smell of frost and woodsmoke in the air. Darkly beautiful. You should go and take a walk. Perhaps go into town, take a look around. Sleepy Hollow gleams in autumn, like a shiny penny."

He gives me a steady look. "You know we can't leave the school. We don't have the same privilege as you."

I ignore the frostiness on the last sentence, even though it was only recently that I learned just how imprisoned the students are. "Have you even tried?"

Paul glances around him warily. The library is fairly busy at the moment, students studying or pulling books off the shelves. The candles flicker at every desk despite there being no draft in the lofty stone building. I think the collective energy of the students agitates the flames.

"No," he says, lowering his voice. "They were very adamant

that we don't leave the campus. Not until after Samhain, and even then, we would go together as a group."

"Doesn't it bother you that they treat you like children? You have to be at least twenty-five. You could be married with children of your own in another life."

"I'm twenty-three, actually," he says, giving me a bashful grin. "And yes, it's peculiar. But who am I to argue or go against their rules? They give us free room and board, and all we need to do in exchange is learn magic." He wiggles his fingers in the air.

"Sounds a little too good to be true," I say under my breath as I dip my raven quill in the tiny vessel of blue ink. Crane is insistent that our handwriting needs polishing too, so he's making us complete the exam in ink instead of pencil. I could use the practice.

"Still, it's silly to keep you here," I add, then groan inwardly when the side of my palm smudges the ink, creating a blue splotch on my skin. "Especially since you won't remember anything of this place when you leave." What are they so worried about?

Though I've been attending school for only two weeks, each day, there are more things and rules that don't make any sense to me. For example, I overheard my alchemy teacher, Ms. Peek, talking about how the linguistics teacher actually has a family back home in India, but he had to leave them behind in order to work here. In general, the school leaders won't accept those who have family since they don't allow students and faculty to bring them, but I suppose he was the exception, maybe because his family is so far away. Perhaps the school wants him to forget his family.

Paul is frowning at me. "I beg your pardon. I won't remember anything of this place?"

My brows go up. Oh. He doesn't know?

"You don't know what happens when you leave?" I ask, and he shakes his head. "You won't remember your time here. Or you won't remember what you learn." I leave out the part where I *do* remember what I learn with Professor Crane for some reason.

Paul rubs his lips together, blinking. "Madness," he says after a moment, flipping another page of the book until we land on an entry about the Five of Cups, a drawing of a weeping figure beneath. "How can they do that? I don't recall signing up for memory erasure."

"I have a feeling it happened when we took our tests," I say. "Though I still can't remember much of mine. Can you?"

"No. But they had said that was normal. They never said that would extend into other areas of our education." He studies my face for a moment. "You must know why they're doing this. You're a Van Tassel."

"Well, don't let that fool you. My mother is very selective with what she tells me. But from what she said, it has to do with the school not trusting the students enough to keep their studies to themselves. They want to keep everything here as secret as possible."

"And when we graduate? Then what?"

"She said the magic is ingrained. All you've learned will come naturally to you."

He gives me a disbelieving look.

"Hey," I go on. "I'm only repeating what she said. I don't agree with it."

"And yet here you are."

"And here *you* are," I counter politely. I tap my quill on the edge of the vessel to get the excess ink off. "Now, back to studying. You know Professor Crane is going to ask the hard questions."

Paul sits back in his seat briefly, tugging at the ends of his gray suit jacket before straightening up again, newly focused on the book. "All right. Write down five things the Five of Cups represents."

This one's easy, I think as I write down the word *grief*.

I wasn't wrong when I said Professor Crane was going to make his test hard. The moment class started, Crane handed out the test paper and silently pointed to the chalkboard, which had the questions scribbled on it as well as the words: *You may leave when you're done.* At least, that's what I think it said. For a teacher, his penmanship is far worse than mine.

Regardless, I took my time with the test. I still feel like I have to prove I should be here, so the last thing I want is to rush through something and fail because I got too confident or lazy. I have been playing with tarot cards since I was young, but the little booklet that came with the stack (which I had stolen from a box in my mother's closet) didn't go into much detail. Some of the cards I had been interpreting the wrong way completely, not knowing all the nuances. The Death card didn't always mean death? That was news to me.

By the time I finish, having taken extra care not to smudge

the ink as I am prone to do, I look up and realize that I'm the last one in the classroom.

I look over at Crane, expecting him to admonish me for taking so long, but his head is in his hands, and his eyes are closed. His black hair is a mess, as if he's been pulling on it, and I notice his socks don't match. He's usually so refined and put together.

I get up and walk over to his desk, delicately placing the test on top of the pile of others.

"Everyone's done," I tell him.

I expect him to jump like he didn't know I was standing there, but instead, he slowly lowers his hands from his face and gives me a tired look.

"Thank you, Kat," he says. Usually his voice is smooth, low, and strong, but now, it sounds faint. Strained. Worried.

I'm about to walk away, but I can't seem to leave him. "Are you okay?" I ask, peering at him.

He sighs heavily and sits back, running a hand through his thick hair. "Is it that obvious that I'm not?"

I give him a tiny smile. "You've looked better. Are we students not shaping up to be the witches you want us to be?"

He gives me an equally small smile in return. "It's not that. It's . . . Actually, I don't even know where to start." He looks away, and I notice the purple hollows under his dark eyes.

"Would you like to go for a walk with me and talk?" I blurt out. I don't know where that came from, but it seems getting him out of this room and talking might help him.

He brings his attention back to me, his eyes raking over my face. "Right now?"

I shrug with one shoulder, trying to appear nonchalant, as if I hadn't come across too bold and eager. "I have a couple of hours before my next class. I usually peruse the library or visit with Snowdrop. That's my horse," I add when he looks confused, "but perhaps some fresh air will do you good. Do us both some good. Sometimes this place can be a little too gloomy." I gesture to the room with its stone walls and narrow windows, the empty cages in the back.

He continues to watch me for a few moments, and I have no idea what he's thinking. Then he gets to his feet. "All right," he says with a conceding nod, patting the stack of tests. "I can always grade these later." His gaze narrows at me. "Just don't think I'll be giving you an A because of this."

"I'm sure I'll earn that A on my own," I say with a confident smile.

He doesn't need to know that I'm bluffing.

"That remains to be seen," he says under his breath as he grabs his coat from the hook and slips it on. He holds the door open wide for me, and we walk down the hall together, our footsteps echoing in the silence until we're through the main doors and outside.

The fresh air immediately feels good. I breathe in deeply, letting the mist that wisps past fill my lungs, my ribs straining against the bones of my corset.

Crane exhales loudly and gives his shoulders a shake. "You're right. This does feel better. In fact, I think until the weather officially turns, we should have more classes outside. Take advantage of it. We could all think more clearly, use the magic of Mother Nature to help us."

I eye the lake and the storm clouds that have gathered at the other end of it. So far, it looks like the rain is staying away from campus.

We walk down the central courtyard path, nodding at students as we pass. They're framed by fading rosebushes and tall stone statues of women holding skulls. The statues look like they've been taken from the graveyards of antiquity, and yet they look appropriate among the flowers. Beauty and death mingling.

"Have you memorized all the students' names yet?" I ask Crane, feeling strangely shy suddenly, like I'm afraid to walk beside him and not talk. I suppose this is the first time I've been with him outside the classroom, not to mention with him alone.

"I have," he says, his hands clasped behind his back. Even when stooped slightly, he still towers over me. He must be at least six foot five. "The school has only forty-two students, and I happen to be good at memorization. Came very handy in med school."

"You went to med school?" I ask. "What happened? Why did you become a teacher instead of a doctor?"

He glances up at the gray sky for a moment, the color mirroring his eyes, before looking back at me. "Would you believe me if I said that teaching is a far more noble profession?"

"No."

He laughs, and the sound pleases me. I think I would like to make him laugh more.

"Fair enough," he says, his eyes focused on the lake as we approach, our footsteps now meeting the fine gravel of a smaller path and crunching beneath our shoes. "It turns out that med school wasn't for me. You know the gift of bestowal I possess?

Well, I didn't know I had it at the time. I didn't know I had the capability to pass on energy. So when we started to work with cadavers—dead bodies—from the morgue to practice, I discovered my touch had the ability to . . . well . . ."

My eyes go wide. "To what?"

"To cause the dead to come awake. Temporarily, of course."

"You're a necromancer," I say in a hush, clutching my hand to my chest.

"No, no," he says quickly. "Not a necromancer. I didn't bring them back to life. I merely just . . . pushed my energy into them." He makes a pushing motion with his hand. "It lasted a second, but it gave me quite the scare. Not to mention, I was surrounded by very sane and normal people. They already thought I was odd with the way my brain works. I couldn't afford for the dead to start speaking to them, or me to the dead. So I quit."

I try to imagine what that must feel like, to have that sort of power to bring the dead back to life, even for just a moment. *He must have felt like a god*, I think. *Perhaps that's why he claims to be one in the classroom. I wonder if that attitude extends to the bedroom.*

My lewd thoughts surprise me, and I immediately shove them away and force myself to pay attention.

"It took me a long time to figure it out too," he goes on. "When you give your energy to someone alive, it's not so noticeable, not to the one giving it. When you give it to someone dead, completely devoid of life force, well, that's a hard one to miss. Nonetheless, I decided I would be better off as a teacher. I'm told I made the right choice."

I mull that over as we continue walking out of the courtyard and away from the buildings. Eventually, the gravel gives way to dirt and a layer of fallen leaves—red, orange, and gold—that ring the shoreline of the lake. Strands of mist hang just above the water like cotton ribbons.

We stand beside each other, our shoes sinking into the earth slightly, and stare at the lake. Its surface is black, reflecting back the surrounding forest like a nightmarish version of itself. I have to look away after a while, as if the lake would pull me under if I didn't.

"So why haven't you been feeling yourself?" I finally ask.

He stiffens, and when I glance up at him, I see a muscle in his jaw tic. "I'm afraid if I tell you, you'll think less of me."

He cares if I think less of him? The admission makes my stomach flip.

"I don't think that's possible," I admit quietly, giving him a shy look. "After all, you just told me you have the power to make the dead come alive, and I don't think I've ever admired you more."

He stares at me in surprise, then furrows his black brows together. "Ah. Well, that's good to know." He licks his lips and turns his attention back to the lake. "I haven't been sleeping well since I got here. At first, I thought it was because I haven't been allowed my drink or my drug."

"Your *drug*?"

"Opium," he says, then eyes me, reading the concerned look on my face. "Don't believe the things you've heard about the opium dens—or joints, as we call them in the city. It's a good drug, and it does a lot to calm the mind, bring you peace and harmony. But your aunt Leona was adamant that I stay sober while at the school, and, well, let me tell you that withdrawing from opium isn't very pretty. So the first few weeks I was here, I was barely sleeping, tossing and turning all night, just praying for a pipe or a tincture. Alas, I had no choice but to deal."

"That certainly explains a lot," I say. Smoking opium? I had heard the stories of men overseas and in the bigger cities smoking it in lurid dens, but I had never pegged someone as proper as Crane to be one of them. It was a dangerous drug; he should know that.

He certainly has many sides to him, I think. *What else does he keep hidden?*

"One would think," he goes on, stooping down to pick up a rock from the shore. He peers at it and turns it over and over in his hand in a rhythmic motion. "But that isn't what's been bothering me. It's what's been happening to me in the middle of the night."

A chill coasts down my neck, and I pull at the edges of my sleeves, wishing I had gloves for warmth. "What's happened in the middle of the night?"

He steps away from me and grasps the rock in his hand and then, with a burst of power, whips it across the surface of the lake, where it skips six times before sinking. Ripples slowly expand. "I've been waking up in a cold sweat, which might be part of the withdrawal, and then hearing my name being called. Or someone crying."

I shiver. "That's unsettling. Is it your neighbor in another room?"

"It's a woman's voice," he states, bending down to pick up another rock. "And in the men's wing, no women are allowed. Of course, I thought perhaps it was Professor Daniels having an affair with the school nurse or something to that end. But that never explained why she called my name. So, of course, I assumed it was Marie."

"Who is Marie?" I ask carefully, ignoring the strange taste of jealousy when I said her name.

"My ex-wife," he says. His expression is blank.

My brows rise. "Oh, I'm sorry. I didn't know you were married. Are you . . . divorced?" I glance down at his hand as if expecting to see a ring, even though I know he doesn't wear one.

"Widowed," he says, winding up and skipping another stone across the water. "She died."

"I'm so sorry," I say again, feeling like my words can't mean enough. The poor man.

"Mmm," he murmurs with a small nod, watching as the ripples spread. "Yes. She died, and, well, sometimes I hear her voice in the night."

"No wonder you haven't been sleeping."

He gives me a pained look. "That's not the worst of it. The voice wakes me up, but then lately, there's been a . . . a . . ."

"A what?"

He sighs and runs his hand over his face. "I don't know. I just don't. I heard this sound outside my door. It wasn't Marie. It was the sound of something heavy dragging itself down the hall. I opened the door, and lo and behold, I saw a trail of blood going down the hallway and a body pulling itself along."

I gasp, nearly falling backward.

Crane is quick. His long arms shoot around my waist, holding me up. "Perhaps I shouldn't be scaring my students so that they faint," he murmurs, and his face has never been so close to mine.

I'm shocked by his story, scared, and yet my eyes are sweeping over his features, noting all the little things I didn't notice at a distance, such as the scar at the end of his left brow or the slightly crooked tip of his nose. I definitely didn't notice the mahogany brown that's flecked in with the gray of his iris that gives his eyes such warmth and depth.

"No," I squeak, conscious of how close my mouth is to his. "I'm fine. I'm fine."

His eyes drop to my lips for a moment, and then he frowns. "Good."

He pulls back and straightens me up, his arms dropping away, distance coming between us.

"Tell me more," I say quickly before he has a chance to change his mind.

He thinks that over and then nods at the buildings. "I will, but only if I can walk you back inside. I'm afraid it's getting a little chilly out, and you don't have a coat."

I want to tell him that I'm always hot, since I'm always wearing so many layers, but I just nod, and we walk away from the shore.

"Not to mention that lake makes me feel uncomfortable sometimes," he adds.

I glance at it over my shoulder, at the darkness. I have to agree with him.

"The energy is palpable."

"Strange energy," I say, nodding.

"Too fitting for a ghost story," he says.

"So what happened?" I prod, our feet on the gravel path again. "You saw the body. Was it a woman? A man?"

"A woman in a nightgown. Always crawling around the corner." He makes a face at that, and I suppress another shudder. "And yet I could never catch up with her. Finally, I saw her go inside my room, but when I went in after her, she was gone. And the blood, which had been very real on the floor, was all gone. The only tangible thing that was left behind was a row of lit candles on my windowsill and a dead snake on my desk, stabbed with sewing needles. Someone had written *Welcome to Sleepy Hollow. May you never leave* in blood."

"My goodness," I say through a gasp. "That's . . . that's . . ."

"Cruel? Horrifying? Diabolical?" he provides. "I thought so too. But when I brought it up with Sister Sophie, she passed it off as a prank. Some students are illusionists, especially second-years, and it's not uncommon to haze the new teachers."

"But the woman in the hallway," I point out. "The blood."

"The blood disappeared," he says, "so that points to illusion."

"But you don't believe that."

He gives me a curious look. "No. You're right. I don't believe that. Especially as it happened again last night. I woke up to hear Marie's voice, her . . . laugh"—a dark look comes over his eyes—"then I heard the . . . body. As it went down the hall. But this time, I didn't want to invite trouble. I stayed in my room with the door locked and waited for the sound to disappear. It took a while, sounded like it was going up and down the hallway for hours, but I refused to open the door. Still barely slept after that."

We stop in front of the building that holds his classroom. "I'm afraid this is where we'll be parting ways today," he says with a slight bow.

"You can't leave me now," I protest. I reach out and grab the collar of his coat. "I want to know more."

"And I have papers to grade," he says, eyeing my hand until I let go of him. "But I promise if it happens again, I'll let you know." He swallows and looks around the grounds. "I have to admit it's nice to be able to tell this to someone who doesn't dismiss the whole thing." His gaze comes back to me, this time with intensity. "You're nothing like the rest of your family, are you?"

"I hope not," I find myself admitting.

He gives me a knowing smile. "Take care, Kat."

Then he turns and walks off, and I know there is so much more he's not telling me.

11

Crane

I'm not sure if it was the talk I had with Kat that helped, someone to listen to what I was saying and not dismiss me as Sister Sophie did, but I finally had a good sleep last night.

Or should I say, I at least managed to ignore the sounds. Marie's accusatory cry and her insults, followed by the thump of the thing in the hallway. But I just put the pillow over my head and counted backward from one hundred, and then, by some miracle, I was out.

Suffice it to say, I woke in the morning feeling in good spirits. Part of me wants to leave the ghosts as practical jokes and move on, while the other has the energy to investigate into Vivienne Henry further. I don't know why the teacher I replaced is of such interest to me. It sounds like she had a nervous breakdown and killed herself. That happens. The isolation probably got to her. The stress. She had been here for far too long.

Yet because I know that ghosts exist and that she did die on the school grounds—in the lake—and I did replace her in a technical sense, I wouldn't be surprised if the ghost outside my door is Vivienne.

Unfortunately, if that's true, it probably means she's out for revenge. A lot of ghosts seek those with magic because our energy is such a draw for them, like moths to a flame. Only on rare occasions are those ghosts actually able to cause harm. If the ghost was also magically inclined before they died, well, that's something I don't want to find out.

Nonetheless, I bathe and get dressed for the day, and before I head out to the dining hall for food, I decide to pull a card from one of my decks.

I pull the Ten of Swords.

To those who dabble casually in the arcane, the Ten of Swords doesn't always mean calamity. A man on the ground with ten swords on his back might mean you're starting over at rock bottom, not certain doom.

But when I pull the card, I see myself on the ground, mimicking the knight drawn on the card deck, my face caked in dirt while I scream for mercy. There is something dark above me, monstrously tall and large, a big black figure that seems to stretch into an endless night sky, the sound of a horse whinnying and galloping hooves. The echo of a blade being drawn.

I push the deck away and sit back in my chair. I certainly wasn't expecting that.

So much for waking up in good spirits.

I take in a few long and deep breaths, flexing my fingers as I calm myself down, reminding myself that my visions aren't always reliable. Then I head out into the hall, expecting to see the body there.

I don't see the body, of course, just Daniels locking up his door. I wave at him and trot over, wanting company on the way to the dining hall so I don't get trapped in my own thoughts again.

"Crane," Daniels says to me with a jovial smile. "How are we this morning, boy?"

He slaps me on the shoulder, his mustache bristling as he talks. Daniels is probably only ten years older than me, but he treats me like a kid. I'll take whatever flattery I can get.

"I haven't quit yet," I tell him as we walk down the hall. "So that's a good sign."

"Aye," he says. "It's a hard place to be at times. But they do take care of us here."

"You've been here for two years, haven't you?"

"That I have," he says as we go down the grand staircase.

"Do you go home in the summer?"

His brows raise. "Home? This is our home, Crane. Where else would I go?"

I shove my hands in my coat pockets as we step into the cool, misty morning, the path slick with fallen leaves. "I don't know. Perhaps the city. Maybe even Sleepy Hollow itself."

"And risk losing my magic?" he asks. "I don't want to forget anything I've learned here."

"They say it comes back," I tell him.

"Have you put that to the test?" he asks. "What if it doesn't, and then I'm useless as a teacher?"

"But you teach philosophy and literature," I point out with a laugh.

"It doesn't matter. My magic is getting stronger here with each passing week. I'm not giving that up. The power, Crane. It's better than fucking."

When he puts it that way . . . "Don't you think that keeps the teachers here indefinitely?"

He shakes his head. "Eventually, they leave. But you might as well put off the inevitable."

I stop outside the doors to the dining hall, touching his arm briefly to pull him to a stop. "Did you know Vivienne Henry well?"

His face goes slack, his mustache pulling down at his mouth. "Not well, no. I suppose there are no secrets here, are there?"

I keep my voice down. "Do you think she killed herself because she wanted to leave? Or because she wanted to stay?"

He lets out a deep harrumph. "I think she was a very tragic woman suffering from hysteria. Sometimes there just isn't much of a story. Now, let's go inside and get some coffee. The weather is far too gloomy for this kind of talk."

"*Did you want* to go for another stroll?" Kat asks me. It's at the end of our mimicry class, and she's hovering by my desk.

I look up from my papers and stare at her for a moment. She's standing here in her pumpkin-colored dress adorned with velvet, a lot more modest than the one she wore on her first day, yet it does nothing to hide her ample curves.

She really is beautiful, I can't help but think. It's the kind of beauty that your brain doesn't process right away because it doesn't seem quite real. Her face is so round and angelic, especially with her blond hair like a halo around her head, but her eyes speak differently. They're full of sass and zest and a maturity that I didn't expect her to have. Not to mention her mouth, which is always talking back and always keeping me on my toes. If it were anyone else, I would have told her off by now, but that smart mouth makes me want to dole out my own form of punishment in the shape of my flat palm on her plump ass.

But of course, I can't afford to think of her like that, sexually or with any affection at all. I wasn't told there were any rules against relations with students, but I also don't want to get myself into any trouble this early in the game. It's a complication I can do without.

I also don't know how she feels about me. She is asking me to go for another walk with her, and she does seem to be focused on me a lot of the time. I'm no stranger to students having their crushes on me. I know that I represent something to them, a person in power and control. But when it comes to Kat, I feel her draw to me might be based on the moments our energies met each other. Her emotions in my body. My energy blocked by hers. It must create a sense of intimacy when you know someone's been sifting around in your brain, in the places you may not even know exist, feeling what you've felt.

"If you're busy, I understand," Kat says quickly, her shoulders dropping slightly, and I realize I've been sitting here and staring at her, not giving her an answer.

"Let's go," I say, and I'm on my feet, grabbing my coat.

We go out the doors and into the autumn afternoon. The

gloom of the morning has lifted, and there's even a bit of blue sky peeking through the high clouds. The fog that hovers around the campus is thinner today, letting enough light in to make you squint. A light breeze blows from the north, smelling of frost.

"Are you not cold?" I ask her, since she's not wearing a coat, though I notice she's at least wearing gloves today.

"I run hot," she says.

"That much I can tell."

She looks at me askew.

"You're hot-tempered," I explain. "I wouldn't know what your body feels like."

Her brows furrow even deeper.

"What I meant was . . . I mean, I have held your hand before, but . . ."

"Tripping over your own words, Crane," she says with a dainty smile. "How very unlike you. You must have been up late again. Another body in the night?"

Crane. Not Professor Crane, but Crane. I like it. So long as she remembers to call me Professor in front of the other students.

"Actually, no," I tell her. "Well, yes, there were the sounds, but I managed to fall asleep anyway."

We stop in the middle of the courtyard.

"To the lake or to the woods?"

The gardens are lovely, but they are peppered with students enjoying the day, and with all the things we're sure to talk about, I don't want them overhearing. I could use the voice with Kat, but she doesn't know how to use it in return.

"How about the woods today? But we can stick to the edges,

walk around the campus that way," she suggests. "I don't feel like being in the dark."

I'm not about to argue with that. We continue to walk along the main path, then converge onto a smaller stone one that goes between a row of tall orange and peach dahlias, heads like giant pinwheels, buzzing with late-season bees. Being in the city for so long, I'd forgotten how soothing nature can be, even when it's dark and electric and heading toward the decay of winter.

"Do you mind if I ask you a few questions?" I ask as we step away from the buildings to where the grass meets the thicket of sweet-smelling blackberries and bramble at the base of the trees.

"Me?" she asks. "I'm the one with all the questions for you."

We walk alongside the woods. "I already answered some. Now it's my turn to ask you."

"Fine," she says with a sigh. "Ask away. I'll have to warn you, I'm quite boring."

"You're anything but boring, Kat," I tell her. "You seduce me."

Her brows raise. "I seduce you?" A hint of color appears on her cheeks.

"Yes. You make me want to know everything there is about you."

She opens her mouth, a peek of her pink tongue coming out to lick her lips, and I feel my cock stiffen in my trousers. Most unwelcome at the moment.

"That's only because you weren't able to see anything in my mind," she says after a moment, her demeanor going from flushed to cool. "You like the challenge. You don't like being told no."

She's not wrong about that, I think.

"I'd like to start by learning more about your family," I go on as we walk side by side.

"Oh, that figures," she says, sounding defeated. "It's never really about me, is it?"

I reach out and grab her gloved hand, pulling her to a stop. "Trust me. It is about you," I say, staring intently into her eyes.

She relents, and I let go of her hand. "All right."

We continue walking. "Tell me, Kat," I say, keeping my voice down, "how often did you see your aunts while growing up?"

"My aunts? Hardly ever. Aunt Leona and Aunt Ana were around when I was a baby, but I don't think I was much older when they and my mother must have had a falling-out."

"Why do you say that?"

"Just the way my father would talk about them. I was always listening—I was always so nosy."

"Still are, I imagine," I interject with a smile.

"That's true," she concedes with a nod. "My father would say that my mother was better off without them. Sometimes he made it sound like she chose him over them."

"They didn't approve of your father?"

"I don't know how they couldn't have. Everyone loved him. He was the nicest man in town."

"I don't think the sisters care much for whether someone is nice or not. They seem to care whether they have power."

"My father was a witch too," she adds, to my surprise. "But I never really saw any magic with him. Or with my mother. In fact, when I was really young, one night when my mother had gone on one of her monthly trips to the school—"

"Your mother went on monthly trips to the school?" I interrupt. "To here?"

"Yes. The days before and after the full moon. She still does. She'll probably be back soon for the next full moon."

"What does she do here?"

"I have no idea," she says.

"You never asked?"

"I was told not to speak about it by my father," she says. "I assume it's some full moon ritual she has to do with her sisters, but my father made me promise to keep my own magic and all talk of magic hidden."

I frown. "Why would he tell you that?"

She shrugs. "He said it was too dangerous for the world to find out what I am. Said I was never to practice my magic in front of anyone, and that included him and my mother. So I didn't . . . for the most part." She trails off with a wistful look in her eyes, and the energy coming off her deepens in grief. "I had a friend. I showed him sometimes."

Him. How curious this feeling of jealousy that she used to show her magic to a male friend. I shake it out of my head.

"Well, I suppose your father wasn't wrong in that. I grew up with a father who was a pastor for the church in our small Kansas town. I didn't even know I was predisposed to magic until the old native man, John, who ran the general store, pointed it out to me one day. After that, he used to visit me in dreams, and it was there I was able to practice and understand. He warned me that my family would never understand and I'd risk being killed over it or locked up in a mental institution, which is more or less the same thing. But to have parents who are also witches . . . feels like a shame to have to bury it."

She watches me for a moment, taking in the information with hunger in her eyes. "I just did what I was told. My father was so adamant about it. And because neither of them ever mentioned their magic or used it in the house, it was easy to pretend we were normal."

"Except when your mother left the house on those full moons."

"Except for that part. I just told myself she was having family time, even though my aunts stopped coming to see us after a while." She stops and points to the stables, which we're now behind. "Want to see Snowdrop?"

"Would love to," I tell her as we walk around the building and to the stalls at the front. There are quite a few stalls, but it seems most of them are empty save for two bay draft horses at one end and a gray at the other.

She stops at the gray, who immediately nickers when it sees Kat.

"Hello, darling," Kat says to the horse, kissing its dark gray muzzle before running her hand over its white forelock. "Crane, this is Snowdrop. Snowdrop, this is Professor Crane."

"You seem to have a close relationship," I comment, their connection quite visible.

"I talk to her when I can't talk to anyone else. My mother doesn't like to listen to anything I have to say, really, and my friend Mary doesn't understand anything of witches or of this school. I'm not allowed to talk about it, even if I could remember it. But Snowdrop knows. I mean, she really knows. She understands my thoughts."

It makes sense that she would have some sort of telepathic aspect with her horse. "Are you able to talk to all animals?"

She nods. "Yes. It's a one-way street though."

"Even so, that's a handy talent to have," I say. "I must admit, I am continuously impressed by you."

"Thank you," she says, giving her horse another kiss.

And now I'm finding myself envious of a horse.

After we spend a little more time with her horse, we continue on our walk, making our way around the back of the school and back down to the lake. She tells me more about her childhood, then about the other classes she's taking here.

"Must be a strange feeling to go home every night and not remember what you learn," I say as we find ourselves standing on the shore of the dark lake again.

"It is," she says. "But I always remember you."

I get the queerest feeling in my chest, a tightness. I swallow hard, staring at her. "You do?"

A faint patch of pink paints her cheeks again. "I don't know why. But I'll remember this interaction with you later. I remember everything you've taught me."

"That shouldn't be possible . . ."

"That's what my mother said."

"Huh," I comment. "Well, I must say, what you just told me is the greatest thing that I could ever hear as a teacher. That what I teach you goes beyond whatever spells or veils they've put up around your memories. That I break through somehow."

She gives me a shy glance, her hands clasped at her front, before turning her attention to the lake. "I can see why that would boost your ego. But I don't think it's about what you've been teaching me. I think it's just you in general. There's something about you that makes you impossible to forget."

That boosts my ego too. I'm struck with this sudden, hungry urge to kiss her.

But given that we are in broad daylight, on campus, I manage to hold myself back. My sexual impulses have gotten me in trouble in the past. It's something I always have to remain in control of.

"That's kind of you say," I offer.

"I'm not being kind," she says, looking back at me. "Just honest." Then, her attention goes to the edge of the lakeshore, where blue butterflies have gathered, their long tongues licking up the water.

"You see those butterflies?" I ask.

She nods. "*Vlinders.*"

"What?"

She laughs, her eyes sparkling. "*Vlinders!* That's Dutch for 'butterfly.' It's what my father used to call them."

"I see. Let's do a little magic, shall we? Can you call those *vlinders* over to you, make them land on you?"

She rubs her lips together as she mulls that over. "I suppose. . . ."

"You're not being graded on this, Kat," I tell her. "It's not a test."

"Feels like a test," she says under her breath.

"I'm merely curious, that's all."

"When aren't you?" she counters. But then she takes in a deep breath and holds out one hand, pointing it at them. She closes her eyes in concentration, and her mouth starts moving soundlessly.

At first, nothing happens. I don't have the ability to talk to animals, so it's not as if I can give her any coaching or pointers, so I can only stand there and watch.

A line between her brows forms as she concentrates harder, her mouth moving faster, and I want to tell her to not give up. Even from where I am, I can feel the energy inside her, ready to go.

And then it happens. One by one, the blue butterflies lift off the shore and start gathering together in a swarm. They bump into each other, the metallic glint of their wings catching the faint sunlight, and then they start flying toward Kat.

"You're doing it," I whisper, unable to keep the excitement out of my voice.

Kat opens her eyes and gasps as the butterflies fly toward her and circle her head. She looks like a goddess or a queen, with them her moving crown.

Then they delicately land on her head, her shoulders, her arms, their wings occasionally opening but content to stay in place.

"Look at you," I say in awe. "Queen of the butterflies."

"*Vlinders*," she says breathlessly.

Yes. My *vlinder*.

She giggles joyfully, spinning around with her arms out, the butterflies sticking to her like glue.

She truly has stupendous power, I think. All those years of having to hide it, being afraid to show it, and it's finally given a chance to breathe.

How powerful she could become.

How powerful *we* could become if our magic were to combine.

Heat creeps through my veins at the thought.

"Kat," I say as she coaxes the butterflies to leave and watches them fly off. "Would you be interested in a little after-hours project with me?"

Her blue eyes meet mine, startled. "After hours?"

"A secret ritual. Here, with me in the dark."

There's someone I'd like to talk to.

12

Kat

The rain held off until I put Snowdrop inside her stall, coming down in torrents while I groomed the sweat from our ride off her. I've always thought of myself as an elemental witch, given the power I have with fire or wind, but lately, I'm starting to think that I may have some influence over the weather directly. So far, it hasn't rained during my rides to and from the school, always just before or after.

Still, I have to run across her paddock to the house, and I'm soaked by the time I get inside.

"Heavens," Famke says as I shuck off my coat. "You almost missed it."

"Almost," I say, looking around. The house has a feeling of contentment and peace with the fire roaring in both the hearth and the sitting room. "Did my mother go out?"

"*Ja*," Famke says, heading back into the kitchen. "She went to see Dr. Fielding."

"Is she okay?" I ask, quickly undoing the laces on my boots.

"She wasn't eating, so I made her," Famke says, sounding more annoyed than concerned, which is a good sign. "She will waste away to nothing if she doesn't eat. As if my food isn't good enough."

"Your food is wonderful, Famke," I tell her. "You know she's never been the same since my father died."

"*Ja, ja,*" she says with a sigh and jerks her chin at me. "Your mother may not be here, but I am. Go take a bath, get into some clean clothes, and I'll get supper going."

I do as she says, taking a long hot bath and getting into my tea gown. By the time I come out into the sitting room, my mother is sitting by the fire. I hadn't heard her, but I knew she'd come in. I could tell by the way the house tensed up, like all the air was sucked out of it.

"Katrina," she says. She's in the rocking chair, and she gestures to the leather chair beside her, the one my father used to sit in every evening with his drink.

My heart wrings at the thought.

I sit down beside her, enjoying the warmth of the fire on my skin. With autumn in full swing, the nights are getting cold. "How are you? Famke said you went to the doctor?"

"It was just a visit to check in," she says dismissively. "Tell me about your day at school. The one teacher you always remember."

My cheeks go hot, and I face the fire, hoping I can blame it on the flames. "It was good. In my mimicry class, I learned to steal one of my classmate's abilities and use them myself."

Her eyes widen, her hands clenching in her lap. "You did what?"

"Only for a moment. His ability was psychometry. Where you can touch objects and gain foresight. Unfortunately, the only thing I was able to touch that gave me any foresight was my pencil. It told me I would lose it later. Guess what? I did. Still don't know what happened to it."

"Dangerous," she mutters, shaking her head, "to remember such things." Then she exhales heavily and gives me a tepid smile. "Dangerous, but . . . I'm also very proud of you. I never thought you would have such potential. Never dreamed of it. Never seemed possible that you could become a greater witch than me."

That's because Papa made me hide it from you, I think. "I wouldn't say that. Nothing too magical about knowing I was going to lose a pencil. But I think I'm getting there. In time."

"You will."

I cough. "Thank you. See, I wanted to talk to you about something. Crane—Professor Crane—he asked for my help performing a ritual next week. It would take place at night, so it would be after hours."

Her hazel eyes skirt over my face, searching. "What kind of ritual?"

I almost tell her the truth.

He wants to contact a dead woman. A dead teacher who drowned in the lake.

And though Crane never told me not to mention it to my mother, I fear I must be cautious.

"He wants to learn how to fly," I say.

"Fly?" She barks out a laugh. "Gods, that is a lofty goal. He obviously has the wrong idea about witches."

"He says I'm powerful and can help. I think he's lonely too," I add in there. That wasn't a lie. I do sense a loneliness in Crane, something he might not see himself. He's not the man to ever admit it, but I am lonely too. I know what it looks like to feel like you've been set adrift.

She pins me with her gaze. "Are you intimate with him?"

I cough in surprise. "With my professor? No!"

"Do you want to be?"

I stare at her for a moment. My cheeks have certainly been going red a lot lately. I look away at the fire. "Mother . . ."

"No, it's the right question. If Brom were still here, you'd be married with a child by now, I'm sure of it."

The sound of his name makes me close my eyes. For once, I don't want to hear it.

"It's all right to have appetites, Katrina," my mother whispers, leaning closer. "For a witch, it's to be expected. Sex is an exchange of power. Of energy. Of magic. I want you to be free to explore whatever you want with whomever you want. You are of the age, my dear child, when you should be doing these things. Even if it happens to be with your professor."

I open my eyes and shift in my chair uncomfortably. "The professor and I are just friends."

"But you are a beautiful, vibrant young witch, and he is a strong, powerful young man."

"How do you know these things?" I say, glancing at her in suspicion. "You said you'd never heard of him."

"If he weren't those things, would you be doing a nighttime ritual with him?" she asks simply. "I think not." She sucks on her lip for a moment in thought. "Just remember the tea."

I frown. "Tea?"

"The tea I made you drink last year. When you were having sex with that farmhand. Joshua Meeks."

I gasp, my hand at my chest, my whole body flushing. "You knew about that?"

She laughs softly. "I am no idiot, Katrina. I knew. I knew. I was happy for you."

Good heavens. I don't like where this conversation is going.

"What about the tea?" I ask, remembering now how she used to make so much tea during that time, though she never did say what was in it.

"Just ask me for it, and I will make it. You can't get pregnant that way."

My body tenses like I've been slapped. I hadn't wanted to get pregnant. After Brom left, I never really thought about it, about starting a family. But the idea that she was giving me a magic tea to ensure I wouldn't get pregnant was . . .

"It was for the best," she says in a forceful voice. "Don't you agree?"

She's right. She's absolutely right. But I should have been able to make that choice for myself.

"So," she goes on, "are you mad at me over this now, or did you want to ask permission to stay out late with your professor? If it's the latter, the answer is yes."

And if it's the former? I think. Still, I'm surprised she's saying yes to this.

"What about Mathias?" I ask. "He can't go so late. Besides, I don't think Mathias needs to escort me to school anymore. And if you're so concerned, Professor Crane can ride back with me."

"The professor shouldn't leave the grounds," my mother says. "But you're right."

"I am?" I look at her in surprise.

"Yes." She folds her hands on her lap, grasping them as if to keep them from shaking. "I'll relieve Mathias of his duties. You must carry a torch with you, but I think you'll be safe on your own now." She stares down at her hands for a moment. "I no longer fear you running off."

I stare at her for a moment, not sure that I heard her right. "You thought I was going to run away? That's why you had Mathias escort me?"

She avoids my eyes. "I was too afraid of losing you, Katrina, and I know you didn't want to go to the school. I could sense your soul being pulled to other places, sense your dreams. You wanted to escape. I couldn't afford to let that happen."

I blink. That is a lot to take in. "You know I could have escaped at any other time. The only thing holding me back was you." I reach out and take her hand. It's so cold, her skin feeling like wax. "I didn't want to leave you, and I won't. And if you want me to stop going to school and stay here with you, I will."

I wouldn't want to. The thought of not attending the institute, of not seeing Crane again, or even Paul, or wandering the grounds and listening to students laugh and practice magic pains me. But I would accept that pain if it meant my mother would feel better.

I swallow the thickness in my throat. It tastes like guilt. "Do you think that's why you're getting worse? Because I'm gone?"

She shakes her head. "No. We don't know what is wrong with me. The doctor said I should avoid all physical activity. And eat more, but, of course, I have no appetite. I'll have to save up all my energy to make it to the school on the full moon."

"That's in a few days. I can take you."

"That won't be necessary," she says. "I can still ride. Chester knows the way. I can practically sleep in the saddle if I wish."

Now is your chance, I think. *Ask her. Ask her.*

"Mother," I begin warily, like I'm approaching a spooked horse. "What do you do when you go to the school? What do you do during the full moon?"

She stops rocking in her chair and looks up at me blankly. "What do you mean?"

"I mean, why do you go? Is it for witchcraft? A ritual?"

She stares at me for a moment, and, suddenly, the room fills with a buzzing sound that gets louder and louder, like a hundred cicadas trapped in here with us, and I almost put my hands over my ears and—

It suddenly stops.

My mother smiles at me. "I like to see your aunts, and they don't like to leave the campus. Full moons are the easiest way to keep to a schedule."

My heart is pounding loudly in my head now, my ears still adjusting to the silence. A cold sweat forms along my forehead.

"You're looking a little tired, dear. Perhaps you should lie down." She gestures to the couch. "Have a nap. We'll wake you in time for supper."

I try to protest, to tell her I'm okay, but my feet move, and I'm up and staggering over to the couch, where I lie down. I fall asleep immediately.

A week later, Crane asks me to speak with him after class. By now, the students don't pay us much attention. They see us on our daily walks around the school. They probably think I'm involved with him romantically, and while that's not true, I don't mind them thinking that either. He makes me feel special.

I walk to his desk, a thrill running up my spine. He looks at me, and I look at him, and it's this clandestine meaning that passes between us, knowing exactly what we're about to do.

Although I actually don't know what we're about to do. All he said to me was that he needed help contacting the lady of the lake, the teacher he ended up replacing who had gone mad and drowned herself in it. He had wanted a little more time to study spells and find out more about her before we performed the ritual. Tonight is the night, but what I'm actually doing as part of this ritual is beyond me. He just told me my energy would be needed.

And I—because I'm apparently a sucker for following his orders—am going along with it.

"Well," I say to him, eyeing the clock in the room. "We have a few hours until it's dark."

"Indeed," he says. "Shall we grab supper?"

I shake my head. "I would rather not eat with you in the dining hall."

He looks so comically aghast that I laugh.

"People are already talking about us," I explain.

"Are they now?" he asks playfully, grabbing his coat. "What are they saying?"

"I imagine they're saying that you are the dastardly seductive teacher preying on his young students, in particular, the ravishing Katrina Van Tassel."

He grins at me. "You got everything right except her name. She prefers Kat."

I laugh, and my stomach tickles like *vlinders* are taking flight. This man is giving me butterflies.

"But I do like this business about me being dastardly seductive. Makes me sound like a menace."

"You are a menace," I say as we walk out the door, and he shuts the classroom behind him. "A menace to the supernatural. Why do you think so many women are haunting you?"

He rolls his eyes at that but then grows silent, his thoughts trapped somewhere as they often seem to be. After all that, we still head to the dining hall anyway. Luckily, the both of us are able to sit with Paul and a few of his friends. They all seem to admire and fawn over Professor Crane, so they don't mind him there. I just stay quiet and let Crane answer a plethora of questions over a meal of roast pigeon and turnip.

It's the first time I've eaten here and the first time I've seen the hall in action at dinner. Usually, I'm riding home by now. In fact, Snowdrop is probably getting restless in the stables, and I make a note of visiting her after this. Until then, I just eat the food—it's not as good as Famke's, but it's pretty close—and by the time the dessert of broiled honeyed apricots and ricotta comes out, I feel strangely at home.

This is what I've been missing, I think, feeling a pang in my chest, an ache for belonging. It's foreign and familiar at the same time.

It's too bad my mother would never let me live on campus. She was so obstinate about her sisters not taking me. In fact, since I've been going to school, I haven't even seen my aunts. Neither Leona nor Ana have ever come to my classes to check on me. Instead, I've only seen Sister Sophie and Sister Margaret, both of whom treat me with a sort of quiet contempt. For how often they seem to deride my mother, it baffles me that my mother comes to visit with them once a month. They might not be related to us by blood, but they are still part of the same coven.

I guess she needs them a lot more than they need her.

I just wish I knew what she really needed them for.

13

Kat

When dinner is over, my stomach full and my heart happy from the company and conversation, Crane makes a trip to the faculty dorms to get supplies while I go check on Snowdrop.

"Hello, darling," I say to my mare, but she seems especially anxious tonight.

"I know, I'm sorry. We will go soon," I tell her, scratching my fingers along her neck.

"You're still here."

I jump in fright and whirl around to see the stable boy holding a lantern and staring at me.

"I am," I say, trying to catch my breath. "I have to stay later tonight. Don't worry about tacking her up for me. I can do that later."

"You shouldn't be here after dark," the boy says flatly. He's not blinking at me, and his eyes seem especially black.

I swallow uneasily. "It's all right. I won't be alone."

"You're never alone. Not when you're here. They'll never let you be alone again."

Then he turns and walks away, disappearing into the night.

I glance at Snowdrop, my heart racing. "Gosh. He must have had a rough day."

I have to wonder if that boy sleeps here. He must. But then, who is his mother if no families are supposed to be on campus? Who takes care of him? The coven?

"Kat?" I hear Crane's voice come from the darkness.

I kiss my horse's nose and then walk toward the lantern that's coming closer to me.

"Did you see a little boy walk past you?" I ask him.

"No," he says, looking around. I've never seen Professor Crane in the dark before. In the lamplight, the shadows under his cheekbones and brows are pronounced, making him look chiseled from marble. Or like a skull. It gives him this otherworldliness that I don't think I've really grasped before.

This man is a witch.

This man is magic.

And he wants me to create magic with him.

"Who was it?" he asks, and I realize I've been staring at him, at the way his hair seems to blend in with the shadows, how dark his eyes look, how they draw me in.

"The stable boy," I say.

In the distance, most of the buildings are dark, with the only lights coming from the dorms and the dining hall, where I'm sure a few people are still lingering over meals. There is no sign of another lantern, like the boy vanished into thin air.

Perhaps he knows shadow magic too, I wonder.

"Stable boy," Crane muses. "Can't say I've ever noticed him."

"He's not staying in the men's wing of the faculty dorms?"

He shakes his head. "No. Perhaps he goes into town like you do. Or maybe he lives in the cathedral with your aunts."

It's only now that I notice that in one of his hands, he's holding what looks to be a black tie. "What's that?"

The corner of his mouth quirks up. "You'll see." He holds out his arm for me. "Come on, let me walk you to the lake."

My stomach flips. From nervousness or something else, I don't know. Perhaps it's everything. Two witches walking into the dark together.

I put my arm into his, and we walk down the path until we reach the main one that takes us close to the lakeshore. The air has a bite to it, and I'm grateful for my warm dress and gloves. But it's also peaceful, the sound of our footsteps punctuated only by the occasional hoot of an owl, so soft that it sounds like a dream.

We stand at the foot of the lake, the water as black as anything. It looks bigger here, feels deeper, seems like it stretches on forever. Mist clings close to the surface, but up above, the sky is clear. I suck in my breath as all the stars come into view, as if the clouds just parted like a curtain.

"I don't think I've ever seen the clear sky here," I say quietly, my neck craned as I stare up and up and up. All the constellations spread out like someone had thrown diamonds in the air and they got stuck there.

"Neither have I," he says. His hand brushes against mine as he lets go of my arm, and for a moment, his finger gently wraps around mine, holding it. "I think you brought out the stars," he murmurs.

Then his fingers start to move up against the back of my hand, touching the edge of my glove. "Can I take this off?" he asks softly.

I gulp. "My glove?"

"I would like to bestow you with what I've seen," he says. "So that you know what we are looking for."

My pulse hammers in my throat, and I turn my head slightly to look at him. He has that zealous look in his eyes that I know he gets when teaching.

"Will you promise to give but never take?"

His face widens in a slow grin, showing off perfect teeth. Still, in this light and with the sharp cut of his features, the effect makes me shiver. "Only this time," he says smoothly. "I like to give, but I love being selfish too."

From the husky tone his voice took on, I get the feeling we aren't talking about the same thing.

"I don't want you trying to read my—"

"I won't," he implores, his fingers curling over the hem of the glove.

Then, with one quick snap, he pulls it off, leaving my skin bare, the cold making goose bumps along my flesh.

He immediately envelops my hand in his, and the energy swarms off him. I feel it, I *see* it, a white glow that reminds me of lightning as it travels up my arm, disappearing under my coat.

Suddenly, the black of the lake fades, and then I'm in a shadowy dorm room. I'm sitting up, hearing a woman laugh and cry, and she calls out, "Ichabod." I hear the thump outside the door. I'm grabbing a candlestick. I'm frightened and curious at the same time. Then I'm in a dark hall, the candlelight swaying. There's a trail of blood. There's the body. The limp gray feet that drag around the corner. I follow it.

The flashes come on fast and leave fast, and then I'm back where I am, staring at the lake and Crane's worried face, his arm around my waist as if I was close to fainting again.

"Are you all right?" he asks, his eyes searching mine.

I gasp for air and nod. "I am. I think so."

He lets go of my waist, and I wish he was still holding me. "What did you see?"

"Everything that you did," I say, trying to catch my breath. "I saw it through your eyes. Had your memories. The cries in the night, the body, all of it."

He frowns, a sharpness to his eyes. "And that's it?"

"That's it," I assure him. Though I have to wonder what else he doesn't want me to see. The more time I spend with him, the more I'm sure he has a lot of skeletons in his closet.

"Good," he says. Then he steps back, places the lantern on the ground, and holds the tie out in front of him between both hands. "Time for me to blindfold you."

"What?" I exclaim in horror.

"I will use you as a vessel."

"A vessel?!" This is getting worse and worse.

"It's possible you will be possessed, but only for a minute or two, just long enough for me to ask Vivienne Henry questions." He says this so plainly, as if he told me what the chef is making for dinner.

"You are not blindfolding me, and you are not using me as a vessel, and you are not opening my body up for possession by some crazy schoolteacher."

He leans in. "But what if she wasn't crazy?" His eyes are wild, the light dancing in them.

"I think maybe *you're* crazy."

"She's after me," he explains. "My energy. My energy is now in you. This is where she died. She will come to you."

"Why the blindfold?"

"Because you need to be totally cut off from this world." He pauses. "And I was hoping you could go in the lake."

"Professor Crane," I snap at him, putting my hands on my hips. "I am not going in the damn lake in my clothes."

"Take off your clothes, then," he says with a lopsided grin, a flare of lust in his eyes that makes me feel hot and dizzy.

"No!" I cry out, giving my head a shake. "You want it so badly? You go in the lake. Or better yet, tonight when she's dragging herself outside your room, ask her then."

He stares down at me with complete focus. "I like to do things on my terms. I want to be in control." Then he gives me his crooked smile again. "Come on, Kat. Be a good witch for me."

I hate that his words are undoing me.

Be a good witch for me? How did he know that praise was a soft spot?

"I'll give you an A," he teases, his voice throaty and deep. "You'll pass all my classes with flying colors."

It's tempting to take it. "I would rather earn my way," I say defiantly. Then I sigh. "But I'll do it for you anyway." I reach out and swipe the tie from his hands and hold it up over my eyes. "I'll be a good little witch."

"Yes you will," he murmurs, his voice growing richer as my world goes black. I feel him move around me, taking the ends of the tie and making a knot at the back of my head.

Then he reaches down and takes my hand in his, and when I try to pull it out of his grasp, he says, "Don't. I'm not trying to do anything to you. I'm just trying to touch you."

A warmth spreads at my core, and I relax slightly. His fingers lace with mine, and he holds me there, as if proving that he can do this without any give or take.

"So is it all a conscious effort?" I ask, teetering slightly without anything to see and focus on. "The exchange of energy when you touch someone's skin?"

"Yes," he says quietly, giving my hand a squeeze. "Otherwise, I'd be wearing gloves all day long. I'd certainly never be able to fuck anyone."

My body goes stiff. The way he said *fuck* makes my knees want to give out.

"And wouldn't that be a shame?" When he says the last word, it's a whisper, close to my face, so close I feel his breath on my cheek.

I swallow hard, my nipples hardening under my corset, heat between my legs. What I wouldn't give for him to touch me all over. What I wouldn't give for him to demonstrate just how he fucks. Would he be cool and demanding? Powerful, like a stern god? Both controlling and wild?

Whatever way he does it, I want it.

"I hate to say this, Crane," I manage to eke out, "but you're being awfully distracting from the matter at hand."

"Mmm?" he says.

Then I feel air between us as he lets go of my hand and steps back.

"You're correct about that. I'm distracting myself. Old habits die hard, I suppose."

"Putting blindfolds on girls is an old habit?"

He lets out an amused grunt. "Let's start the ritual, shall we?"

He goes behind me and places his hands on my shoulders, his mouth coming down to the nape of my neck. He breathes in like he's smelling me. "I'm going to hold you from back here so you can keep your balance. I'm not sure what will happen if Vivienne comes in, but you might be disoriented."

Lord, I feel sick. "Please tell me you've done this before."

"I haven't," he admits, his breath causing me to shiver as he briefly presses the tip of his nose against my neck.

"I feel like you should practice on someone else before me."

"There's no one else with as much potential as you, Kat. And besides, this is just practice. I don't actually think she'll come forth. We'll need to wait until Samhain, when the veil is at the thinnest. That's when we can conjure her on our own terms."

"What are you wanting to ask her, anyway?"

A beat passes. I feel his breath on my hair. It makes me want to lean into him. I want him to touch me everywhere. "I want to know the truth."

"I saw what you saw though. Have you seen any pictures of Vivienne? How do you know that the body in the hall is her or that she's trying to communicate with you? Ghosts just scare people sometimes, don't they?"

"And how many ghosts have you seen?"

"None," I admit. "Unless you count the one I saw through your eyes."

"That doesn't count," he says. "Now, close your eyes. . . ."

"I'm wearing a blindfold," I remind him.

"Close your eyes," he says testily. "And imagine you're in black emptiness. In the voids, the spaces between the veils where so many pass through."

I see the place I was when he was trying to read my memories, the place where I stopped him and ran away. "I see it," I whisper.

"Now, think of people you love who are gone. Think of your father. Those feelings will bring him to you."

"I can bring my father to me this way?" I say, excitement flooding through me. I have so many questions to ask him. Forget about Vivienne Henry—I want to know the real reason my father made me keep my magic hidden. I want to tell him I love him. I want him to come back.

"I don't know," Crane says, his fingers strong on my shoulders. "See if you can. This is what the practice is for."

I project myself inside that space. I think of my father, about seeing him again. I think of reaching out for him, grabbing him and pulling him into a hug. Of long nights spent by the fire, him reading from a book to me, feeling so much love.

But try as I might, he doesn't materialize.

So then I try to think about Brom. I don't know if Brom is dead or alive, but if he is dead, I want to see him again. I want to ask why he left. I want to know if he ever thought of me. I want to know what happened to him.

I picture him, the last night I saw him. His face in the moonlight. How troubled he was. How handsome. How good his hands felt on my body, how much pain he caused, but how that pain turned bittersweet. How it changed me forever. How much power I gleaned from us, from our union. How much I craved that connection again.

If you're out there, Brom, let me find you, I think. *Let me find you, please.*

Crane's grip on my shoulders tightens. "What are you doing?" he whispers.

But I can't answer. All I can do is keep repeating those words and thinking of Brom and hoping he'll lead me to him. Even if he's still alive, maybe I can reach him this way.

Come home to me, Brom, I think.

"Kat," Crane hisses. "What are you doing? What do you see? Don't you feel that?"

It takes me a moment to process what Crane is saying. To realize that beyond this void, there is the real world.

But then I feel it too.

A dark, sinister power seeping into the void. Slowly, slowly, coming on hoofbeats that get louder and louder. Coming for us, coming for me.

And then it appears. A black horse leaps across the void, on its back a horseman with no head. It smells of decay and brimstone, and it's coming to me, bringing with it a world of evil. A world where souls are trapped and screaming to die.

The horse gallops right up to me, and though the horseman

has no head, I still feel its eyes. I feel it looking into my heart and soul.

It's looking for something.

Someone.

But it isn't me.

Then it abruptly turns, rears up, and gallops away, disappearing into the darkness.

And I'm falling backward into Crane's arms, the blindfold ripped off my face as I'm placed on the cold ground, his hands tapping at my cheek.

"Kat! Kat, Katrina, Kat!"

My eyes fly open, and I stare up at Crane's anguished face peering down at me.

"I don't know what happened," I manage to say. For some reason, it hurts to talk.

He puts his arms around my shoulders and helps me sit up, crouching beside me. "What did you see?"

I try to think, but it feels like moving through a swamp. "I don't know. Something big and . . . bad. It was very bad. It was *evil*."

A violent shiver rocks through me.

"I knew it! I had sensed it around us," Crane says, talking fast, that excitable look in his eyes, like a mad scientist.

A mad mage, I think.

"I sensed it, and I knew it was being drawn to you. What happened? Did it get you, touch you?" He runs his hand over my cheek. It feels warm and full of life, and I close my eyes to it for a moment until he takes his hand away.

"It just stared at me. I can't even tell you what it looked like anymore, but it looked at me, inside and out. Inside my soul. It looked at me, and it moved on."

"You don't feel it . . . hitched a ride somewhere inside you?"

I shake my head, though that gives me a splitting headache. "No. No, it left. Can't you feel it did?"

He looks around for a moment, at the stars, at the dark lake, and nods. "Yes. It's gone. Come on. Let's get you up and get you home."

"Get me home?" I ask as he lifts me to my feet.

"Mm-hmm," he says, brushing a strand of hair off my face, my skin singing at his gentle touch. "I'm going with you."

14

Crane

I expected Kat to protest when I told her I was going with her back to her house in Sleepy Hollow. But to my surprise, she not only welcomed the idea, but she was insistent I not just walk beside her but ride her horse with her.

A perfect gentleman would have told her that he'd prefer to walk, to keep space between them.

But I am not a perfect gentleman.

Truth be told, I'm not a gentleman at all.

I'm a deviant.

And she knows that too. She knows it and yet invited me to be as close to her as I've ever been. As soon as we walked back from the lake and tacked up her horse, I was swinging onto Snowdrop's back and pulling her up along with me.

"Are you comfortable?" I ask her. I'm sitting in the saddle, and she's basically in my lap, the heft of her backside pressing against my cock, which is painfully stiff. I know she can feel it—I'm a tall man, and my cock is equally as impressive—but she doesn't seem to mind. Still, I don't want to make her uncomfortable. "If not, I can dismount and lead you."

"No, it's fine," she says with a small shake of her head. Her voice is small and delicate, but there's something else there. A rawness. Something carnal that makes my blood run hot.

Is it possible that she not only feels me . . . but likes it?

I try to adjust myself just in case, but it's impossible not to be turned on when she's so close to me and after all the magic we just played with. "Are you sure you're comfortable?"

"Yes," she says softly. She leans back against me, and she adjusts her grip on the reins as Snowdrop plods along the path away from the stable. I lean forward slightly and put my hands over hers, holding them for a moment before I move them out of the way and take over the reins.

"I like to be in control, remember?" I murmur against her ear.

She smells heavenly. Like orchids and sex. I'm sure she's not even aware that I can pick up on this, but when she was in that other place, her body was in a state of arousal. It's not that I have preternatural senses normally, but I feel like having been inside her head—and having her inside of mine—has linked our bodies together. I can smell her provocation, feel the heat coming off her body. I figured it wasn't her father she was looking for between the veils but someone else, someone who made her aroused.

I want to find out who it was she was looking for, who she was thinking of.

I want to make her forget them.

"You don't need to remind me," she says, her voice a little breathless.

I move my nose to the nape of her neck. "Are you sure about that?"

Her breath hitches slightly, and I grin. I enjoy toying with her like this, playing these games, pretending that the energy we have when we're together isn't capable of becoming something powerful. I remember the dark feelings I saw in her head, that lust and arousal, and I want that from her. I want it to swallow us both. I can only pretend to be a proper teacher for so long before the urges come out to play. The urge to be her teacher in other ways.

I guide Snowdrop along the path that heads to the gates, and with each moment we approach them, I can't help but fear what might happen once we pass through.

What if I don't remember her at all? What if all my memory goes, not just of the magic I learned while at this school, but of the ritual tonight, and Vivienne Henry, and how Kat has been making me feel?

What if it doesn't let me leave the school at all? What if there's an invisible force that will hold me back and only let her return home?

I don't want to lose her tonight. I don't want to let her go.

"Who were you thinking about in the veils?" I ask her.

"W-what? Why?" Her body stiffens against me, which in turn makes my cock stiffen against her backside even more.

"Because I'm jealous," I admit, my voice dropping. "I know you were thinking of someone you've lain with. Someone who has touched you, made you come." I whisper the last word.

She swallows audibly, shifts in her seat. The friction against my cock makes me let out a hiss of breath, my eyes closing for a moment, and I take one hand off the rein and reach for where the petticoats of her dress are bunched up at the front of the saddle.

"Does this disturb you?" I whisper into her hair. "That I know this? That it turns me on? That I want to do that to you?" I run my lips along her earlobe, and she shivers. She tastes like sunshine and flowers. "Would you like me to do that to you?"

She lets out a needy yes, so faint that I barely hear it. But I know her body wants it too; it's in her smell, the way she's both tense and soft.

I slide my hand under the layers of her dress, my palm coasting over her drawers, up her thigh, until I meet where the fabric splits apart, lined with lace. "You can tell me to stop," I murmur, my fingers inches away from her bare skin. The heat that's coming off her is like an inferno.

"I won't," she says, leaning back against me, and I place my mouth on her upper neck, my lips kissing and sucking at her skin, reveling in the taste of her. She groans, and when I slide my forefinger along where she's so slick and warm, her groan deepens, her chest rising and falling with heavy breath. "God, please."

I moan, my cock begging for release already. Just hearing those words, I feel close to coming in my trousers.

"You know I love it when you see me as God," I tell her, biting her earlobe. "Let me rule you as one. Let my power revel with yours." I slide my finger farther along her wetness until it's plunging inside of her.

She lets out a breathless cry, a sound I've only dreamed of hearing from her lips. These past weeks, I've watched her and wondered what it would sound like when I made her surrender to me. She clamps around my finger like a vise.

"Yesssss," I hiss in her ear. "Let me rule you. Let me teach you, my *vlinder*. Let me set you free so that you can fly."

Let me make you forget that other man existed.

I plunge another finger inside her as the horse walks on toward the gates. I feel like I'm racing against the clock, that I'll remember none of this when I cross over, and what if I don't remember what happens on the other side? I want to remember the feel, the sound of her coming on my hand, coming because of me.

"Will you let me make you come?" I whisper to her as she starts to buck against my hand.

"Yes," she says shakily.

"Ride my fingers, not the horse," I tell her, and I start driving my fingers in and out as she writhes against me.

We're at the gates now. They slowly swing outward, as if ushering us off into the night. I want to remember this.

I want to remember this magic.

This power.

I slide my thumb over her wet, swollen clit, and then she's crying out, her voice rising in a steam of breath and echoing into the night sky.

"Oh God! Oh my God!"

She's loud enough that it carries across the lake, and I'm sure someone in the dorms is looking out of their windows now, wondering who is up to what. But we're in the dark, and no one can see us, and even if they could, I wouldn't care.

Her body spasms and jerks, and the energy that moves through her and onto me is unlike any I have felt before. I don't see into her mind, I don't see her memories, but I feel her, every inch of her, like a current runs from her to me, connecting us. It brims with power and destiny.

I only felt connected to one person like this before and never had the chance to explore it more. But with Kat, I do.

Lord, I hope I do.

She's still writhing against my hand, grinding against the saddle and my cock, and it's hard not to come myself. I want nothing more than to shove her forward so she's lying against the horse's mane and pull up her skirts, thrust my cock into her as deep as it can go. She's already so wet she'd be able to take me.

But before I can do any of that, we're riding through the gates, through a cold sheet of air that makes the pressure in my head build until it feels like it will pop. It feels like being doused with ice water.

"Fuck," I grumble, making a fist around the skirt of her dress. "What was that?"

"I think that was the wards," Kat says in a small, strained voice, still sounding breathless. "I suppose you'll forget everything that just happened, won't you?"

I brace myself as the horse walks on, the pressure in my ears alleviating until finally it clears. I try to hold on to the memory of her coming on my hand moments before: the sound of her cries, the way her desire dripped through my fingers, how she let me blindfold her at the lake, the way she trusted me to hold her hand, to give and not take.

And then . . .

Nothing happens.

I feel the same as before.

I haven't forgotten a thing.

"I still remember," I tell her, placing my lips at the back of her head. "I remember the soft, wild noises you make when you come. How you made me feel like a god, whether my fingers are inside you or you're in class, gazing up at me with those hungry eyes of yours. What a good sweet witch you are."

I can't see her face clearly, but I know her cheeks are burning. "You remember," she muses softly. "And I remember you. We remember each other, no matter what the coven has protecting the school. What does that mean? Why us?"

She twists in her seat to try to face me, but I drop the reins and reach for her face, holding it back toward me as I kiss her. She's so sweet and hot, her lips and tongue like a taste of heaven.

"I want you," I murmur against her lips. "I want to come inside you."

I want to know what happens when the energy we create inside of each other explodes.

She breaks away from the kiss and looks around, breathing hard again. The lights of the school have faded into the background, and while we didn't bring a lantern with us, my eyes have adjusted enough to see the dark trail ahead of us while it cuts through the woods. The horse can see even better than we can. We are alone out here, and while I don't remember how much time we have before we hit the village of Sleepy Hollow, I know it's more than enough.

I run my mouth down her neck, realizing I may be coming on too strong, despite what we just did. "I'll do whatever you want."

She lets out an amused breath. "Is that so? I thought you always had to be in control?"

"Doing whatever you want *is* me being in control," I tell her. "So long as I'm giving you pleasure."

"Mm-hmm," she muses, resting back against me. "You know, you're pretty good at making someone forget things."

"What do you mean?" I ask, my hands taking over the reins again.

"The ritual," she explains, her voice dropping a register. "I was terrified of the whole ordeal, and yet how quickly you were able to wipe that terror from my mind. How quickly my body moved on under your touch. Is that part of your magic?"

I scoff. "It's not magic, Kat. It's that terror heightens our emotions. Our senses. Our hearts beat like hummingbirds, and all that energy needs a place to go. Sex is the perfect place to put that energy. The terror only makes it more divine. It primes it."

"Do you make a habit of making women climax after they're scared? Do you have a habit of scaring them?"

"Sometimes," I admit. "Men too."

I hold my breath and wait. Witches, as a whole, are open-minded when it comes to different forms of sexuality. I like to sleep with both men and women. But Kat comes from a small town and wasn't quite raised as a witch. It's possible she's not as tolerant as I hope. I wasn't even aware of my sexual preferences until I moved to San Francisco. Ironically until after I was married.

"Oh," she says softly.

"Does this displease you?" I ask, my jaw feeling tight, ready for some form of rejection.

She swallows and shakes her head. "Not at all. I've just never . . ."

"Never been with a woman? Never knew a man who'd been with men?"

"Never to both of those," she says. "But I'm okay with the idea of it." She glances at me over her shoulder, her eyes bright even in the darkness. "At least with the idea of you with other men. You seem so worldly, and I feel so sheltered."

"You won't always be sheltered," I tell her. "One day, you'll move someplace far away from Sleepy Hollow."

A moment of silence passes. An owl hoots from the forest. "Will you come with me when I do?" she asks. Her voice is so delicate and shy that it sends a bolt of anguish through me, this unbearable urge to protect her.

"I would like that," I tell her sincerely. "Where would you like to go?"

"Anywhere," she says, her shoulders relaxing. "Anywhere at all. Manhattan seems nice."

I tense up.

She quickly adds, "But I know you came from there. So maybe that's for some other time." She pauses. "Do you have bad memories from New York? Is that why you came here?"

I sigh heavily, the past feeling too close at times. "New York, no. It was a blur of opium. A lot of being poor. I should have worked, but I didn't. I just wanted to forget everything. I wanted to be someone else."

"Did you break any hearts there? You must have."

I chuckle. "No. No, but I was close to having my heart broken."

"Really?" She sounds so surprised. "By a man or a woman?"

"Does it matter?"

"I'm sorry. I was just curious."

I rest my chin on her shoulder, embracing her from behind. "I know you are. Being curious is the way to my heart. And it was a man. A poor, broken soul on the run from something I didn't understand. He was truly haunted, sick in the head, and yet beneath all his turmoil, I saw someone worth saving. After all, I was running from something too."

Myself.

"Did you try to read his memories?" she asks.

I swallow uneasily, feeling shame. "Yes. I tried. I needed to know what ailed him, what he was running from. But we were only together for a couple of weeks, and I experienced the same thing I did with you."

"What do you mean?"

"He blocked me. I couldn't read him. I could only feel what he felt, and there was a lot to sift through on that alone. I didn't push it. I didn't talk to him about it or whether he was aware he was blocking his mind from me. Then one day, he was gone. On the run again. I still don't know if it was something I did that made him flee or that he had something that was hunting him."

She grows silent at that, and I can tell her mind is working.

"That sounds terrifying," she eventually says. "To feel someone you're with is being hunted."

"It was. But what did I say about terror leading to sex?"

"It leads to magic."

It led to magic. I had magic with that man. He was so wild and unpredictable, wearing every single emotion on his sleeve. He felt everything in the same ways that I feel everything, but I'm always trying to run from it, hide from it, bury it under layers of aloofness. He ran right into it. Embraced it wholeheartedly. He was so damn messy in every aspect of his life.

And he loved it when I ruled over him. He was tall, though

not as tall as me, and his muscles were huge. He was built like an ox, so strong and sometimes dangerous, and yet he'd let me dominate every single inch of him. The man sucked my cock like no one else had ever done before.

But I feel no need to dwell upon it. He was gone.

I've moved on.

"What was his name?" she asks.

"Abe," I tell her. "Never gave me a last name."

"Where did he—"

"Shh," I say to her, cutting her off.

In the distance, I hear the sound of hoofbeats.

"Do you hear that?" I whisper, steering Snowdrop to the side of the trail just in case. Blackberry bushes reach out and scratch along our arms, pull at her dress.

"What are you doing?" she whispers as we duck under a branch.

"I hear a horse," I tell her as the sound gets faster, louder. "They're coming fast. I think they're on the trail, but . . ." I turn my head behind me, seeing only darkness, then look forward again. "I can't tell where it's coming from."

She lets out a small gasp. "Do you think they're after you? For escaping?"

"It's not a prison, Kat," I tell her, but even so, I don't feel so sure. Could it be one of the sisters out to get me and drag me back to the school? If that's the case, I'm not going, no matter what they do. If I have to punch an old witch in the face, so be it.

"You could be in trouble for, uh, what you did to me," she notes. "Maybe they saw or heard."

"Did to you? I'll have to remind them that you were a very willing participant."

"That might not matter," she says, and the hoofbeats are closer now.

She opens her mouth to say something else, but I slide my hand over her lips to keep her quiet and then pull Snowdrop to a stop. Luckily, the horse doesn't make a noise, but its white coat will be noticeable in the dark of the woods.

I think about maybe taking the horse into the thicket and out of sight, and perhaps the rider will pass on by without noticing us. There's also a chance that it's not someone after us at all, but—

"Ichabod!" Kat cries out. She's staring over my shoulder in horror, and I quickly whip around to see a big black horse just feet away, galloping toward us at full speed. Steam rises from its body, and on top of the giant horse is an equally giant man, dressed all in black with an ax at his side.

He doesn't have a head.

He doesn't have a fucking *head*.

It's just like my tarot card vision, I think. *This is what I saw.*

And just like that vision, I know what's going to happen next. Snowdrop will rear, and I'll fall off, and this headless horseman will pull out his ax and take off my head.

This is how I'll die.

"No!" Kat screams at the horseman as he's upon us now, a black creature of death in the night, built from bones of fear, and he brings his ax in the air.

I cover Kat with my body, shielding her from the blow as Snowdrop whirls around and rears. I try desperately to keep us both on the horse while also trying to keep Kat from harm, and just when I feel myself slipping, Snowdrop's hooves meet the ground again.

I glance up, ready to feel the slice of the blade in my neck, only to see the big black horse snort at me, its face inches from mine, and though the man remains headless, I can feel him staring at me.

Then he kicks at his horse, and it spins around and starts galloping down the trail toward Sleepy Hollow.

I straighten up, and Katrina lifts up her head, watching as the horseman disappears into the night. "He's going into town!" she cries out, glancing at me over her shoulder. "We have to warn my mother!"

15

Kat

How quickly things went from a dream to a nightmare. One minute, I was being pleasured by Crane's fingers atop my horse; the next, we were about to be killed by a horseman with no head.

The most frightening, mind-twisting thing about all of this is that I've seen him before. Inside the void, in that place between worlds and dimensions where I was searching for Brom. I saw the headless horseman, this entity of evil. And now he's here.

In this life.

In my life.

And yet, just like it happened in that black, empty space, he didn't hurt me. It seemed like he wanted to, but he didn't, like he wanted someone else instead and couldn't be bothered with me.

"I fear he wants my mother," I shout to Crane after I explain what I saw in the void. We gallop on the dark trail heading toward Sleepy Hollow, Snowdrop with her head down, going as fast as her hooves will take her.

"What makes you say that?" he says, his mouth close to my ear.

"I don't know," I admit. "I just have this feeling that the horseman is after someone I love. Like it's looking for them." I don't have anyone else left that I love. Though lately, I worry I'm falling *in* love with Crane. Which leaves my mother, the only family I have left, plus Famke.

"And you've never seen him before tonight?"

"I think I'd remember if I did," I point out. "This is the first time I've heard of a headless horseman, let alone seen one." And still, that horrible feeling of dread won't go away. *Come on, Snowdrop*, I urge her silently. *Go faster if you can, please.*

My mare snorts in response and somehow manages to pick up the pace, and it's not long before we're thundering past Wiley's Swamp and out of the woods and going across the covered bridge that spans Hollow Creek, her hoofbeats echoing like a thunderstorm. We gallop down the lane past Mary's farm, all the lights in her house off. Beyond the heavy snorts from Snowdrop and the sound of Crane's ragged breath in my ear, I don't hear anything else. No screams, no sounds of another horse or anyone being bludgeoned to death with an ax.

Finally, we make it to my house, the white siding bright under the pale moonlight, a few windows glowing from the inside. It feels like a safe place despite everything.

"Mother!" I yell at the house as Snowdrop comes to a skidding halt, dirt flying. Crane practically jumps off the horse before reaching up and snatching me off the saddle by the waist and placing me on the ground.

The front door swings open, and my mother comes flying out, pulling a scarf around her shoulders. "Katrina!" she exclaims.

"What's wrong? What's happened?" She looks over at Crane, bewildered. "Who is this?"

"I'm Professor Crane," he says, extending his hand. "Pleasure to meet you, Ms. Van Tassel."

She frowns at him and then turns back to me, ignoring his hand. If I wasn't so upset already, I'd be angry at her for being so rude to him.

"Did the ritual go all right?"

The ritual. I pause for a moment, wondering if the ritual caused the horseman to appear.

"It was fine. Nothing happened, but . . ." I glance at Crane, and he gives me an encouraging look. "We saw something on the trail when we were riding home."

Her frown deepens as she looks at him. "Why did you go with her? You know you're not supposed to leave the school."

Crane opens his mouth to say something, but my mother turns back to me.

"You shouldn't be breaking so many rules."

"There's no rule against it," Crane says stiffly. "For teachers, it's merely discouraged. At any rate, I didn't feel comfortable with your daughter riding home alone on a night like tonight, and you should be glad I went with her."

"We saw a horseman," I fill in. "A headless horseman."

"The Hessian," Famke's voice rings out, and we turn to see her standing in the doorway to the house, wringing her hands together. "It's the Hessian."

"Who is the Hessian?" I ask.

My mother holds Famke's gaze for a moment, something unreadable passing between them. Then she looks back to me, her forehead wrinkled. "The Galloping Hessian of the Hollow. He's a ghost, a spirit of a man who died during the Revolutionary War. Was decapitated by a cannon. He's the legend of Sleepy Hollow."

"I've never heard of him before now," I say. I glance at Crane briefly. "Neither has he. Doesn't sound like much of a legend."

"He hasn't been seen in fifty years," my mother says. "There were stories about him aplenty when I was growing up." An odd look comes over her face. Her eyes seem brighter, like this whole thing excites her. "I'll have to tell the sisters."

Strange that she calls them *the* sisters and not *her* sisters.

"Why?" Crane asks. "Because the horseman came from the direction of the school?"

"Yes," she says, pressing her hands together. "Perhaps you opened a window with your ritual. The sisters should know. If the Hessian starts to kill again, they may be the only hope to put him back where he belongs."

"Excuse me?" Crane says incredulously, his brows shooting up. "Kill again?"

I look to my mom with an equally bewildered expression. "What do you mean kill again? He's killed before?"

"*Ja*," Famke says, still hanging by the door and looking around nervously. "They say he cuts the heads off people he meets in the night."

"They say, or he actually does?" Crane asks. "Because fact over speculation is of the utmost importance here."

"And he didn't chop off our heads." I push at mine as if to demonstrate it's still on my neck.

"Speculation," my mother says patiently, giving Famke a warning look. "Don't listen to her."

"No, but it's true," Famke refutes. "I was a child when it happened. You wouldn't remember, Sarah. You were too young." She looks to me and Crane. "It happened when my family arrived from Holland. I remember that one of the clergy at the church had gone missing. No one knew what happened to him. And then the killings started. Two of the other clergymen were discovered with their heads missing, one in Wiley's Swamp, the other in Hollow Creek beneath the bridge."

Crane makes a face. "Charming little town you have here. You left that out of the brochure."

"So then he's back," I say. "What does that mean?"

"It means the both of you will stay here tonight. Crane"—she nods at him—"you can have the guest bedroom. Katrina, you're sharing my bed tonight."

"Whatever for?" I say as she puts her hand on my shoulder and ushers me toward the house. I would have been a baby the last time I slept with my parents.

"This whole thing has me frightened," she whispers. "And I am feeling weak. I don't wish to be alone."

Oh. Well, I can't refute that. I look at Crane over my shoulder, but he's staying behind with Snowdrop, stroking her neck.

"I'll put her away in the stable for you," he says, and starts leading her along the side of the house, and I mouth my thanks.

"You could have been nicer to the professor," I whisper to my mother as we step into the warmth of the house. It smells like honey, woodsmoke, and spices.

"Why should I? He's the one who broke the rules. Be glad I'm not making him sleep in the barn."

"What happened to all the things you said last week about being intimate with him? You were encouraging it."

She gives me a sharp look. "Do you need the tea?"

"No," I hiss at her as I start taking off my coat. "I haven't . . . we haven't . . . there's no need."

She leans in and peers at me closely, then grabs my chin and moves my face around. "Are you certain? Because there's certainly a change in you, Katrina."

"I'm certain."

"Good," she says in a clipped voice, letting go of my face. "Time to adjust your expectations about him. He's your teacher, nothing more. A ghoulish fellow too, at that, with those haunting eyes and cheekbones and skin like a ghost."

I don't know what to say. How quickly she's changed her tune about him. "I don't understand."

She stoops down and unlaces my boots. "There's someone better out there for you." She looks up at me and winks, which is most unnerving. "You'll see."

"I've put on the kettle for some tea," Famke says, coming out of the kitchen. "I'll go make sure the guest bedroom has everything he'll need."

Moments later, Crane comes in, smelling like frost. "She's all settled and happy," he says to me, taking off his coat. "She's a good horse."

My mother just stares at him before she walks off into the kitchen.

Crane comes over to me, leans down, and whispers, "I don't think she likes me very much."

"I'm sorry," I say, looking around to make sure no one is watching before I reach up and place my hand on his cheek. "I don't know why she's being like this."

"She's just looking out for her daughter," he says with a smirk. "I wouldn't trust anyone around a man like me either."

I'm about to tell him that there's nothing wrong with a man like him, but then again, I am his student, and he did just ravage me with his fingers while on the back of my horse.

"A cup of tea before bed?" my mother asks, coming out of the kitchen holding two steaming mugs. "I picked it from herbs in the garden. They'll help calm you down and sleep. I can't imagine the nightmares you might have after such an ordeal."

Crane and I take the mugs from her. I sniff mine. Crane does the same. It smells warm and soothing, cinnamon and orange rinds. It's not the tea I was thinking of.

"Smells like nettle," Crane says before blowing on it. "One of my favorites. Alleviates pain. Soothes the nervous system."

"You seem to know a lot about it," my mother says tritely.

"He went to medical school," I speak up, but Crane gives me a look, wishing for me to stay quiet.

"Oh?" she says, looking a little more interested now. "And why did you go the teaching route instead? You preferred to be poor?"

Crane chuckles at that. "I preferred being able to help people in whichever way possible." He blows on his tea again and has a sip. "So, is this your witchcraft? Herbal teas and tinctures?"

My mother shrugs lightly. "I suppose. It's not very fancy, is it?"

"No, but if it works, it works. It's magic all the same. It's healing people, helping people, wouldn't you say? Tell me, Ms. Van

Tassel, for I've been very curious about you. Why don't you teach at the school? Surely your skills and knowledge would go a long way, given your family name."

That was a question I had wondered too and yet never asked. But Crane gets right down to brass tacks.

My mother presses her fingertips together, and I can see she's thinking. "I'm afraid you think too highly of the Van Tassel family name," she says. "I may be Leona and Ana's sister, but I haven't been part of their coven for a long time."

That takes me by surprise.

"But I'm not a part of their coven either, and I teach at the school," Crane points out.

She gives him a stiff smile. "Yes. And perhaps you're a much better teacher than I could ever be." She nods at us both. "Now, finish your teas, and off to bed. I'll be making the journey with you to school tomorrow. I may not be part of their coven, but the sisters need to know what you saw."

I want to tell her that we can inform them ourselves—it's about time I saw my aunts—but then I stop myself. I want to see how my mother is on campus. I mean really watch her and watch how the sisters interact with her. There's something about their relationship that nags at me, but I can't put my finger on what it is.

"Well," Crane says, bowing slightly to my mother. "Thank you for the tea and your hospitality. I better go get ready for bed."

He turns to me, and our eyes lock. I don't want to be apart from him, not tonight, maybe not any night. I think from the intense look in his dark eyes, he doesn't want it either.

But then he heads toward his room just as Famke comes out of it, showing him around, and my mother steps in beside me.

"There's one man for you, Katrina," she whispers in my ear. "And that man is not him."

The next morning, we rise with the dawn. The roosters crow from the yard, and golden light streams through our windows. I'm curled up in the corner of the bed, alone, forgetting I'm upstairs in my mother's room. I think I slept like the dead; the tea probably knocked me right out.

I get up and slip on my dressing gown, surprised to find Crane already up and reading a book by the fire. He glances up at me as I walk down the staircase and grins.

My heart does a little dance in my chest. I don't care what my mother said about him looking like a ghoul—he's certainly beautiful.

"Good morning," I say to him, feeling stupidly shy at having him see me so early in the morning, despite how intimate his fingers were with me last night.

"Good morning," he says, his smile getting deeper, one that makes me feel weak at the knees.

"Katrina, get dressed and get ready," my mother barks as she bustles out of the washroom. "We need to leave soon."

I roll my eyes and get ready as quickly as I can. Then we have a quick breakfast of a few hard-boiled eggs and bread, which Famke was very insistent we eat.

By the time we're out in the stables, getting the horses tacked and ready, the sun has already burned off the layer of fog that was sitting on our pastures and over the Hudson. The water sparkles now like a mirage.

My mother gives Crane my father's old horse, Gunpowder, a sway-backed dapple gray who is still strong but only gets more stubborn over time, and once she's on top of her sorrel gelding, Chester, we're off and riding toward the school.

It's a brilliant morning, clear blue skies and the air scented with bonfires and the last of the season's blackberries, October only a couple of days away. Goldenrods that dot the lane sway in the breeze, and I'm having a hard time reconciling this bucolic morning with the terror of last night. Is it possible that it all happened? Could it have been an illusion, not an actual ghost of a soldier?

And if it was an actual ghost, this Hessian, where was it going? Who was it hunting?

My mother is riding between me and Crane, and I try to catch his eye, but his focus is elsewhere. I want to talk to him in private about last night, about everything. But even if he did use his so-called voice, where he speaks inside my head, I don't have the ability to respond. And there's a chance that my mother would hear it. There's so much of her magic I don't know about.

Eventually, we reach the school and go our separate ways after handing our horses to the stable boy, who seems a little less spooky now in the daytime. My mother takes off for the cathedral building to talk with her sisters while Crane and I walk toward the center courtyard.

"I know I'll be late, but I need to get changed," he says, coming to a stop. He's close, almost too close if anyone were to be watching, but he doesn't touch me. "Are you all right?"

"No," I admit. "I want to be alone with you. I want to talk to you."

He swallows and gives me a quiet smile. "And I want to be alone with you. More than you know, my *vlinder*. Our afternoon walk will have to suffice."

"Okay," I say with a nod, hating how strangely desperate I'm feeling for him. I feel scared for reasons I can't explain. It's not just that we encountered the horseman last night. It's everything. It's the way Crane made me feel, the power I felt when I came on his hands, this need to grab him and get as close to him as possible. I ache for him, both physically and emotionally, maybe even spiritually.

"I would die to kiss you right now," he says, leaning in closer, his charcoal eyes burning on my lips. "And I would happily accept that death." Then he pulls his head back. "I'm not a patient man, Kat, but it will have to wait. I promise it will be worth it." He gestures to the dorms. "Will you wait for me while I get changed?"

I nod, and he casts a cautionary glance around him before hurrying off to his dorm.

I exhale a trembling breath, my whole body feeling jittery, and stand there on the path as he runs into the building. There's so much to try to make sense of, and I feel like my brain isn't keeping up.

Thankfully, Crane doesn't take long, and he's back in a few minutes. "How do I look?" he says as he takes long, quick strides toward me, tightening the buttons at his collar. "Do I look like I spent the night at the Van Tassel farmhouse?"

I laugh, reaching out and straightening his necktie. "Not at all." Truth be told, all his suits are dark and look the same anyway.

We hurry along toward the classroom, and with my short legs, it's hard to keep up with him—he covers so much ground when he wants to. Crane anxiously checks his pocket watch. "Well, a few minutes late won't kill anyone," he says. "I'm sure one of the teachers has already unlocked the classroom."

He opens the door to the building for me and ushers me inside. By the time we reach his classroom, I'm already out of breath.

Someone did unlock his door for him, and the chatter of the students rolls out into the hall.

We stop inches away, and I look at him to ask if it would seem wrong for the both of us to enter the room together. He taps my bottom with his hand, telling me to go first.

I give him a coy smile and then step into the classroom.

Everything looks the same as it usually does except for one big difference.

There's someone sitting in my chair.

And it's not just anyone.

No . . .

It can't be.

I feel all the blood drain out of me, my vision growing fuzzy, and I fear I'm about to faint.

It's like looking at a ghost.

The ghost of Brom Bones.

He's sitting in my seat and staring right at me with those achingly familiar brown eyes of his, so dark they're almost black. He's older now, with a dark beard, and he's so broad-shouldered and Herculean that he barely fits in the desk.

But it's him.

It's *him*.

He came back to me.

"Oh my God," I say softly, my hand at my lips.

Just then, I feel Crane come up behind me and hear his sharp inhale.

"Abe?" Crane whispers, a gasp.

I twist around to glance at Crane over my shoulder, his eyes focused on Brom too, a look of utter shock on his face.

Abe? I think. *Who is Abe?*

I look back to Brom, but he's still looking directly at me.

"What is he doing here?" Crane whispers, a tremor in his voice.

And then I remember what Crane told me last night.

And I realize that we've both been under the spell of Abraham Van Brunt.

16

Crane

One year ago

I can't stop staring. The man has been coming into the opium joint for the past few nights. He never speaks to anyone, except a few words to the meister, who arranges his pipe for him. Then he takes his pipe and sits in the farthest corner, disappearing into the dark until all you see of him are puffs of smoke and the occasional shine of his black eyes. There's nothing unusual about a single man coming in here and lying down in one of the beds or on a rug on the floor and smoking for hours, and yet, I can't help but be drawn to this one.

It doesn't hurt that he's beautiful. Tall, with wide boulder-like shoulders, and when he takes off his coat, you can see how much muscle he has. He's just brimming with power, the kind that makes me wet my lips. And then there's his longish hair, his beard, those eyes of his that are so brown they're like teak and ebony. All these things call to me. Makes my cock perk up, even when the opium is competing for my body's attention.

But that's not why I'm so fixated on him these past few days. It's because when he's in the corner of the room, he's not blissfully unaware of the world like everyone else seems to be. He's watching. He sits there and smokes, and he watches everything.

He watches me.

Just as I watch him.

Except he looks like he's watching *for* something. Or he's running away from something. The only difference between him and the rest of us users is that he's not running away from himself.

I put down my pipe and get up, moving through the haze of smoke and across the room until I'm standing right in front of him.

"Can't help but notice you've been staring at me," I say.

He tilts his head back and glares up at me. His eyes could cut through steel.

"I think you have it the other way around," he says. His voice is gravelly and rough and stirs something primal inside me.

"Perhaps we've both been staring at each other," I say to him. I crouch down so that I'm at his level. I can't see him much better because of the shadows he's in, but the energy just radiates off him. Dark and wicked and all the things I love, all the things I've neglected.

"What's your name?" I ask.

He puts the pipe to his mouth and inhales. He lets the smoke fall out slowly, his eyes locked on mine. "Abe," he says eventually.

"No last name?"

"Don't need one here."

"Well, I'm Ichabod Crane," I tell him.

"Ichabod," he says through a cough, his dark eyes becoming heavy-lidded. "You don't hear that name too often."

"You can call me Crane," I tell him. "If it pleases you."

And if you want to please me, you can call me Daddy.

"What would please me is if you got the fuck out of my face and left me alone."

I grin at him. "That's a nasty mouth you've got there. Care to put it to good use?"

He lets out a low growl and attempts to get up and perhaps tackle or punch me, but the drug has him in its grip. I merely push back on his rock-hard shoulders until he's against the wall.

"You're new at this, aren't you, pretty boy?" I say, leaning into him. I'm straddling him now, my knees planted on either side of his hips.

He gnashes his teeth together like a rabid dog, but his movements are too slow.

"A pretty little animal who doesn't know his limits."

"Fuck you," he snarls.

I just give him a half smile.

"I'll tell you what, Abe," I say to him. "I'll leave you alone, and you can continue to smoke yourself into a stupor, but answer me this one question."

He lets out a raspy growl as an answer.

"Are you in any danger?" I ask gravely.

He goes quiet at that, blinks at me like he doesn't really see me. I know questioning people when they're high isn't the best way to get information, but I can't help myself. Something in me wants to find the threads that are barely holding him together and unravel him.

"Why do you say that?" he manages to say thickly.

"Because I see it in you," I tell him. "I see many things in you. I know you're running away from someone. Something, perhaps? And that you're having a hard time finding peace, thinking that death and danger are lurking around every corner. It doesn't have to be that way."

He watches me for a second, his eyes growing heavy. "It is that way."

Hmmm. I shouldn't be surprised he's not giving up his secrets to a stranger. Against my better judgment, I reach out and grab his hand and try to read him.

His eyes go wide as they stare into mine, big black pools that I'm drowning in, and I feel so much all at once. Fear, anger, shame, and something dark and terrifying, enough that I almost let go. But try as I might, I can't see into his mind, can't see his memories. I can only feel him and all he's going through. It is a *lot*.

"What are you looking at?" he asks me, swiping his hand out of mine in a clumsy manner.

"Truth," I tell him. "What are you looking for?"

He wiggles his jaw back and forth, his breathing becoming more labored, but remains quiet.

I don't think I'll get anything else from him tonight.

"If you're on the run from someone, you better take it easy on the opium," I tell him, getting to my feet.

"You're here all the time smoking the same as I am," he grunts.

"Yes, but unfortunately, I'm only running from myself, and I have a lot of experience. It takes time for your body to adjust to the drug. Until it does, you're a sitting duck. Tell me, where are you staying?"

"None of your business."

I shrug. "None of this is. But if you want to make it my business, you can always stay with me. I have a hotel room not too far from here. It's small but clean, and I lucked out with a bathtub and hot water. You could get yourself cleaned up, soberish, and we could talk about what to do with you."

He continues to stare up at me, eyes hard and disbelieving.

"Why? What are you planning on doing to me?"

"Oh, me? I don't plan on doing anything," I tell him. "I might be a man of various appetites, but I'm also a man who looks out for another in need. I think you need help, Abe. And it would please me greatly if I could help you."

He makes a low noise in his throat, and for a moment, I think he may yell at me. But then he closes his eyes and leans back against the wall. "I don't need any help," he says, his words drifting.

I watch him for a moment as he falls deep into the haze, and then I go back to my pipe across the room and sit on the bed. I smoke a little more, and I watch him as he drifts in and out.

Eventually, I decide to go home. I leave the den and step out into the night. The October air is hard, and it's bitterly cold despite it being hot a few days ago. I pull my collar up against the cold and walk, looking forward to bed.

Then I hear footsteps behind me, stumbling, and a low voice call out, "Ichabod."

My heart leaps in my chest, and I turn around to see Abe coming toward me, shrugging on his coat.

"Well, well, well," I say to him. "Are you here to come home with me or to punch me in the face?"

He glares at me. So much anger in this man. I would love to fuck it out of him.

"I'm here to come home with you," he says gruffly, as if he hates the idea and is doing it anyway.

I just smile and put my hand on his shoulder. "Good choice, my friend."

We walk to the hotel and don't say a word to each other. This is not the first time I've brought a man back to the room. The ones I meet don't care where we go as long as we both get to fuck with abandon.

Still, as we go through the hotel to my room, I feel a hint of shame at how threadbare and plain the place is. I sold the house in San Francisco years ago, and that money is almost gone now. What I should have done was try to get into the real estate market here in New York City, but I was too afraid to put down any roots, and my lifestyle has eaten its way through my funds. I tend to change hotels every few months, and they keep going down in quality. At least with this one I still had enough money to splurge on a private bathroom.

But Abe doesn't seem to mind or notice. Of course he doesn't—he's still high, which works out well for me because when we go to my room, I realize I left it a disaster. I quickly putter around, cleaning things up, but Abe is already in the bathroom and running the bath for himself.

I decide to give him privacy. I have a bottle of whiskey and find a clean mug and glass among the mess, and I sit on the corner of my bed and wait. And drink. And wait. I don't hear any slosh of water, nothing. It's just silence.

What if he's drowned? Or found my razor and killed himself? I don't know the man and what he's been going through.

I can't shake the troubling thoughts, so I call out, "Abe?"

I put down the drinks, get to my feet, and open the door to the bathroom.

He's in the bathtub, just staring at the wall. His eyes are so dark against the white room and brimming with intensity that it makes a shiver run down my back. This is generally the opposite of a drug comedown.

"Abe?" I ask again. I'm starting to wonder if it's even his actual name. "Are you all right?"

He doesn't say anything. Doesn't move.

I slowly walk over to him and perch on the side of the tub. I can't help but stare into the water at his body. Every inch of him is hard-packed muscle. I'm strong, but I'm lean, not a lot of fat on me, but his body is thick and tight all at once. He must weigh a ton, and I imagine pushing his body into the floor as I ravage him from behind, how good it would feel to shove him around, make him obey my every command. His cock is especially magnificent, even when it's submerged and half-hard, and the soap that's floating in the tub bumps into the tip of it.

Finally, he looks at me with a slow turn of his head, and I make sure he knows I like what I see. I let my eyes linger on his body, let him feel the heat in my gaze. His cock twitches under the water, growing large, stiff, and magnificent under my watch.

"I was worried," I say after the tension in the bathroom seems too thick to bear. I meet his eyes, and I'm startled by what I see. How utterly focused and carnal he looks. Gone is the sullen scowl or the simmering fear or the fog of the opium.

"I have the feeling you worry too much," Abe says.

I let out a small laugh. "You'd be wrong. I used to worry. I came to New York so I wouldn't have to."

I think you're the first person I've worried about in a very long time.

He reaches into the tub and wraps his fist around the meaty base of his cock.

"As you can see," he says in a throaty voice, sliding his hand up and down his shaft with deliberation, "you don't have to worry about me."

A smirk tugs at my lips. "That's really sweet of you," I croon. "But I'm afraid you have the wrong impression. You're not here so that I can get you off. You're here to get *me* off. And if you're a good boy, I'll give you release too."

I watch him carefully. I'm particular in my wants and needs, and not a lot of men love being submissive. This man certainly isn't the submissive type. He's dominant too, I can tell. But I'm older than he is, maybe by ten years. I have experience, and for all the rawness in his eyes, the jutting swell of his blood-darkened cock, I have a suspicion he doesn't do this often. There's a greenness underneath, one that usually comes with a heavy helping of guilt, a sense that desire for another man is wrong.

"You're free to leave if that displeases you," I say, standing up. I reach down and rub the heel of my palm against my cock, hard and straining against my trousers. "I won't take offense. I'll be glad you at least got to have a bath, got a moment of respite from whatever is haunting you. Or hunting you."

He swallows hard, his Adam's apple bobbing on his thick neck. "What if it's both?" His voice is a whisper now, and that anguish and fear has come crawling back. "What if I'm being haunted and hunted?"

His words drive a stake of need through me. Not just the sexual need that's throbbing throughout my entire body but a need to protect him. To save him. To fix him. This broken, haunted stranger in my bathtub.

I carefully unbutton the fly of my trousers and pull out my cock, the weight of it heavy in my palm, the skin hot and buzzing with want, aching to be touched and sucked.

Abe's eyes stare at my length with fervor, a wildness coming over his face that drains all the fear away. *This will help*, I think. *This is a start.*

"I will take your mind off things," I tell him, making sure he hears it as a command.

Abe's gaze burns into mine as he adjusts himself in the bathtub, the water splashing over and onto the floor as he rotates so he's on his knees. With one hand, he grabs his cock, and the other reaches for mine.

I quickly snatch his wrist, gripping him tight. "Don't touch yourself. That's a rule."

"You can fuck your rules," he sneers.

My cock twitches at his profanity.

I bend his wrist the wrong way, and he lets out a rough gasp.

"I'll fuck your mouth," I counter. "You want it, you're going to have to do things my way."

He tries to whip his hand away, but I have a strong grip, and he's still under the influence. His mind might be clear, but the drug lingers in the muscles.

"Now, open those soft lips of yours," I tell him, letting go of his wrist and grabbing his chin while I ready my cock with the other. "And open wide. I know I'm a lot to swallow."

He keeps his eyes locked on mine, but he's faltering. He finally gives in and lets his gaze drop to my cock, taking in the sight of me. He reaches out—both hands this time—and his lips part, the inner rim dark pink and wet.

I let out a growl of impatience and let go of his chin, grabbing a fistful of hair instead and forcing his head forward. My shaft slides in past his lips, hitting the back of his throat. To his credit, he doesn't flinch nor gag; he just takes me in, his teeth grazing the underside of my cock until pleasure spikes through me, a heady, incapacitating kind of pleasure that I haven't felt in a long time.

God, that's it. That's *it*.

Abe starts off slow, and even though I'm the one in control, from the way my fingers have made a knot in his thick, silky hair, I let him take the lead. Because when he does, he brings me in deep. He sucks me off with fervor, like I'm dessert he's been looking forward to all day, hell, all year. His eyes go from the task at hand to my eyes and back, and I know he's enjoying this as much as I am. It almost feels cruel to watch him work me like this, shaft wet with his mouth, brow furrowed in concentration while he bucks his hips against the edge of the bathtub, trying to get purchase, trying to get release.

His will come. I'll make sure of it.

"You look like an animal, you know that?" I murmur, giving his hair a sharp tug. "You suck me like one too. Some wild, feral creature I picked up off the street."

Abe grunts at that, glaring up at me now. He gets mad when I insult him, and yet he's still running his tongue around my tip, still fisting my base with both hands, taking his anger out on my dick.

"You're doing good," I encourage him, though I'm not smiling. "So good. Keep going, pretty boy."

Another glare, another graze from his teeth that makes my toes curl against the wet bathroom floor. Eventually though, I have to close my eyes and surrender to the sensations, letting words of praise fall from my lips to his ears.

You're doing so good.

Look at how I'm fucking your tonsils.

Such a quick learner, such a good boy.

That's it, that's my boy, deeper now.

I've got you.

He takes direction like a dream, this big, brutal man bound to me for the evening, and it's not long before I'm telling him to gulp me up as I spray down his throat. I come hard and long, my eyes going back in my head, the knot inside me exploding like a grenade.

I grunt and let loose a stream of expletives, and he doesn't falter, he doesn't stop, until he's absolutely milked me dry.

I stare down at him and yank his head back, a string of spit running from my spent cock to his wet mouth. "You did so well," I tell him. "I think you deserve a reward. Tell me what you'd like."

He stares at me with unreadable eyes. At first, I think they're still heavy with lust, at not having gotten his release. I would be willing to grant him that. But then I realize it's not lust at all but a different kind of need. One that pains him.

"A place to stay for a few days," he says in a strained voice. "A bed and someone to share it with." He pauses. "I don't want to be alone."

Shame. It had been a while since I felt it, but I suppose I was due.

Did this man just suck me off in exchange for a place to sleep? Nothing else?

I clear my throat, tucking my cock back into my pants after he lets go. "Of course. You can stay here as long as you like."

His eyes brighten briefly at that. Relief.

"Truth be told, I haven't had anyone stay the night for a long time," I admit. "Man or woman," I add.

He just nods, taking that information in stride. "It would be nice for me too."

I go and grab him a towel, holding it out for him as he climbs out of the bath, and then I wrap it around his shoulders, gathering the ends at the base of his throat. I place my hand on his cheek briefly, his beard soft and wet, and give him a kind smile. "Let's have a drink."

17

Kat

Brom is back.

He's back and in my classroom, of all the places to show up.

How is this possible?

Crane meets my eyes, and it's more than obvious that he knows Brom, except he knows him as Abe. Crane's expression is torn but then quickly melts into his teacher mask, chin raised, eyes turning a cool gray, though the curiosity in them can't be quenched. He never looks so alive as he does when he can't figure something out.

I look back at Brom, meeting his eyes now, and though they don't seem to acknowledge the professor at all, I realize I can't just stare at him open-mouthed like this, frozen in time.

"Brom?" I manage to say, my voice coming out high and squeaky.

He gets out of his seat, and my goodness, has he grown. Not

just up—he's still around six feet or so—but in terms of muscle. He's really earning that moniker of Brom Bones now.

"Kat?" he says, and the sound of his voice brings relief flooding through me.

This is him.

This is *him*.

The entire class is watching as he strides toward me and envelops me in a huge hug, his arms wrapping around me with near bone-breaking strength. He smells like he always did, like bonfires on an autumn night, warm and cold at the same time. He smells like my childhood, my teenage years. He smells like a home I thought I'd lost.

"Oh God," I whisper against him, burying my head in his chest, the scratchy wool of his coat harsh on my skin, tears threatening to come down my cheeks. "It's really you."

"You've changed," he says, his large palm at the back of my head, cradling it. "You're a woman now."

I laugh, joy flowing through me like a river. None of this seems real.

"Is this a dream?" I ask.

He pulls back and grabs me by the shoulders, those black eyes skirting over my entire body, looking impressed, an impish smile on his face. "You look like a dream," he says. "So maybe it is."

I feel my cheeks go pink. "Brom, I have so many questions."

"Ahem," Crane says, clearing his throat loudly.

We both turn to face him and realize we're not only holding up the whole class but that Sister Margaret is standing in the doorway, grinning at us. I don't think I've ever seen her genuinely smile before, and the effect is disconcerting, like watching a cat try out a human expression for a change.

"May I?" Sister Margaret says to Crane, extending a hand into the classroom.

"Please," Crane says imploringly, obviously wanting an explanation for all of this. Crane may not know that Brom has been missing, but he's at least wondering how he came to be in his classroom suddenly.

Sister Margaret walks into the classroom and steps up on the platform in front of Crane's desk. Her hood is down today, but she's in the same long black cloak as the sisters always are.

"Students," she says, her voice bright and carrying across the room. "We have a new student joining you today. He's born and raised in Sleepy Hollow and just came back after a four-year absence. Everyone, say hello to Abraham Van Brunt."

She gestures to him with an even wider grin. I had no idea that Sister Margaret knew anything about Brom, but she's treating him like he's a star pupil. In fact, Brom never showed an inkling of witchcraft while I knew him, but perhaps that's changed. I mean, it has to have—why else would he be attending the institute?

The class gives a lukewarm welcome with a few hellos. Brom may not be a Van Tassel, but the fact that he's from Sleepy Hollow and the fact that Sister Margaret is positively glowing over him means that they're also placing him in the same category as they put me. Not the same. An "other."

Brom gives an awkward half bow, his eyes darting over the room briefly before finding mine again as Sister Margaret turns her attention over to Crane.

"You should have a little chat with Brom after class to try to get him caught up with what he's missed. Perhaps a few private tutoring classes should do it."

Crane's brows rise briefly, but his face quickly goes neutral. "Very well."

But Brom is still staring at me as if he can't believe I'm really here. That makes two of us.

"Brom," Sister Margaret says. "Can I speak with you out in the hall? Katrina, your presence is requested too."

Brom and I exchange a bewildered look but follow her flapping cloaks out into the hallway. I meet Crane's eyes as we go, but they're still unreadable. I can only imagine what he's thinking right now. Is this really the Abe that he had been talking about? Is it possible he met Brom while in New York or San Francisco and he changed his name slightly? But if it is Brom, then why is Brom acting like he's never seen Crane before? It's like Crane barely exists to him.

Of course, it might all be an act. It's not as if their affair would be allowed publicly anyway, so he could just be pretending he doesn't recognize Crane. And didn't Crane say that Brom nearly broke his heart? Perhaps it ended badly enough that Brom feels guilty. I have no idea, but every second that passes, I'm getting more and more curious and more and more confused.

We step out into the hall with Sister Margaret, and she closes the door to the classroom. She looks at him, then at me, her smile coy, her eyes dancing. "How wonderful to see you again, Brom."

Brom gives her a faint smile, the confusion clear on his face. "Have we met before?"

"You wouldn't remember," she says.

"No," he says, his smile faltering. "I don't remember anything."

"Be that as it may," she says, clapping her hands together, "it's so nice to finally welcome you to the school. Did you ever imagine you would be here alongside your sweetheart?" She looks to me now as if suddenly she's glad I'm here too.

"Brom!" my mother's voice rings out through the hall, and for a moment, I'm gobsmacked by the sound until I remember that she rode with Crane and me to the school this morning. That seems like a lifetime ago.

"Ms. Van Tassel," he says to her with a polite nod as she comes running down the hall toward him with her arms open.

"Please, it's Sarah," she says against him. While she embraces Brom like he's her long-lost son, my focus is beyond her.

At the three witches coming down the hall in her wake.

Sister Sophie.

Aunt Ana.

Aunt Leona.

The air in my lungs goes cold at the sight of them, especially my aunts. This is the first time I've seen them (that I've remembered), and they look nothing like the aunts in the memories from my youth. Their faces are nearly identical, which is odd because I didn't think they were twins but perhaps they are, and much like it had happened when I first met Sister Margaret, I can't seem to get a focus on them. It doesn't help that they have the hoods over their heads, casting their bony features in shadow so that they resemble skulls.

The three of them glide down the hallway like a floating

triangle with Leona at the front, her palms pressed tightly together as if in prayer, wearing a smile that's a little too wide for her face.

"Here he is," Leona says. Her voice is also not like I remembered. It sounds projected, as if coming from above and below me instead of in front of me, and it's the coarse voice of a smoker, raspy and drawn-out.

The triangle of sisters stops in front of us, all their attention on Brom.

"We are so glad to see you here," Leona says to him. "To have you back."

She glides toward him and places her hands on either side of his cheeks. "Yes, yes, it is you. We have been looking for you for so long."

"Everyone in Sleepy Hollow was," Sarah interjects.

That was true. For at least a year, search parties would go out, up to Boston or down to New York City, searching for Brom. The odd thing was that it wasn't his parents who seemed to care as much but my mother. I figured it was just because he mattered so much to me.

"We nearly gave up," Sister Sophie says.

You did give up, I want to say. The town may have looked for that first year, but for the years after that, no one even mentioned his name, as if he didn't even exist.

As if hearing my thoughts, Leona's sharp eyes swivel over to me.

"And, Katrina," Leona says. Less of a smile for me, which is fine because it doesn't suit her. "I suppose we owe you a nice welcome as well. I apologize that Ana and I haven't come by to check on you. We hear you have been doing quite well in your classes though. I'm sure in no time you can help get Brom caught up."

Ana just nods at me, her smile tight-lipped and more like the type of greeting I'm used to seeing from the sisters. She really does look like Leona though. The only difference is their hair color—Ana's a graying dirty blond and Leona's dark and streaked with white—plus Ana's nose hooks to the right. How didn't I know they were twins?

"After all," Sister Margaret says, "I'm sure you'll want to get your schooling done before you get married."

"What?" I ask, blinking at her.

Brom coughs, and I give him a look of confusion that he gives back in return.

"The marriage," my mother says, as if we had just been talking about it. "Your betrothal to each other. As it's always been promised. Don't tell me you've forgotten." There's a sharpness over those last words, something hard coming over her expression.

"Mother," I begin, exchanging another glance with Brom. "I hardly think this is appropriate, given the circumstances. He just got back." From where? "And we haven't seen each other in four years. A lot can change."

"Nothing changes," Leona says, her voice going low, her cold eyes bouncing between Brom and me. "Some things are meant to be. You were destined to be with each other from the day you were born."

Brom makes a low, guttural sound, and I look at him. He looks like an animal about to pounce, his jaw set. "I don't even know how I fucking got here," he growls at them, his eyes flashing with petulance. "How about I figure that out before you talk about us getting fucking married."

Everyone looks stunned, their eyes wide. Only Ana looks like she's trying to hide a smile.

He doesn't even know how he got here?

"Abraham!" my mother admonishes him. "I don't know where you were living before, but that kind of language isn't appropriate in Sleepy Hollow or at the institute."

"Sarah," Leona admonishes her with a wave of her bony hand. "Let him be. It's quite all right. He's been through a lot, I'm sure. Let him speak in whatever way he sees fit."

My mother clamps her mouth shut into a white line, shrinking slightly into the background. How quickly she cowers to Leona.

"Brom," Leona says. "That is what you still like to be called, isn't it? Not Abraham or Abe?"

He grunts, and I notice his hands flexing and unflexing at his sides.

"Perhaps it would be best for you and Katrina to get to know each other again," she goes on. "Sarah, why don't you invite Brom and his parents over for dinner tonight."

It was a command more than anything, and my mother nods. "Yes, of course."

"Wait a minute," I speak up. None of this is making any sense. "He just got back, yes? As much as I would like to see Brom, doesn't he need time with his parents alone? I'm sure they want to talk to him."

"Darling," Leona says with a sympathetic tilt of her head.

"Didn't you know that Brom got back days ago? I'm sure it would be fine with them all to join you tonight."

I turn to Brom in surprise. "You've been back for a few days and you didn't tell me? You didn't come by and . . . and . . ."

There was no news of it. Nothing.

He stares at me for a moment, and he must have learned something from Professor Crane already because I can't read his face at all. He doesn't say anything either.

I'm not sure I have a right to feel it, but I feel utterly betrayed that he's been back and he didn't even come by to say hello, to let me know he was in Sleepy Hollow and he was okay. What has he been doing?

"He's been ill," Sister Margaret says. "Have some compassion, Katrina."

I look at the sisters. They're all staring back at me with an expectant look in their eyes, like I'm supposed to shrink into the background like my mother did.

"I do have compassion," I tell them. "*I've* been sick with worry for years, thinking he was dead, and suddenly he's back, my best friend is back, and I'm supposed to just be understanding that this was kept from me for days?"

"I'm sorry," Brom mumbles.

But the fact is I'm not mad at him, not really. I'm not sure what I'm mad at; I'm still trying to get a handle on it. Everything is happening so fast and at once. Me and Crane together, then the horseman, then Brom back in our lives. It's overwhelming, like I've been torn into too many different directions and too soon.

"Perhaps we should let you get back to class," Leona says. "I'm sure it won't take long before you'll be hitting it off like you used to."

She gives the other witches a look and a sharp jerk of her chin, and they start floating down the hall away from us.

"Sarah," Leona barks at her. "Come."

My mother meets my eyes, and for one moment, I see fear. Pure terror, as if she'd just been asked to stride into hell. Then she turns, her head down, and follows her sisters.

And I'm left in the hall with a boy I once knew who has turned into a man I don't.

18

Crane

"Professor Crane." A student named Matilda who always wears her brown, unruly hair in a high bun, puts up her hand and starts waving it once I notice her. She's huddled in the corner with two other students, Josephine and Mark, trying to enter each other's minds and, from the looks of it, not having a lot of luck.

I walk over to them, but my eyes drift to Kat and Brom where they sit with their desks turned toward each other. I've been watching them the entire class, unable to look away. The student they're working with, Paul, has given me a look a few times as if to ask me what my problem is, why I'm staring, but I can't explain it to him any more than I can explain it to them.

How is this happening? How did Abe, *my* Abe, end up in my classroom?

It's him. There's no doubt now that it's him. When I first walked into the room, I thought I was looking at a ghost from my past.

Then I figured there was no possibility this could be the same man I'd been with in New York. Despite looking exactly the same as before, there was one big difference: he no longer looked afraid. That fear was replaced with a blankness. And when he looked me in the eyes for just the briefest of moments, his eyes held nothing in them. They were glass black and empty. He didn't see me at all. No recognition, no nothing. I would have been insulted, as if my cock was that forgettable, had it not been so confusing.

But when Sister Margaret announced him as Abraham Van Brunt, that sealed the deal.

It was him.

My haunted lover.

My hunted lover.

And he's here for reasons I don't understand.

Then there's the fact that Kat knows him. Knows him well. Perhaps even loved him at one point, judging by the fierceness of their embrace.

Jealousy stabbed me like a knife to the heart. I was jealous of him. I was jealous of her. Two humans I craved, and they shared this ease and intimacy with each other, giving each other what I wanted.

But then they were called out into the hall by a Sister Margaret I barely recognized, her face stretched with glee. I don't know much about Sleepy Hollow; I don't know their legends and their ghosts and what has happened in the walls of this school or in the streets of their town, but it's apparent that both Kat and Abe/Brom/Abraham have some twisted history here.

It's absolutely maddening. This mystery I don't understand is like a thorn in my side, one that's disappeared under the skin and impossible to get out. I must get to the bottom of this because none of this makes sense, and in my experience, when things don't make sense, that means something has gone wrong.

I walk over to Matilda, Mark, and Josephine and force myself to listen to their issues. This is psionic class, and today, we're learning about how to block telepathic intrusion. I figured since this was something Kat had learned to do, it might be possible to give other students the same set of skills. The problem with these particular students is that none of them can get into each other's minds, let alone learn how to block such an infiltration. Heaven help me from giving them all Fs.

The class drags on, and by the time I've dismissed everyone, I'm unable to look away from Brom or Kat. They drag their feet, lingering behind, and then I remember that Sister Margaret suggested some after-hours tutoring. How simple that must have sounded to her.

"Professor Crane," Abe says as he approaches the desk, and fuck if that phrase doesn't sound so sweet coming from his lips. He'd never called me professor—I don't even think I told him I'd been one. But now that he's saying it, I never want him to stop.

Though I should probably stop thinking of him as Abe.

"Brom," I say with deliberation, keeping my voice level, staying seated behind my desk so he can't see how aroused I am. It's been a godsend with Kat this past month, and it's coming in handy again. "Or do you prefer Abraham?"

Abe?

"Brom is fine," he says to me, giving me a half smile. Still nothing in his eyes for me. They're friendly—I'll give them that—but it's a friendliness that seems apt to change on a dime. I've picked up on several mood shifts from him already.

"His nickname when we were young was Brom Bones," Kat says. Her tone is light and easy, but from the look in her eyes, she's feeling as bewildered as I am.

Brom Bones, huh? Fitting.

"So you two know each other from long ago," I say, folding my hands on top of the desk.

"Yes," Kat says through a wavering smile. "We were best friends."

I lock eyes with her for a moment, wondering how deep their friendship went. I know it's terribly unfair to be so indignant over their shared pasts, but I am. I'm possessive over her, even though I have no right to be, and I might just feel the same way about him too. This should make the rest of the school year torture, along with the ghosts of dead teachers and a headless horseman running amok.

"I see," I say, steepling my fingers together. "Well, I have to admit, Brom Bones, it's quite a surprise to have a new student in my class a month into the semester. Can I ask why you missed so much already? Where have you been?"

Kat looks to Brom with an eagerness she can't hide, her fingers gripping the ruffles on her dress bodice as if holding on for dear life.

Brom stares at me blankly for a moment, like he's trying to gather all the thoughts in his head and not having much luck. Then his thick black brows furrow, and I pick up on a flash of pain, his eyes seeming darker than ever. He reminds me of the man in New York, the one who would give himself completely to me, a toy for me to do with what I wanted, and how after we were done and spent, the light would drain from his eyes, and they would turn so dark and haunted again.

I was a welcome respite, but the relief never lasted.

"I . . . ," he begins, licking his lips, that wildness coming across him. "I don't know." He looks around him as if to double-check that the room is empty. "I don't remember."

His chin dips at that, and shame wafts off him.

"You don't remember?" Kat asks, reaching out and putting her hand on his arm.

"What do you mean?" I add, leaning forward, ignoring the way she's touching him.

He pinches his eyes shut and lets out a shallow breath, shaking his head. "I don't remember. I don't remember the time I've been gone. I don't remember any of it."

Then he opens his eyes and stares right at me with such desperation that I feel it in my skin. "You're a teacher, right? You know things? Maybe you can help me."

"I don't understand," I say, and his expression crumbles. I splay my hands out. "Try explaining in layman's terms, and then I'll see what I can do."

He looks up to the ceiling for a moment, then says, "Four years ago, I left Sleepy Hollow. I don't know why. I don't remember why I left. I remember a feeling—I remember fear. But I can't remember why I left. I have vague memories of a city—New York, maybe. I don't know. But I know that time passed, and now suddenly, I'm here. I woke up . . . *here*."

"What do you mean you woke up here?" Kat asks, her dainty brows coming together. "Out in the hall, they said you returned a few days ago and that you'd been ill."

"That's what they say. But I don't remember any of that either. That's why I didn't come by to see you, Kat. I would have been to see you right away, you know that." He reaches out and takes her pinky in his hand, giving it a squeeze, and the air gets caught in my lungs.

I swallow my jealousy down. "So you don't remember why you left. You don't remember where you've been. You don't remember how you got here. You just woke up in this classroom today. Is that it?"

He nods. I glance at Kat, who gives her head a shake, a thin strand of blond coming loose from her bun.

"This is impossible," she says.

"I know how it sounds," he says gruffly. "But I'm telling you the truth."

"Crane," Kat says to me, hope swimming in her beautiful blue eyes. "You can help him. Try to read him."

"I . . . ," I begin. I'm about to say that I already have tried to read him once and that I didn't get any further with him than I did with her. But while I'm sure that truth will come out sooner than later, it can wait.

I pause and fix Brom with my gaze. "Are you sure you would like me to try? I can gain access to your memories using magic. You just have to go into it wanting to let me in."

Brom licks his lips and nods quickly. "Yes. You can try. I don't remember anything."

At that, Kat's face flushes slightly, but she doesn't say anything.

And then I realize what he means to Kat. He was the one she was searching for in the void during the ritual, the one that made her feel desperate and aroused. He's the dark, hot lust I glimpsed when I first tried to read her.

He's the thread that we share, the common denominator that has always bound us. I thought it was a shared experience from our past, perhaps grief or something else, but all this time, it was Brom.

"All right," I concede. I get up and move around the desk, glad that my desires are under control. I walk right up to Brom and make myself stop before I get too close inside his personal space. I have to remind myself that he doesn't know me the way I know him.

But did I really know you at all? I think. *Who are you?*

I hold out my hand, palm up, my eyes flickering over his face. "Give me your hand," I tell him.

He meets my eyes and holds them there, and for just a moment, he frowns, not out of confusion by what I'm asking, but in a searching way, like he just had a glimmer of his past.

Brom places his hand in mine, and I wrap my fingers around it.

Do you remember this feeling? This feeling of your hand in mine, of my fingers wrapping around your dick and bringing you to a finish?

He blinks, perhaps a little unnerved at how intensely I'm staring at him.

I close my eyes. I picture my energy welling up inside me like a bubbling pot, heat pouring through my arm and hand and onto him. I'm in the void and see a door in front of me, but it's closed. This is his mind. This is what I want to see.

But try as I might, I can't open the door. I can't get any feelings from him either, not in the way they once rushed through me or in the way it happened with Kat. Instead, I feel like there's something else behind this door. But whatever it is, it isn't him.

I press to the door and listen.

"I will do your bidding," a low, sinister voice says from the other side.

Then I hear other sounds. Cannon fire. Horses whinnying. Cries and shouts and the drawing of swords. People begging for mercy, pleading for their life. The sounds of death. Blades slicing.

I hear war.

There is nothing else beyond this door except war.

And then the door opens, swinging out toward me so that I'm knocked backward into the void, and hot wind smelling of brimstone and rot comes flowing toward me.

"There is no room in here for you, Teacher," the voice says.

Then the door slams shut, and suddenly, I'm being pushed backward, enough that I'm stumbling back into the classroom until my back hits the wall.

"What happened?" Kat exclaims.

Brom's eyes are wide, still holding out his hand. "What did you see?"

I gasp for air, my heart thundering against my ribs. I feel the sulfurous smell sticking to me like a cloak.

"I saw war," I tell him, catching my breath. "I heard it. There is a war inside you, Brom Bones."

He frowns and quickly exchanges a confused look with Kat before coming back to me. "A metaphorical war?"

I have to pause, rubbing my lips together as I think. "I'm not sure. I didn't see it. I didn't see anything, but it's what I felt and what I heard. It was almost as if it didn't belong to you."

There is no room in here for you, Teacher.

That voice hadn't been Brom's.

But right now, something is telling me to keep that close to my chest.

Because this man isn't the same man I had once been intimate with.

That man had been on the run because he'd been hunted.

This man is one who has finally been caught.

19

Kat

That's a lovely horse, Brom," my mother says to him as we're tacking up at the school stable, the strange stable boy running around and trying to help us all.

I absently stroke down Snowdrop's neck, peering over at Brom, who is leading his fully saddled horse out of the stall. It's a magnificent stallion, completely black and shiny like the polished obsidian arrowhead I have in my desk drawer. Its size and strong, arched neck make it look like a Dutch warmblood crossed with a Friesian rather than the thoroughbreds and cobs that frequent these parts. It's not lost on me that it looks exactly like the black horse the horseman was riding last night. The only difference was the horseman's seemed like it was born from the bowels of hell, and this horse is calm and gentle.

"It is a nice horse," I say, leading Snowdrop out. "Where did you get him?"

He swings up onto the saddle in an effortless display of horsemanship and gives me a loaded look, one that says: *I don't remember.*

"I picked him up on my travels," Brom says with forced confidence, fiddling with the reins.

"And what's his name?" I ask, though I know he doesn't know that either.

He's nearly glaring at me now.

"Daredevil," the stable boy speaks up, coming out of the stall with my mother and her horse. "I heard him referred to as Daredevil."

"By whom?" I ask.

Sarah laughs. "By Brom, naturally. It's his horse."

But the stable boy doesn't say anything else. Instead, he meets my eyes, and something blank passes over his expression before he turns and runs back into the stable.

I ponder that as I mount up on Snowdrop, feeling Brom's eyes on my back. So he has a horse that he doesn't remember, and it has a name that he didn't give it. Who gave the horse the name? Whoever gave it the name gave him the horse.

I need time to talk to Brom alone. After Crane tried to read him after class, looking visibly shaken by whatever he said he didn't see—this war inside of Brom—Sister Margaret showed up and gave Brom a tour, much as she had done for me, and I had to hurry off to my next class, spells and chants, which I was already late for. The rest of the day I was locked in a mix of magic and non-magic classes, and I didn't get out until twenty minutes ago when my mother came for me to make sure I was riding back with her and Brom into town.

My mother takes the lead, clucking to her horse, and we follow single file with Brom behind me as we head down the path through the courtyard. The weather seems to have shifted since this morning, but then again, everything in my life has shifted since then. No longer are the students studying and conversing out in the grass. Now, the ground is covered in a layer of dew, and the flowers are drooping. The leaves on the maples, birches, and elms are still bold with color, but so much more has fallen to the ground in decaying piles. The mist is ever present, hovering above the black surface of the lake, and for a moment, it reminds me of Brom's eyes. Black yet veiled. Him but different. Him . . . but not him.

I glance at Brom over my shoulder, wishing that Crane had taught me how to do that speaking-without-speaking thing so that I could talk to him. He's glancing around, a look of strange contentment on his face, as if he's seeing his surroundings for the first time. I must admit, he looks good on that horse, his black hair and eyes matching the horse's black coat and eyes, both strong, muscular, commanding. He looks good out here with the backdrop of the school behind him, like he belongs there, maybe even more than I do.

"So you're a witch," I say to him.

He meets my gaze, brows arched. "Why do you say that?"

"Because you wouldn't be at the institute if you weren't."

"Katrina, don't pester him," my mother says from in front of me. "You know that Brom's mother, Emilie, is a witch. It runs in the family."

"I'm not pestering," I tell her, unable to keep the annoyance out of my voice. "And I know she's a witch; it's just that while growing up, I was the one who had a bit of magic, and Brom never did. I would do tricks for him, and he could never do it in return. We tried—remember, Brom?"

"I was a dud," he admits. "Daffy had all the magic."

My heart warms at the way he calls me Daffy. I haven't heard that nickname in a long time.

My mother twists around in her saddle to look at me sharply. "You performed magic for Brom?"

I remember my father's words, and I immediately feel shame. "I know. I'm sorry."

"Don't be sorry," she says quickly. "I just . . . I had no idea. You never showed any magic around me when you were little. I thought perhaps you barely had any, as if it skipped a generation."

I'm about to confess that Papa told me not to show it around her, but something stops me. Something that lets me know that my mother shouldn't know of that conversation. Something in my father's voice and eyes that had always seemed to say more than he was saying.

That my mother couldn't be trusted.

She couldn't be trusted around my magic.

"It wasn't much," I eventually say.

She stares at me for a moment, trying to read me. Then she looks back to the gates that rise up before us. "We all start small," she says. "The small things add up with time."

The gates open for us, and I wonder if Brom will lose his memories of earlier, if he even knows that it's a side effect of the school. Did he take the tests at all? If so, when?

We ride under the iron arch of the gates, the pressure of the wards reaching into my skull and squeezing, the wash of cold, and then the pressure lifts, and we're on the trail, riding through the dark woods.

I glance over my shoulder at Brom. He's wincing, one hand pushing on the side of his temple.

"What was that?" he asks.

"The wards," I say. "You must have felt them when you rode in." I pause, waiting for him to tell me he didn't remember that either. Unless going through the wards has the opposite effect on him. "Do you remember anything now?"

He shakes his head. "No."

"Do you remember class earlier with Professor Crane? Your tour with Sister Margaret?"

"Yes," he says, frowning.

"He remembers just as I do," I announce to my mother as I face forward, though lately I'm remembering pretty much everything that happens at school and not just Crane's class. "How do you explain that?"

"There's a lot that can't be explained right now, Kat," my mother says in a tired voice.

That can't be explained, I think. *Or won't be?*

When we reach our house, Brom continues riding on, telling my mother that he'll invite his parents over for supper. Brom's family lives on the next farm over from ours, and I contemplate riding with him just so I can have a chance to be alone with him and ask questions, but he's already pushing on his way. Maybe he needs some time to be alone himself to try to figure out what's happening. I can't imagine what it must be like for him. The desperation in his voice when he asked Crane to fix him . . . it broke my heart.

We untack the horses and go inside the house, which smells like soup. My mother finds Famke in the kitchen and tells her to make extra for dinner since we're having company. Famke couldn't look more surprised to hear of Brom's return.

"Is it true?" Famke whispers to me while she's chopping up celery, my mother having gone to take a bath. "Is Brom really back?"

"He's really back," I tell her.

She squints at me through a few strands of frayed gray hair that have fallen across her forehead.

"You don't look happy, child."

I put on my best smile. "I am happy. I'm relieved."

"But?" She presses the knife against the celery but doesn't cut it.

"But he doesn't remember anything," I whisper. "Not why he left, not what's happened while he's been gone. He doesn't even know how he got here. The sisters said that he's been home for days but was too ill to see anyone. But I don't believe that, and Brom doesn't either. He says the only thing he remembers is waking up today in my class. That's it."

Famke searches my eyes for a few moments.

"What is it?" I ask.

"Are they talking about marriage again? Between you and Brom."

"Yes," I say emphatically. "As if he hasn't been gone at all. Don't get me wrong, I still love Brom like I always have, but . . ."

"But now you're with the professor."

I give her a look. "How do you know that?"

"The walls listen," Famke says, resuming her chopping. "They listen and watch."

"Are you the walls?"

She smiles to herself, but it's a bitter smile. "I have been here a long time, Katrina. I have seen a lot."

I've always liked Famke. Always trusted her.

"What have you seen?" I whisper.

Famke's eyes dart to the empty doorway, then back to me. Her expression turns melancholy. "Your father wanted the very best for you. You know that, don't you?"

I nod. "I know."

"But what he wanted for you was not what your mother wanted. He didn't want you to marry Brom."

I blink at her, shocked. "What do you mean?"

Of course he did. That's all they ever talked about. My destiny, how Brom would be the perfect husband, and we would have perfect children and never want for anything.

"He didn't want you to marry Brom because your mother wanted you to marry him. And his parents wanted you to marry him." She pauses, slicing the celery with one hard cut. "And the sisters wanted you to marry him. Because it was never up to you or Brom."

"He wanted me to have my own free will," I muse.

She purses her lips at that, tilting her head. "Yes . . ."

"And?"

"What he really wanted was for you to leave Sleepy Hollow."

I shake my head. No. That goes against everything I've believed, everything I've heard.

"No," I tell her. "That's not it. His dying words were for me to watch over my mother."

Her gaze is steady. "Are you sure he said what you think he

said?" She leans in close. "I came here to work for your father, Kat. He hired me, took a chance on me when I had lost my husband and had no one, no prospects. I loved him like a son. My allegiance in his passing is to you, not to your mother."

"Okay," I say in a small voice, not expecting to hear this.

"There are very few people in this world that you can trust," she says. "Your father was one of them. Your mother is not."

I swallow that down. It's bitter but not surprising. Not even a little.

"What does she do with my aunts on the full moon?" I whisper.

She gives me a wan smile, brushing her hair off her head with a swipe of her arm. "I am not a witch, so I could not tell you what she does. But I do know this. Your mother takes. She took from your father; she'll take from you. And when she goes to the school on those full moons, she goes to something that *gives*."

Then she turns her back to me and starts on the carrots next. "Now, if you please, I have to make all this extra food, which I was not prepared for."

"Sure," I say softly, stewing on everything she just told me. I slowly walk away, feeling dazed, and go to my bedroom, shutting the door behind me and sitting on my bed.

What do you do when the person who is supposed to love and protect you ends up being a shadow? Who do you trust?

A couple of hours later, the Van Brunts are seated at the dining room table with my mother and me. They were insistent that Brom sit at one end of the table and I at the other, like my father and mother used to do. I think it disturbs me as much as it does Brom, but he's hard to read tonight. Then again, there's nothing to be read when it comes to him.

His parents are equally as strange but in a different way. I've known Emilie and Liam Van Brunt my whole life, and they've always been peculiar. I would chalk it up to her being a witch and him a stoic farmer of few words. But their relationship with Brom always felt more like they were distant cousins rather than parents. It was common in these parts of the country, especially among Dutch immigrant farmers, for there to be a coldness and distance in families. Life was about surviving in a new land. Children were often seen as an extra hand to help on the farm. They were never coddled or fussed over.

And yet with Brom's parents, there wasn't any of that. Brom did work on the farm, hence how he got his strong physique, but his father had money and hired people to do most of the work. And they were never cold with him either; they just kind of existed. People he shared a house with, nothing more. They were remote but never cruel. Indifferent but never callous.

Tonight is no different. It should be different. They should be overjoyed, hugging him, perhaps even crying at their good fortune of his return. Instead, they're stiff in their seats and staring at him with stretched smiles on their faces, barely talking, just observing him and, on occasion, me.

The only sense of normalcy in this dinner party is Famke. Despite everything she told me earlier, Famke is busy serving the roast pumpkin and salted pork and making sure everyone is fed and happy, commenting on how it's been such a long time since we had any guests over. That much is true. When Mary first moved to Sleepy Hollow and I had been spending a lot of time with her, my mother had her family over for dinner, but never again after that. Her family was a little too "normal" for us, I think. And other than visits to the doctor and to her sisters at the school, my mother doesn't seem to have a social life or any friends. Even though she's stayed friendly with the Van Brunts since Brom had disappeared, it was never the same. He was the glue holding them together.

Sometimes I think Brom was the glue holding *me* together. After my father died, I turned to him for comfort and company, to his brazen strength. After he left, I had to learn to get those things on my own (after all, my mother wasn't an option). If he'd stayed, I know I would have married him, had children, and become a wife, and I never would have learned who I was without all the glue to fix the cracks.

"I want to make a toast," my mother says, raising her glass of wine. She looks at Brom and smiles at him warmly. "I want to say how absolutely wonderful it is to have you back in Sleepy Hollow, Brom. And not only that, but to be attending the institute. I know the school was never on your agenda growing up, but now that it is, I'm sure we can all agree that it makes a lot of sense."

I snort at that, and my mother looks at me sharply. Brom's brows nearly disappear into his hairline.

"Katrina?" my mother says testily. "Did you want to add something?"

I exchange a look with Famke, who just gives a barely noticeable shake of her head before hurrying to the kitchen.

"I find your choice of words amusing," I say before having a sip of my red wine. "Because absolutely nothing about all of this makes any sense. And you know it. You all know it!"

"Kat," Brom says in his gruff, quiet voice, his expression telling me not to rock the boat.

But I'm sick of how everyone is acting like all of this is normal.

"What? None of this is normal!" I cry out, ignoring him. "Brom has been gone for four years, and he doesn't remember a single thing. He should be at the doctor's, at an alienist. If you want to use witchcraft, then he should be going through regression hypnosis, reverse divination, anything. But you're all just accepting it!"

"Katrina," Emilie says, her hand shaking slightly as she folds her napkin. "We are all in shock, dear. We know it's not normal, but we are doing the best that we can. Brom is back, and that's all that matters now. Doesn't that matter to you? That he's back?"

My heart sinks, as if they think it doesn't matter. I give Brom a pleading look, hoping he knows that it matters more than anything. "Of course it matters! And I'm in shock too. This is all I've wanted for so long, but . . . we have to know what happened to him. There has to be an explanation. I can't just sit here and not want the truth."

I look around the table. Everyone is staring at me with such sympathy it makes me want to flip the table over. Only Brom remains bothered, a fist curling over the knife in his hand, his dark eyes focused on his plate.

"I think you've been spending too much time with that Professor Crane," my mother chides, and Brom's gaze turns sharply to mine. "Always wanting an answer to something and asking too many questions while missing the big picture. I was kind enough to let him stay over, but really, I think your focus should be Brom."

What are you doing? I want to scream at her. *Why are you bringing up Crane in front of Brom like this?*

I dare a glance at him, and his grip around the knife is so tight that his knuckles are going white, his eyes blazing with unmistakable anger and betrayal.

"Professor Crane," Emilie muses. "I've never heard of him. But perhaps with Brom living on campus, he can get to know him too."

"Brom's . . . living on campus?" I say. I glance at Brom, but he's still looking at me with fire in his eyes.

"Yes," my mother says with a smug smile. "Brom will be moving to campus this weekend." Her smile gets even deeper. "And so will you."

20

Brom

Darkness.

For a moment, I see only darkness. Hot. Putrid. Oozing. Black nothing. Black everything.

There's a flame in my heart, dark fire. It consumes all, eats everything, leaves nothing.

Destroy her, the voice inside my head says, malevolence dripping with its every word.

Fuck her.

Capture her and fuck her.

Defile her.

Listen to her beg for mercy.

Make her take your seed.

Destroy him.

Drill a hole in his eyes with your cock.

Fuck his brains until they're coming out his ears.

"Brom," my father chides from beside me. His voice is fearful.

He's always sounded afraid when he talks to me, but tonight, he trembles with it. It's enough to pull myself out of the black ooze, to separate from the thing I fear is inside me.

The other man.

The other me?

I look down at my hand. I'm gripping a knife. So tight my knuckles look dusted in snow.

I glance around.

No one is paying attention to me.

Everyone is paying attention to me.

Kat looks flabbergasted. Her mouth open. She's upset with her mother. She's been upset the whole night. Because of me and not because of me.

"What do you mean I'm going to live on campus?" Kat says, her voice high and brimming with confusion. She's been operating at this level ever since I reappeared.

Reappeared.

As if I'm a magic trick.

Here in one hand, then appearing in the other. A coin behind the ear when there was nothing before. A rabbit in a hat.

Someone has been doing magic on me. The sisters. It has to be. It's always them. Even before I left Sleepy Hollow, I knew it was them.

But is that why I left? Did I leave Sleepy Hollow because of them?

Or was it something else?

Someone else?

My heart pangs with shame. Then lust. Then something like

love but softer and more innocent, like the love you throw around as a child. With abandon, to anyone, anything, not caring where it lands.

I look at Kat.

My beautiful Kat. How she's grown. Changed. And yet it's still her. A woman. A goddess. A witch.

She is the balm on my wounded soul. She soothes where everything burns. She smooths the scars flat until I can pretend I'm whole again.

Now, in this candlelight, with her hair down her back like the smooth, shiny cornsilk we'd shuck during those late, hot summers, she glows. Gleams. She's an angel, and I'm a devil, and that means the devil won't stop. The devil never does. He'll dirty everything he touches.

Her eyes are different now, though perhaps she says the same about mine. I look in the mirror, and I don't even recognize my face sometimes. But her face is older, braver, stronger. Kat was never a meek girl. She may have described herself as sheltered, but I don't think that's true. Her father did what he could to shelter her, and after he died, she turned to me. Yet she wanted to push her boundaries.

She wanted to leave.

And now her mother is telling her she must live at the school.

"I thought that's what you wanted," her mother says, nibbling at a piece of meat that she never quite eats. Her whole meal is a mess of food that never makes it into her mouth. It doesn't sustain her. Her skin is sallow and drawn, and her eyes are greedy, and *nothing* sustains her.

"I did, but . . . but, you were so against it," my Kat says. "And now that Brom is there, you're saying I must go."

I act like it doesn't hurt, but it does, and I'm a bad actor. I wince. Shards of glass in my chest. She doesn't want to be close to me, is that it? Is it this professor? Is he the problem?

My thoughts go to him against my will. I don't like thinking about him. He seems familiar and strange. I don't like the way he looks at me. Like I'm his friend. More than a friend. He makes me uncomfortable with how comfortable he makes me feel. When he held my hand, I wanted to die. I felt him inside there with me. I also felt that other part of me. The one that hunted me. That one hates the professor, and so it makes me want to hate him too.

Was he really with Kat? My Kat?

Does he love her? Does she love him? Did they only fuck? Does he give her greater pleasure than I did?

I'm gripping the knife again.

The rest of dinner fades into nothingness. I feel the dark inside of me wanting to rise, and I manage to keep it at bay. I know it's a foreigner in my system, an intrusion, but as long as I stay in control, it won't infect me. I can hold it back.

Kat is upset. She leaves the dinner table and steps outside into the cold, grabbing a shawl from the rack, saying she's going to check on her horse.

"I don't understand," Sarah says to me with a sorry smile. "All she wanted was to be on campus. I'm sure she'll come around. She has no choice."

I excuse myself. I try to smile, but from the look on my parents' faces, I might look like a monster grinning. I don't explain what I'm doing or where I'm going, but I don't have to.

I open the door and head out to the stable.

It's a cold night. Frost has settled, and the grass crunches beneath my boots. A cornfield stretches from the back of the house to the barn, the stalks tall but wilted and spent, glimmering like ice under the pale moon. I hear her in the stable, cooing gently to her horse, and cross the pasture to her. She has a siren song. She always has.

The lantern hanging outside the stall flickers at my approach. I've noticed this now, how the lights never stay still. All supper, the flames on the center candlesticks danced, the fire at the mantel joining in. No one thought it was strange. Everyone thought it was strange.

"Brom?" Kat's voice rings out, soft as summer air. But there is no mistaking the changing season—everything around her is cold.

I stop by the stall and stare at her. Her horse, Snowdrop, raises its head and snorts, ears back, tail swishing. I look into the gray mare's eyes and see the reflection of myself in them.

For a moment, it looks like I have no head.

Hot steam flows out from the horse's nostrils, and I reach out, gently stroking her velvet muzzle. I feel her calm, and my gaze goes to Kat beside her.

She's standing there, her shawl clutched. Wary. Her soft, full mouth held together tightly.

"Kat," I say. But that's all I can say.

She stares at me for a moment, and then her expression softens, her hand going to Snowdrop's shoulder. "I'm sorry," she says quietly. "I couldn't stand to be in there a minute longer. I know I was rude."

"You don't have to apologize to me," I tell her. I want to go to her. Touch her. Kiss her.

Fuck her.

Defile her.

Spread your seed inside her.

I blink the voice away. "I know how strange all of this is for you."

"And for you," she says, and she's coming to me now, stopping a foot away in the sawdust. She stares up at me, anguish in her pretty blues, her pulse visibly ticking in her throat. "They all act like it's normal. As if the past four years never happened."

But it *is* like it never happened.

I reach out, and I take her hand in mine. Her skin is cold but soft, so soft. I wrap my fingers around it, feeling how fragile her bones are. How easy it would be to crush her.

She must be protected from all of this, I think.

She must be protected from me.

"I think you're right to not want to be at the school with me," I tell her.

Her chin dips. "No. That's not it. It's not that I don't want to be with you. . . ."

"Is it him?" I sound petulant. I don't care.

Her eyes widen.

"Him?" she repeats.

Oh, but she knows who I mean. She is pretending.

"The professor," I say coolly.

"Professor Crane? No. It's nothing to do with him. I don't understand why my mother changed her mind so abruptly."

"Perhaps she didn't want you there alone, but now that I'll be there, she feels I can protect you."

She studies me for a moment. "Do you really believe that?"

"I would like to believe that." But I don't. Because I don't know that I'll be able to protect her from myself. And her mother has never cared to give her any protection. She would offer her own daughter to the wolves if it would please them. I feel she's doing that now.

And I'm the wolf.

Kat shakes her head, gnawing on her lower lip. Her attention goes to Snowdrop, her pale hand on the horse's white coat. "My mother doesn't want what's best for me. I know that now. I always knew it, but I didn't want to believe it. Now I know."

I can't help but give her a fleeting smile, my heart warming with pride. "You're all grown up, Kat. You finally see the truth."

"What do you mean?"

"That your mother has never been on your side," I tell her.

"What do you mean?" she says in a quiet voice, looking uncomfortable. "What makes you say that?"

"I don't know, Daffy. Remember when your father brought you home that pet rabbit for your birthday? You had been so happy, and I think your mother hated that. She said the rabbit was a rodent and unfit to be a pet for a young lady and made you give it up. I think she was jealous of your connection to the animal, same connection you have to Snowflake. I didn't really know what I was seeing at the time, but I knew that your mother never had your interests at heart, let alone your best ones. It was the same with my own parents. I knew they didn't care. They still don't. You see that, don't you? You've always seen that. You could have told me, but you didn't."

She looks down at her shoes, and I give her hand a squeeze. "Neither of us have parents who care. You were lucky you had your father. He was the only one who did. We have to look out for each other."

"Look out for each other?" she says with a snarl and rips her hand away.

Her anger shouldn't surprise me, but it does.

"You should have been here to look out for me! To protect me when I had no one. Instead, you took my virginity, and then you left me! You left me, Brom!"

Her words sting like nettle. As if this is my fault?

"I didn't *take* anything. You gave it to me. And I told you I don't remember why I left," I grind out, feeling anger rising from that dark place, where the thing resides. "How many fucking times must I explain that?!"

"You took my innocence," she decrees, jabbing her finger into my chest. "You took it, and you left me. You used me and discarded me. I spent four years thinking your disappearance was all my fault!"

I reach up and grab her finger, gripping it hard. "I was lost for four years! I don't know what happened. You think this is all about you?" I squeeze her finger harder, feeling darkness flood my veins. "And fuck your innocence. It seems like you've thrown that away like a dirty rag. I know you're screwing your professor."

"Ow!" she cries out, trying to pull her finger away, but I won't let her go. I can't.

"Go to hell, Brom!" she yells, kicking at my shin.

"I've already been to hell," I sneer at her, the darkness bubbling up and up now. It wants to take over. It wants me to claim her. "And hell isn't done with me."

"I'll scream," she says as my grip goes to her wrist. Fury and panic flood her eyes. "I'll scream if you don't let go of me."

"Do you think anyone will care? This is what they want, don't you see?"

And at that realization, the darkness fades enough for me to see clearly.

What I'm doing to her. What I'm saying.

I drop her hand and step back.

"I'm sorry," I say, but my voice is shaking, and the words sound empty.

She stares at me with pure venom.

Venom and sadness.

Betrayal.

"I didn't mean to . . . I didn't mean what I said," I add. "About your innocence."

She glares at me. "Perhaps I'm not so innocent. Maybe you did lead me down that path. There wasn't just you. There was that farmhand. Joshua Meeks."

I picture him in my head. Stocky, blond, always smiling. She was with him too? "You're just trying to hurt me now."

The darkness starts to flood in again, like the tide.

"So what if I am?!" she snaps. "And yes, now there is the professor, but it's not . . ." Her lip curls. "You have no right to be angry about me and Professor Crane. About anyone. You were gone. And Crane is a good man, more than you'll ever know. He wants to help you. He, he—" She cuts herself off, slamming her lips shut, her nostrils flaring. "I think you should leave."

The darkness wants me to stay.

But I am better than that.

"All right," I say to her with a nod. "I'll go."

I turn and walk out of the stall, then look at her over my shoulder. "Daffodil," I say. "I'm sorry."

"Don't call me that." She glowers. "Don't call me anything."

I swallow that down. The rejection.

I grab my horse and ride off into the night.

I know the darkness will come before I get home.

21

Crane

I can't sleep.

Rain falls lightly against the windowpanes, and the candles I have lit in a row on the sill flicker slightly in a draft, a shield against the dark. The clock on my desk ticks loudly as it has all night, counting down the hours and yet never seeming to move. It was one in the morning, and then it was three in the morning, but now it is two in the morning, and I can't tell if I'm awake or dreaming.

I dig my nails into my hand until it hurts.

I'm awake.

I am awake, too awake, my brain bouncing around from thought to thought to thought. I think about Brom walking into my classroom this morning. How it pained me more than I thought that he didn't remember who I was—me, the man who opened his bed to a stranger for a few weeks, a stranger on the run. Whatever Brom had been running from had brought him back here somehow, I was sure of it. None of this makes any sense unless you involve witchcraft, but if the sisters brought him back here for some reason, then the question is why? And why did he leave Sleepy Hollow in the first place?

When I can't come up with any answers, I move on to Kat. My favorite thought. Lovely, beautiful Kat, whose body and soul I feel preternaturally drawn to. I feel like I'm just getting started with her, that I'm just about to plunge headfirst into the abyss for her, ready to drown in all she was offering.

But now I don't know how to proceed. I *want* to proceed—I want her in all my dark and deviant ways—but with Brom stepping back into the picture, that surely complicates matters. There's no doubt this was the man who once brought her pleasure, just as he had for me, and perhaps even a man she was in love with. Maybe still is. Will she even want me now that he's back? Will I be discarded? It wouldn't be the first time.

And then I think about Sarah. I think about Kat's strange witch of a mother and how different she is from the other sisters. She barely resembles them, doesn't seem to have much love for them, seems separate from them in nearly every way.

Staying at the Van Tassel house overnight, I was bombarded by so many emotions, ones that seemed to belong to the house itself, a house with a soul. I felt love. A strong love between a father and a daughter, so unlike the one I had with my own father. But I also felt fear. I felt so much fear hidden in the dust that's swept under the beds. I felt the fear Kat's father had of Sarah, something that didn't surprise me considering Sarah's cold and controlling demeanor, but also fear that belonged to Sarah. Whether that fear is of Kat or of her sisters, I'm not sure. But there is something off about the Van Tassels. Something very, very off. And I'm not even sure Kat is aware of it.

My lids finally droop close, and my thoughts drift back to Brom's dark eyes, to Kat's blue ones, to the inhuman voice inside Brom that was ready to do one's bidding.

Thump.

Thump.

Thump.

I open my eyes, sitting up straight.

It's back.

Am I dreaming?

I dig my nails into my skin again, droplets of blood welling to the surface.

I'm not dreaming.

Thump.

Thump.

Thump.

I hold my breath and listen, shaking my hand, a splatter of blood falling to the bedcover.

Thump.

It's right outside the door. I can feel it there, the energy seeping in. I can almost see it like black tar flowing underneath the doorframe, coming across the floor toward me. Wanting me. Craving me.

Knock.

I jump, my heart bucking wildly.

She's here. She's here.

Vivienne Henry is here, and she's knocking on my door.

Knock.

"Oh Jesus," I murmur, my words sounding far away, like I spoke them in another lifetime.

Knock.

I find myself getting to my feet, even though my knees are shaking. Every part of me is shaking with fear because she wants me, she wants me.

Maybe she wants all of us.

"Watch your head," a voice whispers from the other side of the door, coarse and metallic and faint, barely even a whisper.

I am a dead man.

The doorknob begins to turn.

A slow creak of metal that echoes in the room.

A turn left.

A turn right.

A push forward.

The lock catches, stopping the door from opening.

Sweet Jesus.

I watch wide-eyed, breath shaking, expecting another try, another push, another chance for the creature to get inside.

But there's nothing.

Silence.

Suddenly, the clock starts ticking again, the sound filling the air, making me realize that time had actually stopped. I glance at the clock. It's 1:00 a.m. again.

I run to the bathroom and vomit, sickness rolling through me, the fear eating me alive without me even knowing I was its meal.

Then I splash water on my face from the basin.

I avoid looking in the mirror.

Something tells me to avoid looking in the mirror.

Quickly, I turn around and go back into my room. The only sound is the ticking clock. The doorknob doesn't move. The feeling of something oozing under the door to eat me alive is gone.

But then . . .

Thump.

Thump.

Thump.

Off in the distance. Far down the hall.

I don't know what possesses me, but I slide on my slippers, grab one of the candlesticks, and go to the door. I take a deep breath, and before I can change my mind, I unlock the door with my key and step out into the hallway.

Just in time to see the body disappear around the corner, those gray, dead feet dragging on the floor. I make a point of locking my door behind me and then start walking after the body, following the trail. There's blood again, and I quickly touch some of it, pressing my wet fingers on my tongue.

It's blood. It's disgusting.

I spit it out and wipe my fingers on my pants and continue down the hall.

I should talk myself out of this. I should stop and go back to my room. Lock the door and go to sleep.

But I keep going. I round the corner and see the body going down the staircase.

I follow, my steps quick, and yet by the time I get to the main floor, where the classrooms are, she's already far ahead of me. Down another hall.

I follow, walking faster now, the candle flame quivering as I go, and I pray it doesn't go out. Without that light, I can't go on in the dark. I haven't mastered how to control fire yet; I don't have that skill.

I whip around the corner, my breath heavy now, and a door is open near one of the classrooms, dead, lifeless feet being dragged inside.

It's the custodian's closet, or so I thought. I had never given it a second glance before, but now that I am looking through the door, I see that there isn't a broom in sight. Instead, it opens to the top of a narrow stone staircase leading down.

Thump.

The thumps continue going down, down, down, and harder now. Wet smacks against stone.

A shiver rocks through me.

I reach back and push the door open as far as it will go, the hinges creaking ominously, then take off one of my slippers and place it at the corner so that the door can't close on me and lock me in here. Then I put my bare foot on the first step, and I wait.

You don't have to do this, I tell myself. *The door could still close on you. You'll be locked down here with that thing. No one may ever find you again.*

Part of me is unbothered by that fact. Of never being found.

So I walk down and down and down, curiosity to be my demise.

The farther down the stairs I go, the more damp the air feels, bringing with it not just the smells of wet stone and earth but also something herbal. Sage and tarragon and the sharp bite of cut stems mixed with the rotten smell of sulfur and dead flowers.

I go down the stairs, the light dancing on the stone walls, and I feel I must go on forever, but eventually, my feet touch a dirt-packed floor.

Ahead of me is another hall, but this one is short and rounds at the end. I don't hear the body anymore, and the dirt is undisturbed.

But I do hear something else. A faint wail that puts the fear of God in me better than my father ever could. It's an inhuman cry that's suddenly swallowed up by silence, like the sound was cut in two, producing a strong silence so deafening that I can hear my own blood in my veins, the sticky sound of my cells turning over.

I press my fingers against my temple, trying to get it to stop. Tears run down my face, and I wipe them away to see blood-stained fingers. I want to tear my eyes right out of my head, press my thumbs straight into my sockets, and—

The silence stops. The air pressure in the hall adjusts, and I see light flicker where it curves around the corner.

I'm not alone here.

I never was.

I look down at my hands, and there isn't a drop of blood to be found.

Hell.

I slowly walk down the hall toward the flickering light, unsure of what I'm about to see but knowing I'm unable to stop. I am compelled to discover what's happening to me, compelled to find out the truth.

I round the bend and see that it ends with a large black iron door. The dirt at the foot of the door forms a right angle, meaning it must be opened and closed enough to pack down the dirt in front of it.

I press my hands against it and wince. The metal is hot to the touch.

Please. I hear a whisper, not out loud but in my head. *Please, Professor Crane.*

It belongs to a girl and a boy and so many different people. It's raw and desperate, and I feel the fatalistic sorrow inside me as if it's my own.

I see Marie's face as she died, mouth stretched in an endless scream.

"Can I help you find something?" Leona Van Tassel's voice comes through so loud that I yelp and jump around, the candle falling out of my hands and onto the dirt floor. It's snuffed out, but not before I see Leona standing behind me, wearing a face without skin. Just round eggs for eyes and a row of sharp white teeth.

Then everything goes black, and I think I might die of a heart attack right here.

"Let me," her voice rings through the darkness, and suddenly, there's light again.

She's holding the candle in her hands now, her fingertips black and dipped into the flame. Her face is normal again, and her expression is more bemused than angry.

"I'm sorry," I manage to say, my teeth clacking together.

"Don't be," she says coolly, lifting her chin. "You're only in a very private part of the school that's off-limits to anyone who isn't part of the coven." She raises her brow, and I realize it's one of the few times I've seen her without her cloak on her head. "Are you interested in joining our coven, Ichabod?"

I can barely swallow. "I was following someone." *Like hell I would want to be part of your coven.*

"Yes," she says dryly. "Sister Sophie told me about your situation. You mustn't let the students get the best of you. You're their professor, after all. You have the higher ground."

I stare into her eyes, the darkness in them growing as if her irises are spreading. "I'll try to remember that," I manage to say. "Still, don't you think it's strange that the students would lead me down here? Where are we, anyway?"

The corner of her lip twitches. "We are in the soul of the institute. We first broke ground here in 1710 and built the foundations of this very building. But when we were digging, we discovered this place right here had already existed, deep underground. Like it was waiting for us."

I stare at her for a moment, processing that, before looking around at the walls. They aren't stone or wood but packed dirt like the floor, covered in a thin veil of what could be oil. "What was it?"

She shrugs. "We don't know," she muses. "The town of Sleepy Hollow existed for only seventy years prior to the construction of the school. This is an old place, older than New Netherland, older than America, older than the natives, perhaps even older than what you call God. But it sustains us, and it will sustain you. You can feel it, can't you, Ichabod? The power here, how it moves like worms through the earth, feeding on your soul."

"On my soul?" I ask.

"Ah, I forget. Sometimes you wonder if you have one. Well,

I'm here to inform you that you do. And it is very, very sweet." She grins. Once again, her teeth are a little sharper than they were before. She waves a hand in front of my face. "You will eeep-sim see dorec fly fantasm, Mr. Crane. Let vorus vim alone."

Half her words don't even make sense.

But it doesn't matter. Because I'm losing my balance and falling to the left. I expect to have my shoulder slam into the sticky dirt wall, but it doesn't. Instead, I keep falling and falling.

And falling.

I wake up in my bed. It's a slow awakening as pieces of the night slowly slip out of my grasp. My head pounds like I have a drastic hangover.

My ears adjust to the ticking of the clock, and I look over in the dim morning light to see the time. Six forty-four. My alarm will go off in a minute.

Everything that happened is nearly lost. I remember I stayed up late, couldn't sleep. I was thinking about Brom and Kat and Sarah, and then I was thinking about . . . Vivienne Henry? Of voices trapped behind walls? Of Sister Leona's row of sharp teeth?

I rub my palm down my face. "What is happening to me?"

I take in a deep breath and try once more to grasp the fragments of the night, but they melt away like dreams. Were they dreams? Thoughts? Did the dead teacher make an appearance again?

I've got nothing. Nothing but questions and never any answers.

Some teacher I've turned out to be.

22

Kat

The next morning, I wake up with a heavy heart, anger and shame settling over me like the low fog outside my window. The first thing I remember is fighting with Brom in the stables, the last person on earth I want to fight with. He had been so cruel and callous, but I had lost my temper. I know it's not his fault that he doesn't remember anything, and I know that's also why he's not himself, why he's become so rough and volatile. I should have been more understanding.

But then again, I didn't deserve for him to compare me to a dirty rag. I didn't deserve his jealous outbursts. I'm trying to help him, and it feels like I'm the only one who is.

Except for Crane. I have to talk to Crane. When we left his class yesterday, he had promised us he would read up on any magic or spells that could work to reverse memory loss. I thank God that I have him, the only other person who seems to care as much as I do. For once, I feel like I'm not alone.

I get up slowly, looking around my bedroom, at the stack of

books on the desk, the dried flowers in a vase, my stack of tarot cards that I now feel brave enough to leave out in the open. On the wall is a framed picture of rudimentary art, wet leaves pressed onto canvas until they left colored outlines, but I had done it with my father one autumn afternoon, sitting outside on the porch, not realizing I was creating a moment in time that would live forever.

Will I be able to take it with me to the school? How much of myself am I allowed to bring? Where the idea of living on campus thrilled me weeks ago, now I feel sick to my stomach over it. Because it isn't my choice, and I don't know why my mother wants me to be there. Is it truly because she wants me and Brom to be closer because she—and everyone else—still thinks we're going to get married? Or is it something else? After what Famke told me and after Brom confirmed my own secret beliefs, I know my mother doesn't have my best interests at heart.

With that in mind, I get dressed for the day. When I head out to use the washroom, I smell a hearty breakfast of fried pork and eggs mingling with the rich scent of freshly ground coffee and chicory, and hear Famke and my mother speaking in Dutch in the kitchen. I wish I could understand what they're saying—my parents didn't bother trying to teach me their mother tongue—but I at least know from their tones that they're having a disagreement over something.

When I'm finally ready, sticking the final pins up in my hair, I make my way to the dining room table, where my mother is seated reading the weekly newspaper. She glances up at me but doesn't say anything. I take my seat across from her as Famke comes in and gives me my breakfast.

"Thank you," I say to her, and while her smile is warm for me, she turns frosty again as she glances at my mother and heads back to the kitchen.

After my altercation in the barn with Brom last night, I stayed with Snowdrop for a while. Her energy had changed after him being there, becoming anxious and pawing at the ground. It took time to calm her, and I was in no hurry to go back inside and face my mother and the Van Brunts. By the time I did go back in the house, the Van Brunts had left, my mother had already retired to bed, and Famke was cleaning up. I wanted to talk to her more about our discussion earlier, but I was tired, and she seemed a little closed off, like she'd already said too much.

"They're having the annual bonfire this Friday," my mother says as she scans the newspaper, her pair of spectacles held at her eyes. "If we move you to the school on Saturday, it would be a nice way to spend your last night here. You could go with Mary."

Mary. I feel a pang of guilt. I've neglected her ever since I started school. In the beginning, she would often be waiting by the fence to meet me and Mathias on the way home, and after Mathias stopped riding with me, I saw her only once or twice. I should reach out to her and soon. She's the only thing in my life that is relatively normal, and I'll be even further removed once I start living at the school.

"I'll make sure to ask her," I say. Then against my better judgment, I say, "I'm sorry about last night. I didn't mean to lose my temper."

My mother lowers her glasses and gives me a small smile. "It's quite all right. I know things are overwhelming right now. In time, everything will make sense again. Just focus on your studies and on Brom."

"Can I ask you something?"

Her expression stiffens slightly, wary of what I'm going to ask. "Of course."

"Why do you want me to marry Brom so much? Why did you and the Van Brunts promise us to each other at such a young age?"

She lets out a laugh. A nervous laugh. "Oh. To be honest, it was all your father's idea."

Lies. She's lying right to my face.

"Why?" I press. "We were wealthy. We had far more money than the Van Brunts. Why would he want me to marry someone lower-class?"

"Katrina," she admonishes me. "Lower-class? Just because your father had a lot of money when I married him doesn't make us any better than them. Really, after the way you treated them last night and now these haughty thoughts, I think you should be directing these questions at yourself. Look inward for a change, hmm?"

And at that, she gets up in a huff, placing her glasses and paper on the table.

I watch as she goes over to her bedroom and shuts the door behind her.

Shutting me and any of my questions out.

I let out a growl of frustration, and the coffee cups on the table start rattling violently, the dregs of coffee spilling over the edges, even though I'm not touching anything.

Goodness me. What the devil is happening?

Famke comes into the dining room and eyes the mess.

"Did you do this?" she asks.

"I guess so," I say.

"Your magic," she says, lowering her voice, her eyes darting to my mother's room. "It's coming out in times of duress. It's unfocused."

"I thought you didn't know anything about magic," I say.

"I said I'm not a witch," she explains in a hurried whisper. "But as I told you, I listen, and I watch. I know what magic looks like when it's waning and when it's coming into power. If I were you, I'd bring this up with your teacher. Professor Crane. Him and no one else. I think he'll know what to do with you."

Another thing for me to worry about, I think as I get to my feet and try to help clean up, but Famke shoos me away and tells me to get on with my day.

I glance at the clock. I wanted to get to Crane's class early so I could talk to him, which means I'm going to have to rush.

Luckily, it doesn't take long for me to tack up Snowdrop and lead her out of the stable, but then I see Brom mounted on Daredevil outside the house, talking about something with my mother.

Shoot. I really thought if I left early enough, I'd also miss having to ride with Brom. I'm still not sure what to say to him. Do I apologize? Do I stay mad? Is he still the friend I always had? Is he someone else now?

With a heavy sigh, I mount Snowdrop and guide her toward them.

"Good morning," Brom says, as if last night never happened, as if the past four years never happened. And yet, seeing him wearing a black suit and coat astride that magnificent black stallion, I can't help the butterflies in my stomach, especially when the corners of his mouth lift just a little, bringing the slightest bit of light to that stony gaze.

"Good morning," I say with a nod, my smile matching his, though perhaps a little less forthcoming. Especially with my mother staring at us like we're two prized cows on the auction block.

"Well, you better not be late for class," she says, a smile plastered on her face. "Are you both in the same one this morning?"

Brom shakes his head. "History, if you can believe it."

"Energy manipulation," I say.

She looks crestfallen at that. "Oh, well, I hope—"

"Excuse me, Ms. Van Tassel?" a deep Bostonian accent rings out from across the lane. The three of us look over to see Constable Wesley Kirkbride riding up on his horse, a grim expression on his face.

It's not every day that the police want to have a word with you. I immediately get a sour taste in my mouth.

"Yes?" she says with a wary expression. "What can I do for you?"

The constable pulls his horse to a halt right in front of us and nods at both me and Brom before facing my mother. "I'm investigating an incident that happened around midnight last night. Do you know of your whereabouts at that time?"

"I was asleep," she says. She looks to the two of us. "I'm sure we all were."

He looks at Brom. "And you?"

"I was asleep," he says. "You can ask my parents."

He sighs. "I believe you, boy." He runs his hand over his face before straightening up, a look of weary horror on his face. "I've never seen anything like this in all my life, even up in the cities."

"What happened?" Brom asks.

The constable stares for a moment, gauging us, then shrugs. "You're going to hear about it sooner or later. This will make news all over the state, maybe the country."

My stomach drops, ice filling my veins with dread. "What?" I whisper.

"A Sleepy Hollow man was murdered last night."

My mother and I gasp in unison.

"Where?" Brom asks.

"Meeks farm. Found in the middle of the cornfield. All the stalks around the scene trampled like someone running from a horse."

"Meeks?" I repeat, my heart going cold in my chest. "Who was murdered?"

"Joshua Meeks. Had his head chopped clean off him."

The world seems to fall out from under me, and I lean forward, clutching Snowdrop's mane. My mother proclaims her shock, and the constable describes the scene further, but I'm not even listening.

Joshua Meeks. The man I had an affair with last summer. Always had a smile for me, kind green eyes, hair like the sun. A man with gentle hands who made me discover things about myself, what I liked and what I wanted, who helped me come into being a proper woman.

He was dead. His head sliced off in a cornfield after being hunted by a man on a horse.

Why him? Why Joshua?

And why after I happened to tell Brom about it?

The sour pit in my stomach gets bigger. I look over at Brom, and he meets my gaze.

He knows what I'm thinking, but he just gives the faintest shake of his head. His dark eyes gleam. *I didn't do it*, they say. *It wasn't me.*

And I believe him.

But I'm not sure for how long.

23

Crane

Crane, you look terrible," Daniels says as I stagger into the dining room and swipe a mug from the stack by the door.

"Thanks," I say as I stand beside him as the cook takes the metal carafe off the wood stove and pours us both some coffee. If I have to give this school some credit, it's that their coffee is the best I've ever had, no doubt because some sort of magic has been used in the process. "I feel like death warmed over," I add.

"Perhaps you're working too hard," Daniels says as we walk together toward a table in the corner. Daniels leans in, the scent of pipe tobacco clinging to his tweed jacket. "Did you hear what happened to Desi?"

"The linguistics professor?" I ask. "No. Do tell."

We sit down, and he gives the room another sweep of his eyes before he whispers, "He's gone."

"Gone?" I pick up my mug, but my hand is trembling enough for me to put it back down. Must be the lack of sleep, the nightmares, the everything. "He quit?"

"We don't know. Yesterday afternoon, they were looking for him. Searched his room. All his possessions are there, his bed made. But he never showed up for class. I think they searched the campus for him, and there's no sign of him."

Aman Desi. Smart man, always talked of his family back in Bombay. "He probably left in the night. Wanted to escape."

"It's not a prison," Daniels snorts. "Besides, he left his papers behind."

My stomach churns uneasily, and when I take a sip of my coffee, there's a bitterness there. I wish I could separate the images I have from last night to figure out what's real and what's a dream. But I've got nothing. And as much as I want to discuss it with Daniels, he obviously doesn't see the school the same way I do. If I were him, I wouldn't be so trusting about a school for witches run by a coven.

Then again, I'm still here. I'm still here because of Kat and now Brom. And I'll be damned if I don't help Brom get to the bottom of what's happened to him.

I have no appetite this morning, so after the coffee with Daniels, the conversation switching over to more genial topics, I decide to skip breakfast and head to the classroom. I have no idea if Brom is in my energy class this morning, but I must speak to Kat.

Though the sun has risen, the morning is still dark with heavy clouds when I walk to the classrooms. The tone of the campus has changed in such a short time, summer surrendering completely to fall. The chill in the air is damp, the kind that seeps through your coat and lives in your bones, and I have to shake it off many times before I get inside the building.

To my delight, I see Kat waiting outside the classroom's locked door.

"Kat," I say, my voice coming out hoarse, echoing faintly in the hall.

"Crane," she says, and to my relief, there's just as much desperation in her voice as there is in mine.

I stride toward her and embrace her without any thought, wrapping my arms around her and holding her tight, breathing in her smell of sun-soaked meadows, letting it fill me with light. She lets out a soft sigh that warms my heart, and I pull back, placing my hands on her cheeks, searching her face. She's as beautiful as ever, but there are dark circles beneath her azure eyes, and her skin looks paler than normal.

"Are you all right?" I ask. And then I catch myself. Should I be touching her like this now that Brom is back? Is whatever we had, whatever hint of relationship that was about to bloom like a rose, now doomed to wither on the stem?

"I'm sorry, I should . . ." I take my hands off her sweet face, but she reaches out and grabs my wrists, holding them.

"Please," she implores. "I need you right now. I need to talk to you."

"And I need to talk to you."

And I need to be with you. I need to know if you're still mine.

I hear the door to the hall open, and she drops her grip on my wrists, and I automatically take a step back from her. A couple of other students file in, and before they have a chance to see us together, I quickly reach for my keys and unlock the classroom door, ushering Kat in.

"Come see me after class," I whisper to her.

Of course, as one student passes me, he gives me a smirk, like he knows exactly what's going on between us. The humorous thing is he really has no idea. Even I don't know myself.

It turns out that Brom isn't in this class, which is for the best, since he's a distraction on his own, and together with Kat, I wouldn't be able to get anything done. So I'm somehow able to push the mysteries of him behind me and focus on our subject for the day, which happens to be how energy manipulation can be aided by spells, crystals, and rituals, including blood magic.

"Blood magic," I explain to the class, "has everything to do with fusing energy together. We've practiced with using our energy to influence others and how to block others from using that energy against us. Now, I want to talk about fusing one's energy with another so that you are connected. Think about fungi. Your biology classes should be touching on how marvelous fungi are."

I notice a few eyes glazing over at that, but I push on. "Mushrooms are connected to each other through underground pathways. What happens to one affects another. As witches, we know they can communicate with each other. This is what blood magic does when it's applied to each other and our energy. Spilled blood fuses us together, connecting us on another plane, one we can't see unless you're looking through the veils. With the right spells and incantations, we're able to become one with another, our energy combining to become something extremely powerful."

At that, I feel Kat's eyes on me. Perhaps she's thinking the same thing as I am. If we practiced blood magic on Brom, is it possible that we could break through whatever blockages he has in his memories? After all, I feel the reason that I'm able to retain my memories of the school when I pass the gates is due to my connection with Kat.

She gives me a little nod. Something to think about.

Too much to think about.

I get through the rest of the class, and I can tell the students are relieved that I didn't ask any of them to take out a knife and start cutting themselves up.

When class is over, Kat goes straight to my desk. "Do you have a class after this?" she asks.

I shake my head. "No. But I know you do."

"It's just philosophy," she says. "I'm skipping it. Meet me at the stables when you're ready."

She turns and hurries out the door. Even though everyone suspects there's something going on between us, the last thing I want is for someone to see us walking to the stables together, especially with what we're about to discuss.

I wait a few minutes, gathering up the textbook I had pulled from the library on blood magic and rituals, then set out after her. A light drizzle is falling, peppering my shoulders with tiny droplets by the time I slip into the shelter of the stables.

I poke my head into Snowdrop's stall, the horse giving me a welcoming nicker. I stroke her muzzle for a moment before moving on to the next stalls until I notice Kat's coat hung up outside one of the empty stalls at the end, furthest from the school, closest to the woods.

I peer inside and see her there. Her back is against the wall, hidden in the shadows, but the moment she sees me, she runs forward through the hay floor and pulls me deeper inside.

"Thank God," she says, holding on to my arms. "I was afraid you wouldn't come."

"Why wouldn't I?" I ask, my hand sliding down to hold hers, wrapping around it. Her skin is cold and soft, and it does something to me, makes me feel like the more I hold on to her, the more I'll fall through the earth.

She gives her head a shake, a strand of blond hair coming loose. "I don't know. I just thought maybe after everything, you would want some distance. There's just so much . . . it's too much."

I reach out and brush her hair off her face, tucking it behind her ear, and she closes her eyes at my touch. "I'm not going anywhere," I murmur, running my fingers over her jaw until I'm gripping her chin. "You have me, my *vlinder*, no matter what happens, no matter what you're about to tell me."

Because I can tell she's carrying something heavy on her shoulders, something I might not like.

"It's Brom," she says warily.

"I know."

She gives her head another shake, rubbing her soft lips together, and fuck, do I ever want to kiss her. "No. You don't know."

I run my thumb over her lip, fighting the temptation to place my lips on hers and make everything go away. "Tell me, then."

"Brom came over for supper last night with his parents," she says. "They're making him live on campus now."

"All right . . ."

"And my mom says I'm to live here too."

I can't help but smile. "So you'll be closer to me. I don't see how that's a bad thing."

"It's a bad thing because my mother was so adamant that I not stay here. Now she's completely changed her mind about it, and all because of Brom. They want me here only because he's here."

"I see." Damned if I don't feel the deep cut of jealousy again.

"Crane," she says gravely, her eyes searching mine with trepidation, "they want me to marry him."

My heart feels like it's dropped out of my chest and into a bloody mess on the floor.

"Marry him? Did he ask you?"

"No. He hasn't."

I sigh with relief.

"But it was always that way. Ever since I was born, I've been betrothed to him. We grew up knowing we'd be married to each other one day. And he was my best friend, and I . . . I didn't mind the idea. I don't think he did either. But when he went missing . . . that was all forgotten. Until now. Now, they're talking about us getting married like he never left at all. They all act like the past four years never happened."

I mull that over for a moment, but all I really care about is how she feels.

"Do you love him?" I ask point-blank.

She swallows hard, the sound audible. "I did. When I was younger, I did. I was in love with him, even though I was a silly teenager who didn't know the meaning of the word."

"And now?" I say stiffly, afraid of the answer.

"I don't know," she says, and the air hitches in my lungs. "I can't tell . . . because it's not Brom. It's not him."

"What do you mean?" I think of the locked door inside his mind, that other voice, the war that belonged to someone else.

She takes in a deep breath. "I left supper early. My parents and his parents were pushing for the marriage as they always have and—"

"Do you know why?" I interrupt. "Do they ever tell you why they want you to be married?"

"No," she says emphatically, her eyes flashing. "And that's the thing. I can't get any answers. My mother says it was something my father wanted, but Famke told me secretly that all my father ever wanted for me was to leave Sleepy Hollow and that he didn't want me to marry Brom at all. It's just that my mother overpowered him on everything."

"Kat," I say gently, taking her hand in mine again. "Tell me . . . how did your father die?'

She frowns at me. "Why?" Then her mouth forms an O in shock. "You don't think my mother had anything to do with his death, do you?"

"I'm thinking a lot of things," I admit. "It's part of my job to examine all the angles. Is it possible that—"

"No," she says sharply. "No, that can't . . . I won't entertain that notion."

Then, a look dawns on her face.

"Think about it, Kat," I say softly. "Tell me how he died."

"Heart attack," she says, her eyes going glassy as she looks away from my gaze. I give her hands a squeeze. "I was there. I saw him die. He was in bed. It was the morning, early. My mother had run out into the hall and yelled for me. Said there was something wrong with him. I ran into the bedroom, and he was gripping his heart, gasping for breath. I ran to his side while my mother went to call for help."

She closes her eyes, and a single tear runs down her cheek. I feel another thread inside me unravel while my sense of protection over her tightens, becoming something raw and fierce.

"He stared up at me, and in his eyes, I saw so much sorrow," she goes on quietly, her voice breaking. "He was so sad that he was dying, and I . . . I knew from that moment on I'd never have something good in my life. I was losing the one person who loved me. But even in his last moments, his words were for my mother, not for me."

I frown. That doesn't seem like the man she'd been describing, the one who would do anything for his daughter, the one who created all the love I felt when I was inside her memories. "What did he say?"

"He said for me to watch over my mother," she says. Then she stops herself, her brows knitting together as she meets my gaze. "No. No, it wasn't that. It was 'Watch for your mother.'"

"As in watch *out* for her?" I venture.

She swallows. "I don't know," she whispers. "I always took it to mean that I would have to watch over her. She became so weak after he died it's like he knew that she would wither without him."

Something about that turn of phrase tickles something at the back of my brain, but I don't know what it is. "Like he was keeping her alive," I muse quietly.

"Yes," she says, a sharpness coming over her expression. "It was like he was keeping her alive. After he died, she was never the same. She still isn't. It's like her life force is . . . gone. No one can figure out what's wrong with her."

I cock my head. "Well, what do you make of that?"

"I don't know. Maybe their magic was fused together. Con-nected. Like the mushrooms you spoke about. Maybe there was something in him that kept her alive."

"Hmmm." There's something more to it than that, but we're on the right track. Least I think we are. Frustration coils inside me yet again. "Damn it, I was hoping I could solve one mystery before moving on to another."

"Maybe if you solve one, you solve them all," Kat says. "You can start with Brom. Because last night after supper, I was alone with him, and he started acting really strange. Getting mean, getting . . . violent."

"Violent?" I exclaim, rage flickering inside me. "Toward you?" I'll fucking kill him if he hurt her in any way.

"He didn't really hurt me, but he was . . . physical in a way he hasn't been before," she says. "He wasn't himself. I was looking into his eyes, and it was like they became so black they belonged to someone else." She pauses, her gaze drifting to the ground. "He insinuated I was a whore for sleeping with you."

My teeth grind together as the rage continues to flame inside me. "Guess it wouldn't help to point out we haven't actually fucked."

Her chin jerks in at my choice of words.

"Sorry," I say quickly. "That was not very gentlemanlike of me." I pause. "Well, you can tell Brom that won't be an issue if you're currently betrothed to each other."

She gives me an odd look. "Don't tell me you're actually jealous?"

"Jealous?" I let out a sour laugh. "Of course I'm jealous. Here I am falling for one of my students, against all reason and logic, and meanwhile, she's betrothed to another."

"Falling for?" she repeats softly, a tenderness in her gaze.

I raise my chin in defiance. "You may be getting under my skin, sweet witch. I won't hide that from you. You're unraveling all the threads that have been holding me together."

She blinks. "Oh," she says, a small smile appearing.

It would be nice to hear something like that in return, but I'm not sure I'll be so lucky.

"Well, I'm not betrothed to Brom," she goes on. "I still have free will. And he's not just another. You were with him. He was your Abe."

I swallow uneasily. "Yes, well, that certainly complicates all of this, doesn't it? As if this needed more complications."

"There is one more thing," she says.

"Oh Lord, what now?" I say with a sigh, running my hand over my jaw.

"A man was murdered last night," she says, and my eyes go wide. "Not just any man either, and not just any murder. It was Joshua Meeks, a farmhand who I had a little . . . relationship with last year."

"How did he die?" I ask cautiously.

She grimaces and runs a finger over her throat.

Head chopped off.

"Run down in his cornfield by a man on a horse," she says. "And the worst of it is that I had told Brom last night about my time with Joshua. Right after I told him about my time with you."

Fantastic.

24

Kat

Crane runs a hand through his messy black hair and starts pacing back and forth in the stall like a restless horse. I know the information I just gave him is probably overloading his system, his brain working overtime to try to put all the pieces together.

"So you told Brom about your tryst with this Joshua Meeks, and then the next morning, Meeks is dead. Apparently, a victim of the headless horseman. Correct?"

I nod, tugging on the ends of my blouse. "Yes."

"And you were with Brom when the constable was there?"

"Yes. I looked at Brom, and he seemed surprised by it all, yet he knew what I was thinking. When we rode here together—"

He stops, his eyes fierce. "Just a minute now. You rode with Brom to school?"

"Of course. He had stopped by the house to ride with me."

"Well?" he asks, coming closer. His hair is wild now from his hands constantly tugging on it. "What did you talk about? And how could you ride with him after everything that happened last night?"

I shrug. "I didn't want to."

"You weren't afraid?"

On one hand, how could I ever be afraid of Brom? I've known and trusted him my whole life. On the other hand, I don't know what the past four years have done to him.

"After finding out about Meeks, I was wary," I concede. "But I didn't know what to say or do. And anyway, Brom knew what I was thinking. After we were on our way, he told me he didn't have anything to do with it."

"And you believe him?"

"I have to. It's Brom."

"People change, Kat. That's when they're the most dangerous, because you're easily fooled."

I throw out my arms, frustration rolling through me like thunder. "I don't know what to believe anymore! What does this mean? Is he connected to the Hessian soldier? Is it a coincidence? Why else would Meeks be dead? Is Brom . . ." The lessons from this morning's class come into my head. "Are Brom and the Hessian connected like the way you were talking about? Could there have been some blood ritual that bound them together?"

Of course, that only leads to the questions of who and why.

"Maybe," Crane says, tapping his fingers against his chin. "Maybe. Or maybe it's more simple than that." He pauses, his eyes lighting up. "Maybe it's possession."

I nearly laugh. "You think Brom is possessed by the ghost of the headless horseman?"

"Do you have a better idea?" he says, narrowing his eyes at me.

"No," I admit. "And no, I don't think he's possessed. When I was riding with Brom earlier, it was Brom." A bewildered Brom who was adamant that he had nothing to do with Meeks's murder. It was impossible not to take him at his word. I knew he was telling the truth, and I just have to make a decision and trust that, otherwise I'll go insane.

"You yourself said he's been different. Violent." The muscle in his jaw tics. "Cruel."

"At times, but that doesn't mean I think he's possessed. I think he's confused and angry and . . ."

"It's not a coincidence, Kat. Those two are linked. Brom might not even realize it, or perhaps he does now. But if he truly doesn't remember anything, then I don't think this can be explained." He looks away, trapped in his thoughts. "We need a way to reach him. I need to get inside his head." He glances at me. "Is he still on campus now? I don't know if he's in my afternoon classes today, but perhaps . . ."

"Now that he knows about us, I doubt Brom will want to talk to you again," I tell him.

He gives me a dry smile. "So I'm not the only one with jealousy issues, then?"

"No," I say, and I hate the little thrill that runs through me and makes my stomach do somersaults. The fact that Crane is jealous of Brom and Brom is jealous of Crane is both overwhelming and intoxicating. Both men I care about deeply, both men carrying darkness in them. The biggest difference is that one man makes me feel safe, and the other is starting to terrify me. And yet, I want them both the same.

What a dangerous path desire is.

Crane's eyes turn molten for a second as he stares at me. "What are you thinking about?" he asks, his voice going low.

I shouldn't tell him. I should stay focused on Brom and what we need to do about him. But there's so much energy and anxiety coursing through my veins right now that I fear what will happen if it doesn't have a place to go.

I hold his gaze and let the fire burn between us.

Then I take a chance.

"I'm thinking about you," I tell him carefully. "About how safe you make me feel. All I ever wanted was to feel safe and protected and to have someone on my side and looking out for me and . . ." I pause, feeling more and more vulnerable, like my ribs are opening up so he can get a glimpse of my heart. "And I do. I have you. Or at least I think I do. Do I?"

He stares at me with disbelief in those stormy eyes, and for a moment, I'm afraid he'll say something that will make all sense of safety disappear.

Then he takes two long strides across the stall and grabs my face in his large, warm hands, and instead of holding me there like he did this morning, he leans down and kisses me. It's a hard kiss, a surprising one that nearly knocks me off my feet, and his hands are so strong, fingertips pressing into my cheekbones to keep me in place. His tongue is demanding, slipping into my mouth, and I open to him, and he takes all he can get. He moans at my taste, and I gasp as his tongue probes deeper, velvet soft and hard, and it feels like he's using his tongue like he'd use his cock inside me, and I'm hit with a wave of desire that nearly drowns me.

My toes curl, and heat floods between my thighs, and suddenly, my clothes feel suffocating, the high neck of my blouse too tight around my throat, my skirt too long and bulky to feel any hardness from his body as he presses it against mine until I'm flat against the wall of the stall.

He pulls his head back, breathing hard, and rests his forehead against mine, the tip of his nose brushing against the tip of mine. "Here's the thing about feeling safe, sweet witch," he says, his voice rough. "It's a baseline. A starting point you can always go back to. I will always take you back to where you feel safest. You can trust me on that. Will you trust me?"

I don't know what he's talking about, but I nod anyway because I do trust him. After the way he protected me when the horseman came after us, I know I can trust him with my life.

"Yes," I whisper. "I trust you."

A wicked smile curves his lips, and I'm struck by how easily this man vacillates between being a good and proper teacher and a man who's a slave to lust. "That's what I needed to hear. Just remember that you trust me, and I trust you to let me know when you're uncomfortable with something."

I blink at him as his hands wrap around me to the back of my neck, fingers curling over the edge of my collar. He fingers the buttons there gently. "What would I be uncomfortable with?" I ask, my voice shaking slightly, but I'm scared and excited, my heart rate increasing.

"Letting me use your body," he says, his gaze dropping to my lips. "Letting me fuck you until you're rendered senseless. Letting me be in control of how you come and when you come and trusting that I'll never let you leave unsatisfied."

With a sudden display of power, he rips the collar of my

blouse at the back, the sound of buttons popping and fabric tearing as the cloth falls away down my arms, leaving me exposed in my corset and chemise.

"Crane!" I admonish him. "What are you doing?"

"Being impatient," he says, and with my neck exposed, his mouth goes to my skin, and he starts sucking. I gasp, my eyes fluttering back, my body immediately flooded with sensation. "I can't stand how many layers you women wear, but I'll rip them all off you if I have to."

"Is this where I tell you I'm uncomfortable with this?" I ask.

He glances up at me, his eyes glimmering and devious. "Oh, no, my sweet witch. This is nothing compared to what I'm about to do to you."

But instead of ripping my chemise or tearing through the laces of my corset, he just yanks them both down until my breasts bounce free. My nipples harden in the cold air, and his lips are on them in seconds, warm and wet, giving long swirls of his tongue.

"Oh my goodness," I cry out, my head going back. I gasp for breath and squeeze my thighs together as electricity flows from my breasts and through the rest of my body, tightening a hot coil in the center of me.

He takes my moans as encouragement and switches between my nipples, biting and sucking, making me squirm and writhe under his touch. His hands trail down my body, squeezing and kneading over my corset until they reach the waistband of my skirt, where he raises it up, bunching it up around my waist, and I'm left in just my stockings, garters, and drawers.

I blush, feeling exposed and vulnerable, but the heat between my legs is impossible to ignore. Crane gets down on the ground and kneels in front of me, his eyes dark with desire as his fingers trace the lace of my undergarments, teasing the slit in the crotch of my drawers where I'm bare underneath.

His gaze flicks up to mine before he leans in and disappears under my skirt. He presses a kiss to my inner thigh. I gasp, my hands scrambling to find something to hold on to as he trails kisses up my thigh, getting closer and closer to the heat that's pooling between my legs.

Then he pulls his head out from under my skirt, his hand kneading into the tender flesh of my thighs.

"Do you want this?" he asks me, black hair a mess, staring up through his dark lashes.

"Please," I beg, my voice barely audible. I can feel energy swirling through me, potent and hot, wanting to do magic, waiting impatiently to be released.

"Has anyone ever tasted you like this before?" he asks, his voice dripping with lust.

"No," I pant. "Never."

"Good," he growls, and lowers his head between my thighs. His mouth finds my center, and he begins to lap at me with long, slow strokes of his tongue. I moan and arch my back against the wall, the pleasure so intense that I feel like I might burst at any moment.

I can't believe he's doing this. That he's tasting me, savoring me like I'm his last meal. I feel so completely vulnerable and exposed, and yet the fire that's building in my veins with each pass of his tongue is addicting.

He continues to feast on me, alternating between gentle sucking and teasing flicks of his tongue. My body responds to him like a bucking horse, sending sparks through me with each touch of his lips.

I lose track of time, lost in a world of sensation. His skilled mouth brings me to the brink of orgasm over and over again, but each time, he pulls back, denying me release.

"Please," I beg again.

I feel him laugh against my wetness, his breath so hot that I fear I might die on my feet from wanting something so badly.

"I love to hear you beg," he murmurs against me, his voice muffled. "But only I get to decide when. Do you understand?"

"Yes," I gasp.

"Such a good, sweet witch."

Finally, when I can just about take no more, he plunges his tongue up and inside me, pumping it in and out like a cock, and then I'm teetering over the edge. I cry out his name and surrender to the overwhelming pleasure that washes over me. He continues to work me through my orgasm, prolonging the experience until I am weak and shaking with sensation, almost falling to the ground. The energy my orgasm creates flows through me, and if only I could use my brain for just a moment, I know I could do something with that energy, create something from nothing.

He finally pulls back and looks up at me. I can barely focus on his face, the wild mess of his hair, the way his mouth glistens with my moisture on him.

"You taste like magic," he murmurs. A look of molten darkness comes over his eyes, and I shiver despite myself. "Now, get on your knees."

I stare at him in surprise. "What?"

But then he's grabbing my arm and pulling me down until I land on my knees in the hay. Before I can say anything, he's moving fast, suddenly behind me, one hand shoving my skirts up to my waist, the other pushing down between my shoulder blades until my chest is pressed against the ground.

"Stay there," he commands. "And wait for it."

I hear him walk off into the stable, the hay pressed against my cheek, loose bits of it scattering as I breathe hard, not knowing what he's about to do.

You can get him to stop, I remind myself. *He won't let you feel unsafe.*

But I don't want him to stop. I like feeling afraid with him, knowing in the end, he'll still protect me. It's the best kind of danger, the one I feel my energy feeds on.

His footsteps echo as he comes back, and I only now realize the sound of rain falling outside the stable, the patter of it on the roof and the maple trees.

"Good girl," he croons. "Waiting so patiently. So trusting." He pauses. "Do you still want to continue?"

I try to lift my head to look at him, but suddenly, I hear a loud smack of something hard against his palm, and I jump.

"Keep your head down. Don't look at me."

I do as he says, my body tingling all over with anticipation.

Then he reaches forward and pulls down my drawers and stockings until my bottom is exposed.

He lets out a low moan. "What a prize student you are," he says. "You're about to find out about a saying us teachers have."

I try to swallow. I can barely speak. "What's that?"

"Spare the rod, spoil the child," he says. "But you are no child, sweet witch. And you will not be spared."

With that, I feel a sharp sting on my bottom as he spanks me. Hard. Not with his hand but with what feels like a riding crop. I cry out, not expecting the sudden pain, but then he hits me again, and again, and again, each time harder than the last, until I'm jerking against the ground. My hands clench into fists as I try to process the sensations, the mix of pain and pleasure causing my body to react in ways I never thought possible.

"Are you all right?" he asks, his breath labored. "I can stop."

I make a noise.

"Is that a yes?" he asks.

"Yes," I manage to say. "I'm all right."

"Very good."

He continues to spank me with the crop, alternating between hitting each cheek until tears are streaming down my face and my bottom is on fire. I can feel the wetness between my legs increasing with each strike, and I know he can too. But even as the pain becomes almost unbearable, the pleasure is still there, lurking just beneath the surface.

"You like this, don't you?" he growls, his hand coming down harder, the crop stinging.

"Yes," I gasp out. "Please don't stop."

He chuckles, the sound sending shivers down my spine. "I thought you might. I'll only stop when you say you've had enough." He emphasizes that with another hit of the crop, and my body jerks. "I can go all night watching the marks I'm leaving on your perfect skin."

Eventually though, my skin goes numb, the sensations flattening me, and my core pulses with a greedy need for release.

"Crane," I say through ragged breath.

"What is it, my *vlinder*?" he says. "Had enough?"

I nod.

He leans down and whispers in my ear. "You're doing so well, sweet witch," he says gently. "Shall I fuck you now? Is that what you'd like? My big cock filling up that tight pink cunt of yours."

I both blush at his scandalous words and moan in response, my body arching up toward him in anticipation. He takes my response as encouragement and flips me over onto my back. My breath hitches as he undoes his trousers, his eyes burning into mine as he brings his cock out of his fly and onto his palm. I can't look away from the brazen sight of it, and he gives me a satisfied smirk as he runs his hand up and down his length, coating it in his own arousal. I knew he'd be large based on the way he felt earlier and how tall he is, but I didn't think he'd be that big. He's huge, long, and thick, and I feel sweat beading on my forehead at the thought. I may have had a lover or two, and Brom certainly was a big boy, but now I feel flush with nervousness.

"It will fit," Crane says smugly, stroking it with easy slips of his hand. "In case you're worried about that."

I gulp down air as he comes forward and towers over me. Then he gets down on his knees, his eyes dark with desire as he leans down and kisses me deeply, his tongue tangling with mine. I taste myself on his lips, salty and strange, but I don't care. I want more of him.

"It's okay," he murmurs against my lips. "I'll take care of you, I promise."

He positions himself at my entrance, teasing me with the tip before pushing in slowly. So slowly. His length fills me up in a way that makes me feel like I'm splitting in two. I cry out, the sensation almost overwhelming, but then he's kissing me again, his tongue soothing and coaxing as he moves inside me. The stretch of him is almost too much to bear, but the pleasure overrides any discomfort. He fills me completely, his cock throbbing inside of me as he begins to move in and out, slow at first but building in speed and intensity with each thrust.

I cry out as he hits a spot deep inside of me, sending sparks of pleasure shooting through my nerves. He grunts in response, his forehead pressing against mine as he continues to pound into me, his fingers digging into my hips.

Our bodies move in perfect sync, a dance of pleasure and desire. The hay beneath us rustles and crunches with every thrust, adding to the raw, animalistic feeling of it all, as if we're just two animals rutting in heat.

"Kat," he groans, his pace becoming erratic as he approaches his own release. My name sounds like a spell coming from his lips. "My sweet little witch, you feel so good."

I wrap my legs around his waist, urging him to go faster, harder. I'm on the edge of another orgasm, the pleasure building and building until it's almost unbearable.

"Would you like to come, my dear?" he whispers. "Would you like me to touch you where you're most desperate for me, that slick little bud that's just crying for release?"

I nod frantically, my body aching for it.

"Tell me, Kat," he says. "Tell me what you want."

"I want you to touch me," I gasp. "Please, Crane, I need it."

He grins down at me, his eyes dark with desire. "Anything for you," he says.

He shifts his weight and takes one hand off my hip, moving it down between us until his fingers are rubbing circles around my clit. I cry out again, the sensation almost too much to bear. But he keeps going, his fingers working me faster and harder until I'm shaking with the force of my orgasm, my body clenching around him as I come.

He doesn't stop moving though, even as I'm coming down from the high. He keeps thrusting into me, hitting that spot deep inside over and over again until he's coming too, his body jerking against mine as he spills inside me. He lets out a deep, guttural moan, his forehead resting against mine as his body shudders with the force of his release.

We stay like that for a few moments, our breathing heavy and labored as we come down from the intensity of our pleasure. Then he pulls out of me, his seed spilling onto the hay as he does so, and collapses onto the hay beside me, pulling me close.

"Thank you for trusting me," he murmurs, brushing my hair off my face. "Believe it or not, I was easing you into it. Into the way I like things. My sexual appetites have often been called . . . deviant."

I let out a light laugh, feeling joyous and dazed. "That was easing me into things?"

"To be honest, I thought of putting a bit in your mouth and riding you like a horse. But perhaps that's something for another day."

My eyes widen. "You really are a deviant."

He grins, a rare show of perfect white teeth. "There are worse things." Then his expression turns grave. "I have specific tastes, and I know it's not for everyone. The fact that you accept me, that you like it, that means something to me. It means a lot." He runs a finger along my lips. "You have me under your spell, sweet witch. With every waking moment, I'm always coming back to you."

"And Brom," I say quietly.

He gives me a soft smile. "Yes. I think about him too. Perhaps as much as you do." He pauses. "I know you feel caught between the two of us. I just want you to know that you don't have to worry about me. I know I have you. You've proven that you're mine. And if that means you're his as well, then that's something I'll just have to deal with."

Oh. What is he saying? "I thought you were the jealous type," I tease.

"I am jealous," he admits, his eyes darkening as he presses his thumb between my lips. "And I am possessive. But I respect the history you have with him. And I suppose I respect the history I have with him as well. Makes it a very complicated knot, doesn't it?"

I swallow hard, anxiety rising in my throat. "I'm afraid," I admit. "I'm afraid for him, and I'm afraid for me."

"I know," he says. "But I'll protect you from him. And I'll try to protect him from himself. I won't give up until I figure this out, Kat. Brom, the horseman, the school, your mother. It's all connected, just one big web and . . ." He trails off, concentrating on something.

"What?"

"Nothing," he says, blinking hard for a moment. He leans in and leaves a soft kiss on my lips. "You're safe with me, my little butterfly. Remember that."

I let the words sink in and let out a peaceful sigh, nestling against him, wishing I could spend all day here. Forever here. Feeling the safety and strength of his strong arms, everything I've always craved.

Except . . .

"You ruined my blouse," I remind him. "Now what am I supposed to wear?"

He chuckles. "My apologies. I'll go fetch you one of my shirts, and you can make do for now if you wear it under your coat."

"You're thin," I remind him. "There's no chance my breasts will fit in there."

He grins at me, his eyes dancing. "You say that as if your breasts are a hindrance. I think they deserve to be worshipped."

I watch as he leans in and places his mouth on my bare breast, his hand going to the other one until I'm sighing with pleasure.

Here we go again.

25

Brom

I have blood on my hands.

I'm sitting on my bed, staring at my bloodstained hands.

Then I blink, and the blood is gone. Wiped clean.

"Brom?" my mother's voice rings out. I look up to see her standing in the doorway to my bedroom. "Is everything all right?"

I nod. But no. That's a lie. Nothing is right. Everything is wrong.

"I've been calling you for supper for the past few minutes," she says. "If you don't have an appetite, that's fine."

"I'm not hungry," I mumble, the words sounding foreign.

"It's normal," she says to me.

I give her a sharp look. "What's normal?"

"To not have an appetite after all you've done."

"What have I done?"

She just smiles at me and closes the door.

26

Crane

I chabod," the voice whispers through the darkness.

For a moment I can't tell if my eyes are open or closed.

"Ichabod," the voice says again. Marie.

I sit up in my bed. The candles I had lit on my desk have gone out. It takes a moment for my eyes to adjust to the black, the moon's light faint.

The last few nights I've heard Marie's voice, heard the thump of the woman outside in the hall. At this point it's obvious it's not a prank. I wish it was. That would be so much easier to deal with.

"You can't hide from the truth," Marie whispers, and I feel cold breath at my neck.

I yelp and scramble out of bed, whirling around to see nothing at all.

"What do you want?" I ask, my voice shaking slightly. It's a stupid question. She never answers. Neither does the woman I am certain is Vivienne Henry.

There's only silence now. Only darkness.

I sigh and sit down in my chair, putting my head in my hands. A man could be driven to madness this way. I have to wonder if any of the other teachers are haunted by ghosts here, whether ones from their pasts or ones from the school. Is that why Vivienne Henry killed herself? Did they drive her to madness?

But Marie's ghost has always followed me. The opium kept her at bay for a long time, but now that I'm clearheaded, she's back. Taunting me. Reminding me of what I did to her. Of what I can never ever escape from.

It's enough to dig my nails into my bare thighs. What I wouldn't give for some opium right now. Just enough to let me sleep, to help me escape for just one night. But I know that if I did leave the school to find some, that I probably wouldn't be allowed back in. I'm sure the sisters have a way of finding out. They don't seem to be paying much attention to me while I've been here, but I wouldn't risk losing my job over it.

Besides, it would only cloud my brain. I need to be thinking as sharply as possible if I want to protect Kat and help Brom regain his memories. I feel like I'm a waste of a human being if I can't be useful at all times.

I need light, I think. I don't want to sleep, don't want to be in the darkness anymore. That's where my demons live.

I get up and strike a match and light the candles along my desk.

I drop the match.

Outside the window, between me and the lake, is a woman dressed in white. She's twirling on the shore, her head back to the sky, long dark hair whipping around her, lost in some sort of frenzied worship. She looks young and familiar, but I can't quite place her.

Then, three people in hooded black cloaks come out toward her. I assume they are the sisters, but I can't be sure. They are moving fast, urgently. They grab the twirling girl, and the minute they put their hands on her she goes still. Her head dips down as if she's fallen asleep on her feet, her hair falling over her face.

I watch as they lead her away from the lake and bring her to the left, possibly toward the cathedral, until they disappear from my sight.

I get up, a prickle of unease on my scalp, and bring out my salts and black tourmaline from my drawer. It wouldn't hurt to ward the room tonight, just in case.

When I get to my morning class I'm on edge; I didn't sleep for the rest of the night. The black tourmaline works well for protection, but the properties of the crystal are intense and not always conducive for rest.

But the moment I lay my eyes on Kat, sitting in the front row, the exhaustion leaves me.

How stunning this woman is. How lucky that she's mine.

Except she is talking to Paul with a rapturous look on her face. Jealousy spikes through me. I had told her I could share her with Brom—*if* it came to that. I feel the selfish urge to claim her as mine. I know better, of course, being her teacher, but if I had no shame I would march right over to her and kiss her so deeply there would be no doubt in anyone's mind of what we are to each other.

My sweet witch has consumed my soul.

I manage to hold it together, reminding myself that she's allowed to talk to the other students and that there's no reason to lose my sanity over it. It's just the depth of my feelings for her is starting to surprise me. Ever since we had sex in the stables it's been torture to stay away from her. We've come together in secret a few times this week, but it's only made me want her more. She's become more addicting than any drug and far more dangerous. She's reaching the deep and terrible places inside me. The places I hide from.

As if she hears my pining, she meets my eyes and gives me the shyest of smiles, quick and delicate, and I know it's going to be an especially long class today.

Thankfully it's over before I go insane. I've locked the door, and it's just the two of us in the classroom. I have her spread out over my desk like a feast.

"Tell me what you want, Kat," I say to her, her dress bunched around her waist, her hips at the edge of the table where I'm prepared to lick every inch of her.

"You usually tell me what you want," she says through a breathless laugh.

"I know," I say, running my fingers up her thighs, teasing her soft, sensitive skin until goose bumps appear. "As I said, I can be selfish, but I want to give you what you need." I lower my chin until my mouth is inches from her sweet cunt. "You've been far too generous with me, indulging my desires."

"Well, you can start by not teasing me," she says breathlessly as I blow air on her, making her writhe.

"I won't," I say, parting her swollen flesh with my fingers, feeling her wetness roll down so that I have drops of her desire in my palm. "I will give you what you want. You only need to tell me."

"I want you," she says, clearly aching for me to touch her. "I want you."

"I know," I say, my mouth hovering over her pussy. "But I want to hear the words, sweet witch." I run my finger through her wetness, and then I lower my mouth to lap at her.

God, she tastes heavenly. I reach down into my trousers and bring out my cock while she lets out a moan as I eat her completely, a ravenous man.

"I want to come," she says. "I want you to make me come."

I grin at how bold she's being. She's asking and taking and it feels good to give for once on her terms. I take my tongue and drag it across her clit while I start pumping my cock into my fist, the heat and desperation building inside me.

I pull back, sliding my fingers of my free hand inside her tight hole. "Do you want to come on my hand? My tongue? My cock?"

"All of it, anything," she gasps, her head rolling back and forth on the desk.

"Then I'll give you all of it," I rasp.

With a grunt I thrust my fingers into her tight hole, finding each of her pleasure points in turn. My tongue swirls around her clit as my cock slides in and out of my fist, my hips rocking to the rhythm of her moans. I feel her body tense as she reaches a crescendo, and then I release her, awash in a sea of pleasure. She shudders and cries out, her orgasm crashing through her like a wave and I keep my fingers deep inside her, working her hard as I pull back to watch. The way she clenches around me, dripping with her lust for me, the pink of her skin blooming deeper—it's my new fixation.

"Oh God," she whimpers, the orgasm coming to a slow, her hands clenched around the fabric of her skirt.

I straighten up, staring down at her. I want her naked, not always in this half-dressed state of affairs, drawers pushed down, skirt up, dress unbuttoned hastily. I want her soft, sinful body under mine, to feel every single inch of her. I want her closer than ever.

I glance at the clock. We have time.

"Take off your clothes," I tell her, unbuttoning my shirt. "Do it now."

She raises her head to look at me. "How quickly the tables have turned," she says with a wry yet sated smile, her cheeks flushed. "It was all about what I want and now you're ordering my clothes to come off."

I toss my shirt to the floor and grab a pair of scissors from my desk drawer, holding them up. "I'm going to fuck you with my cock like you asked. But you didn't specify how. Now take off your clothes or I'm cutting them off your body."

"You will not," she declares, her eyes sparking. She's beautiful when she's outraged.

"I'll buy you new ones, I promise," I tell her.

She lets out a huff and starts hastily undoing the top of her dress. I put the scissors back down but pick up my ruler instead, then finish removing my pants until I'm completely nude.

She pauses. She hasn't seen me like this before. My cock gets even harder from just the lustful awe in her eyes.

"You're beautiful," she whispers, her gaze skirting over me from head to toe.

"And you're not naked enough," I threaten her with a wave of my ruler.

To my surprise, once she undoes the top of her dress and the sleeves fall away, I see she's not wearing a corset underneath, just a chemise. I go to her and lift the linen over her head until she's topless, then stare down at her body.

Her breasts are full and pale and gorgeous, her nipples pale pink and pebbled. I cup them in my hands, relishing their heaviness, run my tongue over them while I pinch and squeeze in all the places she likes.

Then I pull down her drawers all the way until she's completely nude.

"You are made for sinners," I murmur as I stare, one hand on my cock, running my arousal over the tip and back. "You were made for me."

Her face flushes at that. I like making her blush. It's the same color of pink that my hands make when I spank her. Or in this case, the ruler.

"Spread your legs. Hold them wide for me. I want to punish that sweet little cunt of yours," I tell her.

She swallows hard and then reaches down, her hands on her thighs and pulling them apart.

I bite my lip in anticipation and run the edge of the ruler up and down her thighs, tapping it sporadically until I get to where she's pink, wet and waiting.

Then I give her a quick hit of the ruler right on her pussy.

She cries out but I grab her face with my other hand and kiss her deeply, my tongue licking inside her mouth, dancing with hers. A moan runs from her and through me and I swat her again, my hand behind her head, holding her in place.

"Is this something you like?" I murmur against her lips as I briefly pull back.

She makes a tight noise of want, and I know I have her approval.

I continue to swat her, and kiss her and she continues to get wetter and wetter.

Then, when I can't stand it any longer, I push her hips against mine and I shove my cock up inside her, tossing the ruler to the floor.

"Kat," I rasp, sucking at her neck while one arm hooks around her back so she's pressed as close to me as possible. "You're so damn wet I think you might drown me."

Then I drive into her harder, deeper, desperate to get closer to her. Eventually the desk starts moving, squeaking loudly across the floor, so I pick her up, her legs wrapping around my waist, and I spin her so she's slammed back against the wall.

Sweat pools between us, her full breasts pressed against my chest, and I fuck her harder, hips driving up to get deeper. It's good like this, too good. She's so sweet and easily corrupted and yet I feel like she's the one in control most of the time, no matter what I do.

I'm starting to think I'll do anything for her.

But soon I can't even think.

There's only the energy and magic that's building between us, mixed with the deep, animalistic desire to fuck her as hard as I can, get in her so deep she doesn't know where she ends and I begin. We are connected. We are one. Our skin slick, our chests heaving, breath panting, hearts racing. Our moans fill the classroom, too loud, but I don't care if I even get fired over this because giving myself over to my sweet witch and having her give herself to me is worth everything.

My orgasm comes on fast and strong, and I'm slipping my fingers in a messy swirl around her clit as I spill into her. She comes quickly, her cries joining my own, our bodies moving in unison until we finally come to a stop.

"Crane," she whispers to me, her forehead pressed against my shoulder. I'm still holding her against the wall. I don't want to let her go, I don't want to slip out of her. I just want to stay inside her for as long as possible. I'm worried that I'll never have her like this, mine and naked and raw, ever again.

"Kat," I say to her, still catching my breath. I place a kiss on the top of her head. "What happens if you become my new addiction?"

She lifts her head to give me a lazy smile. "I'll be naked a lot more."

27

Kat

Friday night is upon me in a flash. The entire week was a blur of sex with Crane, which happened as frequently as possible, most often in the school stables, though once on his desk in the empty classroom and once against a tree in the woods. With each and every time that I submitted to him, succumbed to his wants and desires and deviant ways, I felt that energy inside me grow. I felt it bond me and Crane together, fusing us. It may not have been blood magic, but it was an exchange of something almost as powerful that is binding in its own way when two witches in the throes of ecstasy join together.

But where I've felt more than connected to Crane, Brom has remained an enigma. He's already moved into the dormitories. I suppose it's easy when you don't have a lot of things to bring with you, but regardless, it did feel quick, like his parents couldn't wait to get rid of him. Which might have been the case. As a result, I haven't seen him around all that much aside from being in a few classes with him. Honestly, I don't know what to do or say around him, at least not until Crane comes up with a plan, so I've been avoiding him and feeling awful about it.

Because it's *Brom*. He was my best friend, the boy I shared everything with, the piece that had been missing from my life for four years as I moved from girl to woman, and he is back. I should be spending every waking moment with him, but there's that disconnect there. He sees it when he looks into my eyes, the wariness, and I see the hurt reflected in his. But I'm not pushing him away. I'm doing all I can to give us back what we once had.

Tomorrow, my mother wants to put my belongings in the buggy and move them up to my dorm, but until then, I'm trying to hang on to my last sense of normalcy. Thankfully, when I stopped by Mary's after school one day, she seemed happy to go to the town bonfire with me. I was afraid she wouldn't want to be my friend anymore after spending so much time apart.

Mary appears outside my door at eight, carrying a pouch with one hand and a lantern in another, a cheerful specter in the dark night.

"What do you have in there?" I ask her as I walk toward her, nodding at her satchel. I feel a little shy, as if I'm getting to know her all over again.

She laughs. "Oh, this? Mathias wants me to fill it up with as many treats as I can find. Candied apples, caramel corn, roasted chestnuts, and soul cakes."

"I'm getting hungry already," I tell her.

We start walking down the road side by side, the lantern swinging shadows on the decaying stalks of sunflowers and corn that line the road. It's cold now, the promise of frost in the air, and I pull my shawl tighter around my neck, wondering what to say to Mary, wondering how much I *can* say.

But she cuts to the core of it.

"I hear Brom's back," she says, shooting me an inquisitive glance. "I can't imagine how you're feeling. Are you happy?"

I try to give her a reassuring smile. "Very."

She raises the lantern to peer at me, and I wince at the light. "I don't believe you."

"I'm happy," I tell her, pushing her hand back down. "Really, I am. It's just a lot to take in."

"Are you still going to get married?"

I hesitate, trying to figure out what to say. "I don't know. To be honest with you, I don't even know how I feel about it. All I wanted for the past four years was for him to come back, and now that he's here . . ."

"He's not the same," she says.

I raise a brow, wondering how much she knows, if anything. "You could say that."

"People change," she says lightly. "That's the way it goes. You're not the same person you were back then either, I'm sure."

She's right about that.

"I know I'm not the same Mary who lived in Providence. Sometimes you change in different directions," she goes on. "It happens. Nothing is in stasis. We are always changing."

"Where did you learn that?" I ask.

"Well, it wasn't from you," she jokes. "Here I was thinking you were going to share all your studies from the school with me, and you've barely said more than hello."

I rub my lips together, guilt panging me. "Listen, Mary, I know—"

She bumps her shoulder against mine in a skip. "I'm just pulling your leg, Kat. I know you don't have any time, and . . . I know you don't have a choice."

"A choice?"

A knowing smile flits across her lips. "I know what you go to school for."

Oh no. "You do?" I ask uneasily.

"I might be new to Sleepy Hollow, but I'm not dumb. This is a peculiar town, and the people are even stranger. I could tell you were a witch the moment I first laid eyes on you."

I stop dead in my tracks. "What are you talking about?"

She turns to face me and starts walking backward. "You don't know this, but the first day I saw you, you were crouched by the sweet pea patch at the side of the road. We'd just moved in, and I was looking around the new neighborhood. I heard your voice. You were talking to something. I looked over at you in the field and saw you crouched down and commanding a frog. Telling it what to do. It hopped from the ground to your finger and back again, onto your shoulder. It seemed to delight you, and from that moment, I was delighted too."

I don't remember any of this. Then again, I was often playing with animals, talking to them. I had no idea that Mary witnessed any of that. "That doesn't mean I'm a witch," I tell her.

"Okay," she says, the lantern lighting up her big smile. "Then what are you? A normal, average human being?"

I could lie. I could tell her yes, I was normal and average, and act like she thought she saw something she didn't. But I'm so damn tired of the lies. "I'm a witch," I tell her.

She claps her hands together. "I knew it. And then Mathias was telling me all about the way the school looked and how spooked out he was, and I couldn't help but put it all together."

I glance at her as she walks beside me now. "And yet you still wanted to come to bonfire night with me?"

"Of course," she says. "You're just more interesting than you were before."

With a grin, she hooks her arm around mine, and we walk the rest of the way to town like that.

It's been a while since I've been in Sleepy Hollow proper, and it feels quite different now. I'm not sure if it's because I haven't been around such normalcy in a long time or the fact that it's a crowded beehive of activity. It doesn't help that so many of the townspeople stare at me as we walk down the main street. At least, it seems that way.

"Why is everyone looking at us?" I whisper to Mary as we go along the town square, where the giant bonfire is lit in the middle, the flames leaping high into the sky while townsfolk are gathered all around with hustlers and merchants selling their wares. Carved pumpkins lit with candles line the path around the fire, their lopsided smiles setting the festive mood.

"Because it's a small town, and you're a prize, Kat," Mary says.

Her words echo something Crane said to me during sex, that I was a prized student. How confident that had made me feel. Yet now, I only feel like I'm being judged. There are a few men on the other side of the fire leering at me, something insidious in their eyes. We were at bonfire night last year together, but I don't remember the men looking at me this way then. Am I just paranoid now, looking for danger and the macabre everywhere?

"Besides, everyone is on edge because of the murder," Mary adds.

My heart drops. Joshua Meeks. For a moment, I had forgotten. Being at the school, it's so easy to become insulated, and with what's happening with Brom, it's easy to forget how real the problem is. But the man I was intimate with last year was murdered and gruesomely so, and I feel terrible that it left my mind. I still don't know how Brom plays into it, if he does at all, but I can't help but feel like I brought this death upon Joshua.

"Weren't you friends with him?' Mary asks gently.

"We were friendly," I say, "when he first moved to town."

"Didn't seem like a guy who had a lot of enemies."

"No. He wasn't that type." He was kind and gentle and didn't deserve any of it.

I have to wonder if any of the townsfolk knew about me and Joshua. After all, my mother somehow did. And, if they knew, whether they're pitying me or if they're thinking I had something to do with it.

I make a point to ignore the attention as we walk around, getting candied apples for ourselves, plus all the extra treats for Mathias. Despite the strange atmosphere, it is nice to feel a part of the town again, the air filled with fried goods, apple cider, roasting chestnuts, and hickory smoke. Mary and I find a bale of hay to sit on to watch the fire, the children running around at the base of it. Despite the caginess in everyone's posture, the children at least seem to be having a good time.

My mind drifts back to Brom and the way we used to play as children. I remember being here at the bonfire with my parents. My father had given us extra money for treats, and both of us were full of sugar, running around like animals. How innocent we were back then. How little we knew of what lay ahead. How quickly all of that would change.

"Good evenin', ladies," a man says as he staggers drunkenly toward us. He's my age, maybe a little older, stubble on his cheeks and drink glazing his eyes.

"Good evening," Mary says stiffly, turning her body toward mine and eyeing him discerningly.

"What are ye pretty ladies doin' here all by your lonesome?" he slurs, plopping down on the hay bale beside me and nearly falling off as he does so. He smells of whiskey and horseshit.

"We were just leaving," I tell him, gathering up my skirt and getting to my feet. As I do so, the man reaches out and grabs my elbow.

"You afraid of me or somethin'?" he asks, holding me in place. "I'm here to keep the big bad wolf away. Don't you know we have a murderer running loose? Cutting people's heads off with an ax."

"It was probably a scythe," Mary speculates. "He was a farm-hand, murdered with his own instrument. Have some respect."

The guy snarls at Mary and yanks me closer to him. I try to pull my arm away, but he doesn't let go until Mary marches forward and shoves her hands at his chest.

"Scram!" she yells at him, enough that he lets go of me. A few heads turn toward us, murmuring, and the guy starts to back away, holding his hands up like he's innocent.

We watch him disappear into the crowd, hopefully to somewhere where he can sleep it off.

And it's at that moment I think I see a familiar face among everyone else.

Dark hair, deep black eyes, a beard on a handsome face.

I see Brom staring at me.

But when I blink, he's gone, replaced by another dark-haired man who has his arm around a dark-haired girl.

"Don't worry," Mary says, putting her hand on my shoulder. "I don't think he'll be back to bother us."

I can't tell her that it's not him I'm worried about.

Katrina.

I groan and roll over onto my back. I hear my name being called, a whisper on a breeze, but I don't think it's real. I must be dreaming.

Katrina Van Tassel.

The voice again. A little deeper now. More urgent.

I open my eyes and stare up at the ceiling at the wood rafters. The room isn't pitch-black; there's light coming from some-where, but it's not outside. The shutters are closed.

I slowly raise my head and look. There is light streaming in from under my door. It flickers in and out, so someone must have the fire going.

What time is it? The middle of the night? How long was I asleep?

After the incident with the drunk at the bonfire, we decided to leave. It wasn't just that he ruined the mood, more that Mary was sincerely worried about the murderer still at large and thought the earlier we headed back home, the better. She made a joke about me being a witch, and so I'd have a better chance at protecting myself if I wanted to stay behind, but the joke fell flat.

Because somehow, I think my being a witch makes things worse. It makes me a target.

Needless to say, she dropped me off at home early, and I went straight to bed while she went straight home to deliver the treats to Mathias. My mother was just leaving with Famke—they had decided to go to the bonfire after all and said they would be back late.

Now I have no idea what time it is and—

Katrina. Kat.

Kat.

There it is again.

That voice.

Unlike any voice I have heard before. Low and guttural and yet also a whisper. It makes my scalp prickle, sending sickly shivers down my spine.

Then I hear a thump. Another thump.

The sound of footsteps inside the house. They echo, shaking the floorboards that reach under my door. Whoever is out there is coming straight for me.

They stop outside my door.

I try to sit up, pull my sheets over my body, but I can't.

I can't move at all.

I'm stuck, frozen, paralyzed. I can only stare as the doorknob turns.

I gasp, but no air moves. It's like I can't even breathe.

The door opens slowly, inch by inch, with a low, long creak.

Until it reveals a man standing on the other side.

He is seven feet tall, and he has no head.

I open my mouth to scream.

I can't.

I try to get out of bed.

I can't move.

I can only watch in pure, utter horror as the man places something down by the door and slowly walks across my bedroom toward me. This giant man in a black cloak that seems to blend with the shadows. This man with no head.

Unlike the other times I had seen him—in the void, on the trail—I don't get the sense that he's looking for someone else. Instead, I know he's looking for me.

Katrina Van Tassel, he says, his voice flowing through the air and over my body like the wind. It settles over me, a physical thing, ripe with desire, and I see him reach down to his crotch, stroking something large and long and dark as sin.

I open my mouth to cry out, but nothing, there's nothing. My scream is choked in my throat, and I can't even breathe as he stops in front of me. With a raise of his other hand, the bedsheets are ripped right off me, leaving me exposed in my nightgown.

I don't know what to do. I can't defend myself; I can't call for help. I'm prey caught in a trap, and he's the hunter coming to finish me off.

It's like he was saving me for last.

He's at me now. Heavy, cold hands on my thighs, and I pinch my eyes shut and try to pull up whatever power I have inside me, whatever means I have to get over this enchantment.

I think of the energy between Crane and me.

I think of its power, of how infinite it made me feel. I focus on that.

And then I use that energy to open my mouth.

And I scream.

The sound reverberates off the walls, and suddenly, I can move. I'm scrambling backward on the bed until my back hits the wall.

And the headless horseman turns to leave. Slowly, as if he's not in a hurry, not afraid of being caught.

He strides out of the room, picking up the thing he left by the door, and then he's gone into the house, past the fire, and out the door.

And I'm getting to my feet, I'm grabbing the knife I keep in the drawer of my desk, and I'm running after him to make sure he's gone, so I can lock the door, as if that will keep him out.

I nearly slip before I reach my own door, something wet and slick beneath my bare feet.

I look down at the floor and see a trail of blood, his footprints still in it.

28

Crane

The clock in the library strikes midnight, but it feels like I'm just getting started. I have a stack of books at my side, a bottle of red wine with a metal goblet, and a row of candles lighting my desk like a beacon in the dark. It's taken me most of the night perusing the stacks, trying to find the right books that can help me figure out Brom, and after rummaging through a few duds, it finally seems I have the most promising ones.

I lay them out in front of me on the desk and have a sip of wine. There's an old tome called *Blood Magic and Other Rituals*, one called *How to Communicate with the Dead*, another called *Personal Exorcisms*, and finally a worn one called the *Book of Verimagiaa*. I pick up the one on blood magic first, since that's been on my mind all week. This particular book has an English title but inside is written in Greek. I don't know Greek.

I sigh and bring out my anointing oil from my pocket, rubbing it on my wrists while I close my eyes and repeat the polyglot spell, which gives the magic wielder the ability to speak and read any language, a godsend when you're a teacher. Then I open my eyes and turn the page.

A cold breeze comes at my back, making the candles around my desk flicker, threatening to go out. I whip around in my seat. Beyond the glow of my candles, the library is completely empty and dark, the moon hiding somewhere behind the trees. Generally, the library is closed to students after 9:00 p.m., but exceptions are made for teachers. The librarian, Ms. Albarez, who is from Mexico City, said that I could stay here all night if I wanted to, and it might end up being that way. I don't plan on leaving until I get what I came here for. All my lesson plans for this week have taken up too much of my time as it is. Being a professor at this godforsaken school might be my job, but Kat and Brom have become my obsession.

My eyes scan the library's crevices and shadows, and I hold my breath, my ears straining to pick up on any errant sounds, any source of the icy wind. There's nothing. Just the tick of the clock.

I turn back to my books and have another sip of wine. I can't help but feel there's something else in the library with me, a presence, but that could be my imagination running wild. It's been doing a lot of that lately.

My thoughts drift to Kat. My beautiful, sweet witch. As much as my natural curiosity and my ties to Brom have me fixated on getting to the bottom of things, I'm doing this for her more than anything. I want her to have her Brom back, even if it might cost me her heart in the end. I am still jealous of their past; I'm possessive over her mind, body, and soul, but because it's Brom, because I've been inside that man, I am willing to share her with him and only him.

And if he's not open to sharing, I'm taking her for myself.

An image enters my mind. One of the three of us together, naked and worshipping Kat in all her ethereal beauty. My stiff cock in her wet, soft mouth, full lips enveloping me with gusto, my fists in her messy hair, driving her head forward until I'm crammed down her throat. Behind her is Brom, pumping his hips like an animal, driving into her hard from behind, her breasts swaying with each hit. She moans around my cock, the vibrations making my balls feel heavy, and I lean forward slightly, reaching out for Brom's neck, placing my hand around it and holding tight. I demand for him to kiss me. He snarls in response, but his eyes tell me that I'm his.

The image fades, and I'm hard as stone. In all my sexual conquests and affairs over the years, I've never come close to being in that situation, a ménage à trois.

But there is no use fantasizing about something that might not be. What if we can't get Brom back to his old self and restore his memories? There is no doubt in my mind that he is connected to the Hessian soldier, but in what way?

My body doesn't care for questions at the moment. I reach down into my trousers, making a fist over my length, hot and already twitching for release. With a groan that seems to fill the library, I lean back in my chair and bring my cock out. I know the tight, hot feel of Kat's gorgeous pink cunt as I squeeze inside her. I know the velvety glove of Brom's ass, plied with slick oil. I hear the sound of her breathy moans and the guttural tremors of his deep grunts as I fuck them both with abandon. I want both of them, everywhere. I want to fuck them in every way. I want this more than I've ever wanted anything. I want to lick her tiny cunt until she's screaming while Brom sucks me off with his pretty mouth until I'm shooting my seed down his throat, until he's so filled with it that it's spilling out of his lips. He swallows while staring up at me with those deep black eyes.

My orgasm slams into me, taking me by surprise. I cry out hoarsely, my ejaculation spurting out in hot waves onto the books, leaving a sticky white mess.

I chuckle at the results of my fantasy, watching how my seed drips off the volumes and onto the desk. That certainly took me by surprise.

Then I get an idea . . . blood magic is one way to form a bond through individuals. The act of sex itself, the exchanging of bodily fluids, is another. What if we were to combine the two? What if we created a ritual where we would mix our blood and seed together, the three of us moving in unison, creating literal magic?

I grab my handkerchief and wipe away my mess from the books before flipping through the pages. Hopefully, the librarian won't notice the stains. I'm sure I'm not the first witch that's gotten carried away while reading the books in here—there's a surprising amount of magic tied to the act of sex itself.

I'm not sure how much time I spend going through the books, but eventually, I find a few promising suggestions. There's a binding ritual that involves blood and sex magic between the participants who wish to be bound. It seems relatively easy enough with some incantations, certain oils, smudging, and a protective salt circle so that we aren't inviting any other lurking spirits inside, which could become bound to us in the process.

And then there's a more intense ritual that must take place at night during the full moon. That one has to be by a body of water, which permits easier passage to the veils, and given what Kat and I did by the lake, that won't be a problem to access. This ritual isn't so much about binding as it is about an exorcism. If the horseman is possessing Brom, he will need to be expelled for him to finally become free. Even better if it happens on Samhain.

Of course, they say it's possible the first binding ritual will be enough. If it's strong, then it might force the horseman to leave anyway. Our connection to each other might sever him, especially if Kat and I are able to manipulate our energy through Brom.

The only problem is everyone involved has to be willing. Which means Brom has to be willing. If he doesn't remember our relationship before, then I'm not sure if he'll want to open up to me in that way, so to speak, and he doesn't even know he's the horseman. I suppose that will have to be Kat's job, unless I see an opportunity for persuasion.

I take out my quill pen and ink and start jotting down notes in my book, including as many details as possible. I finish the rest of the bottle of wine, then go through the book on types of spirits. By now, the moon has risen above the trees, casting a faint glow into the library, not enough to light it but enough to deepen those shadows.

Eventually, I come across an interesting passage about retrieval spirits. They aren't always easy to conjure—you often have to have one that wants to be used in some way. Sometimes, these spirits are angry or have done terrible things since that malevolent energy is what keeps them bound to the earthly realm, unwilling to move on through the rest of the veils. A witch can summon these spirits to retrieve people who have gone missing or have run away, with the spirit finding and possessing the person and physically bringing them back.

Could that have happened to Brom? His parents, or Sarah, or the coven, did they conjure the Hessian and send him on a mission to find Brom and bring him back? And if so, was it because they were worried about him or for some nefarious purpose?

I keep reading, my heart thudding in my head as I'm filled with that enigmatic feeling I'm always chasing, that high that's greater than any opium, that sense of being on the edge of *discovering* something. The text goes on to say that in rare cases, the spirit might refuse to leave the person. In even rarer cases, the spirit can hold a tether to both the corporeal body and their ethereal body, possessing the former at will but only after dark. The spirit can influence the host, or the host can influence the spirit.

That has to be it, I think. That has to be what's happened to Brom. And if it's not, I can at least use that as a starting point for this diagnosis.

Eager to learn more, I continue reading, turning the pages until I feel that cold wind buffet my back again.

The candles flicker indignantly.

"No, no, no," I cry out softly, pleading for them to stay lit, even as the wind snuffs them out for good. I'm plunged into a mix of smoke and darkness.

I twist around in my seat just in time to see the front doors to the library slam shut behind me. Even in the dark, I can see the tall figure standing between me and the exit. The air fills with the smell of sulfur and rot.

The Hessian soldier strides toward me, his heavy boots echoing on the floor. The world seems to bend to his favor, power and energy churning through the air. I feel my cells respond to him in the same way, a sickening sense of want and desire alongside debilitating fear that has my stomach clenching, my body frozen in place.

Then my gaze drops to his hands, where he's carrying a man's head, blood dripping as he comes toward me. He tosses it on the floor, and it rolls ahead of him for a bit before teetering off to the side.

I should run. I should get behind the desk. I should grab my anointing oil and chant repelling words, anything to keep him at bay.

But I can't.

Because I'm fascinated.

And curiosity is what killed the cat.

In this mystery that's been wrapping around us, the headless horseman is the cog in the wheel. If I could disarm him here and now, then Brom could go free, go back to being the Abe that I knew.

"I'm not afraid of you!" I yell at him as he marches toward me. "I know what you are! I know who you are!"

The horseman lifts his other hand, an ax that gleams from the faint moonlight that comes in through the windows.

He aims to chop off my head.

I should probably move.

I scramble, going behind the desk just in time as he brings the ax down, slicing both the desk and the books down the middle.

The problem with a man with no head is that he can't communicate with you. It's a very one-sided relationship. I think about Kat and how she's able to speak to the animals and wish there was something I could learn from that, but I doubt that will happen before my head is hacked off here in the school library.

"I know you can hear me, Brom!" I cry out. "I know you're tethered to him and him to you!"

Which means the reason he's here is because of Kat.

Because he wants me out of the picture.

"She doesn't just belong to you," I say as the horseman picks up the ax again and strides powerfully around the desk toward me. "She belongs to me. And I belong to you too."

The horseman doesn't seem to care for my blathering, his presence an unstoppable force.

"Fuck," I swear, reaching into my other coat pocket for a vial of salt rumored to be from the lost city of Atlantis. I take it out and uncork it, tossing the salt at him just as he's about to swing the ax again.

The white granules hit him and fizzle, steam rising, and the Hessian lets out an inhuman roar despite not having a face. He waves his arms around in distress, and for a moment, I think it's enough to keep him at bay. He is a spirit, after all.

But then he keeps on walking as I race around yet another desk, my hands patting down my coat, trying to find something else I can use.

I have nothing but words.

Nothing but my own energy.

I put my hands out.

"*Non potes me nocere!*" I command.

You can't hurt me.

The headless horseman pauses.

"*Me tangere non potes!*" I yell.

You cannot touch me.

He comes to a stop, raising his arms as if shielding himself.

I know that spirit words don't last forever; it's just a spell, a temporary bandage for the witch to get to higher ground. But here, I will take what I can. If I run now, he'll only catch up with me. The trick is to convince him not to kill me.

"You know who I am, Brom!" I yell. "You remember, deep down in that secret shadow side of you. You remember what we had together!"

The horseman straightens up, marching toward me again, and I back up until my back hits a wall of books.

Nowhere to go.

Nothing to protect me but my magic and my wits.

The horseman stops right in front of me, the stench of sulfur overwhelming, a sense of chaos taking over. His body is so hard, his cloak and armor seeming to swallow the world with its darkness. He presses it against mine, like he aims to crush my bones first before removing my head, the wall of books unyielding.

I'm staring right at his missing head. He's got at least five inches on me, if not more, making him taller than seven feet. The wound there looks cauterized, red and grimly glowing. The closer I look, the more it seems like something is wriggling in the stump. I avert my eyes, not wanting that to be the last thing I ever see.

One of his hands goes to the top of my head to make a fist, yanking on my hair.

"You know that's not how this works," I tell him, my voice shaking, but I don't care if he knows how terrified I am. I'll do what I have to do to reach him.

I manage to buck my hips against his with the little leverage I have, even as he keeps his fist in my hair.

"That's what you want, isn't it?" I say with a sneer. "That's why you're here. Not to kill me. Not to have my head. Because you remember what I gave to you. Don't you, pretty boy?"

The horseman stills at the use of his nickname.

I know he remembers.

I reach down with my hand, squeezing it between his crotch and mine, flipping my wrist around so that my palm is pressed against his cock.

"This is what you want," I whisper harshly, my grip tightening over him. He's extremely long and hard and huge; my hand feels small in comparison. But he's aroused by this, pressing his hips against my hand and grinding.

"I can give you what you want," I say hoarsely, keeping my eyes away from his missing head. "I can give you what you've forgotten about. What you won't let yourself think about. I know you want me, Brom. I see it in you."

The horseman stills again. I grip his cock tighter, rubbing faster over the leather pad at his groin.

"Want to beg me to let you come?" I go on. "You know I love it when you beg. You know I'm good with my promises."

He lets go of my hair.

I think he might just come right here.

But he staggers backward instead.

Turns away and starts marching toward the doors, his cloak flowing behind him as he goes, boots echoing with each hard step. He passes by the decapitated head and kicks it backward with his boot so it goes bouncing toward me.

Then he pushes the doors open and disappears into the night.

My legs threaten to give out, and I slide down to the floor, my hand at my chest as if to keep my heart in place.

I've never been so close to death before.

He had come here to kill me.

And yet I was able to reach him, enough to get him to stop, enough to even scare him. He's scared of his own feelings for me, feelings for a man, sexual or otherwise.

But I know what it's like to feel that way. How complicated it gets. How those complications lead to confusion and how that leads to anger and that anger can lead to violence.

I think about Marie.

I think about the night I found out she was having her affair with our neighbor Ray.

About how for so long I had tried to bury my attraction to him. How angry I was that she was able to cheat on me with him.

I think about how I went to visit Ray, how I confronted him like any angry husband would.

And how that anger morphed and changed.

Because I wanted Marie. But I wanted Ray more.

And coming to terms with that meant tackling everything the church and my pastor father had taught me was wrong while growing up.

Sometimes you can't face the fire until you're pushed right into the flames.

I get to my feet quickly, panic taking hold of me.

Because I know how Brom feels, I know what he's going to do.

I know who he's going to seek out.

He's going to go after Kat.

Unless he's already seen her first.

29

Kat

After the headless horseman came into my bedroom, I immediately went to find my mother, wondering why she never heard my scream. But she was nowhere to be found, and neither was Famke. It turns out that I hadn't woken up in the middle of the night by the intruder. It was only 11:00 p.m., and they were probably heading back from the bonfire at any moment.

But I couldn't just wait for them. I contemplated running over to Mary's and telling her what I saw, but I didn't want to risk leaving the house. When the fire burned out, I didn't even want to head out to the woodshed to get more logs for the fire, so I went around lighting all the candles I could find with sparks from my fingers.

Then I got on my hands and knees and washed the blood out of the floor, trying not to be sick. The terror still has a hold on me, and if it wasn't for the blood, I would think that I dreamed the whole thing.

But it was real. He came into the house, wanting me. Whether to defile me or kill me or both, I don't know, but it was me this time that he wanted. It was only by pure luck that I was able to conjure that energy in time.

And yet, it's not like he turned away and ran. He walked off like I had just asked him politely to leave. Which meant he might come back. So I decided to gather up all the salt in the house and start sprinkling it around all the entrances, hoping it might bar him.

Now I'm sitting on the chair in the living room, a lit candlestick by my side, jumping at every noise. By the time the clock ticks midnight, my mother and Famke are still not home. I'm starting to get worried. What if the horseman attacked them too?

But the idea of leaving the house and looking for them in the cold night is too terrifying to bear, so I stay where I am.

Then I hear a tap.

Another tap.

I slowly get to my feet, picking up the candlestick. The flame dances. The house seems to seethe with darkness, the shadows thickening. My skin tingles with fear all over.

What is that?

I hear it again.

It's coming from my bedroom.

My chest tightens with fear.

Another tap.

There's something at my bedroom window.

I stand in the sitting room, filled with fear so acute that it makes my knees shake.

Another tap, louder now.

A rock hitting the pane.

Could it be?

I dare to take a step forward, then another, until I'm pausing in my doorway.

At my window, underneath the elm tree with its autumn leaves, is Brom.

Despite my reservations, I find myself being pulled to the window like a magnet. I push it up, cold air flowing in.

"Brom," I say in a breathless gasp.

He stares at me, his eyes midnight black, and I'm brought back in time to the last night I saw him before he disappeared. How could this man be any different? How could this not be the Brom who I know?

"Can I come in?" he asks. His voice is gruff, but the tone is soft.

I hesitate, my mind reeling over Brom's counterpart, the headless horseman.

"Please," he says.

There's desperation there, and with one look into his eyes, I see how tortured he is. My Brom, who always felt too much, wore his heart on his sleeve. I can't say no. I've been pushing him away all week, leaving him in the cold, and the guilt is getting to me.

I step away from the window, and he climbs through with ease. Gets to his feet beside me in the bedroom, and I feel all will and resolve, even fear, melt away. Because this feels like us. His large body, that immense power in his muscles and bones, the darkness inside him that's always been there from day one.

He sucks in his breath, the candle in my hand flickering, and I feel the air leave my lungs. The tension between us is a tight line of energy that crackles like a lightning storm, the intensity rising until I can't breathe at all. The hair on my arms rises, heat building in my core.

This man is my thunderstorm.

"I've missed you," Brom whispers, taking a step forward, his hand at my cheek.

I close my eyes, leaning into the familiar feel of his palm. Warm, calloused, protective. This is him. This is the man I know. This is the man I've been waiting for.

"I've missed you so much, Daffodil," he says.

My eyes fly open at the sound of my old nickname. I gaze up into his eyes, and I'm swept away by the storm in them, how dark they are, how beautiful.

He leans in, brushing his lips over my cheek. "I've missed you so much," he whispers again, his voice raw, and the candlestick starts to tremble in my hand, the flame flickering.

Goodness. How will I survive him?

"Brom," I say, but then he's kissing me. His mouth is warm but tentative, unsure, as if he's holding himself back. He parts my lips with a dip of his tongue, and I can't help but moan into his mouth.

The candlestick falls to the floor, the flame going out, and Brom runs his hands up into my hair, holding me in place. His kiss deepens, licking into my mouth, long, slow strokes of his tongue that give me goose bumps, that make my whole body shake.

He's so different from Crane in this way. While Crane is composed and aloof most of the time, he is wild in his fucking. While Brom is wild and moody most of the time, he is sensual in his kiss.

And it feels so good to be kissed by him. Something both familiar and new. I grab his shirt, my fingers wrapping around it and holding tight as I realize I finally have him back. My insides are burning up as he kisses me deeper now, this slow pull of our mouths, like we have all the time in the world. I never want this kiss to end. I want to drown in this sweet desire. I want to revel in our return to each other.

"Kat," he says against my mouth as he pulls back slightly. "I never stopped thinking about our night together."

Our lips break away, my breath hard, and I look at him in surprise. "What do you mean? Do you remember thinking about me?"

He gives his head a small shake, his eyes squinting in anguish. "No. I don't remember. But I know. I know I was. How could I not? I've been thinking about it nonstop since I came back to Sleepy Hollow." He presses his forehead against mine, his hands leaving my hair and ghosting over my neck, my collarbone, over my breasts, my nipples pebbling under my thin nightgown. "We were so much younger than we are now, but you left your mark on me. And now you're fully a woman, Kat, and I want you. I want you like I've never wanted anything before. You make me such a desperate man."

He continues to slowly rub my nipples through the fabric until the heat between my legs pulses hungrily, and he leans in, kissing my collarbones. It feels like being brushed by butterfly wings. "I think I might die if I can't have you for my own," he murmurs against my skin.

My eyes roll back in my head. I swallow hard, unable to stop from speaking the truth. "You can't have me for your own. I belong to Crane too."

He tenses, his fingers pinching my nipples hard as I bring my gaze to meet his. His nostrils flare, eyes flashing with contempt. "I had you first."

His mood is like mercury.

"And you will always *be* my first," I tell him. "But you know I'm with Crane."

His upper lip curls. "I will make you forget him."

I nearly laugh at how possessive he's being. "You can't make me forget him, Brom. You're the one who . . ." I stop myself, licking my lips.

One hand goes to the back of my neck, gripping me there, the other grabbing my waist. "The one who what?" he says, his voice hard, his grip harder.

"You're the one who has forgotten," I tell him, feeling like this should be something Crane tells him, but at this point, I'm not sure how that will go. "You know Crane. You've met him before. In New York. You were in New York City, and you were calling yourself Abe, and you were with him. You were *with* him."

His eyes widen briefly, like two black moons, and then his brows meet, and he shakes his head. "No. No. You're mistaken. He's mistaken!"

"Brom," I say as his hand grows tighter at my neck. "I know you don't remember, but that's what happened. You were his lover."

"Shut up," he sneers, letting go of my neck and pushing me to the side. He goes to my bedroom door and closes it, and my heart jumps. He turns to face me. "I don't know what game you're playing."

"Me?" I cry out. "You're the one playing games here! Just before you showed up tonight, the headless horseman came into my room! He came in holding a head. Am I going to find out tomorrow that it was a result of your jealousy?"

His chin jerks in, indignation working his brows. "You think I'm the headless horseman? You really think I'm the murderer?"

"Well, are you?"

He strides toward me, and I back up until the backs of my legs hit the bed.

"Whore," he snarls in my face.

"What?" I exclaim in shock.

He growls and grabs me by the throat, squeezing. "Dirty fucking whore," he says.

Then he kisses me. The tenderness of earlier is gone. This kiss is deep and brutal. He's taking and taking, tongue plunging in deeper, fucking my mouth.

My body betrays me. I should push him away for calling me that word, but some hidden part of me likes it. It wants to feel his wrath. It wants to be insulted. I can feel how wet I am already, the inside of my thighs damp. The thrill of danger is too beautiful.

He pulls at my neck until our mouths break apart and I can barely breathe, and in his eyes, I see a storm of lust that terrifies me.

"You couldn't even wait for me," he rasps. "You had to get someone else's cock to satisfy that greedy hole of yours." He brings me forward again by the neck, the pressure getting tighter, and I gasp, our eyes inches away from each other. "I'll fuck them out of you. You belong to me, only me. And tonight, I'm claiming you as mine."

My stomach twists, and I'm panting under his grip.

"You like that, don't you?" he growls. "Little slut."

And then he pushes me onto the bed. Before I can right myself, he's lifting me by the neck and flipping me around so that my knees are on the bed and I'm pressed with my breasts against the wall.

"Put your hands up on the wall," he warns, his voice gruff and hard. "Don't move."

With shaking arms, I do as he says, my heart pounding in my chest and head. I lay my palms flat on the wall, and I hear him behind me, taking off his clothes. I could stop this. I could at least try. But I don't want to. I want him to give himself to me in all his fury. I might belong to Crane, but I still want Brom to belong to me.

"Fuck," I hear him say through a gasp. "You're going to feel this. You're going to feel me so deep that you'll forget you've been fucked before. You'll never be rid of me."

Behind me, the bed sinks as he kneels on it, and I feel his wild energy at my back. It's hot and immense and seems to grow more powerful by the second, and I feel like I'm about to lose my mind.

I jump, startled, as his hands find the bottom of my nightgown and tug it up around my waist. Then he pulls down my drawers, sliding them over my feet, discarded on the floor somewhere.

"How perfect you are, Daffodil," he rasps, the lust making his voice raw as I feel his eyes on my bare skin. "You're so wet. You're dripping for me."

I gasp as a hand slides up between my thighs and rubs over

where I'm soaked and swollen, and I can't help but let out a deep moan that rattles my lungs.

"All of this is mine," he rumbles. "All of this for me. Did Crane make you gush like this?"

I know better than to answer that question, but then he shoves his fingers inside me and with his other hand makes a fist in my hair, yanking my head back. I cry out, and his mouth is at my ear, his breath hot.

"Answer the fucking question. Did your professor make you this wet? Did he fuck you with his fingers too? Did you squeeze them like a vise?"

"Yes," I manage to say.

"Did you like it?" he says, licking up my earlobe, making me shiver. His fist in my hair tightens painfully, his fingers fucking me.

"Yes," I whisper.

He pauses, pulling back slightly.

"What a little whore you are," he says.

Then he spits on the back of my exposed neck, and I flinch. The spit slowly rolls down my spine and under the back of my nightgown, and I feel his eyes burning on me.

"But you're my whore," he adds as he removes his fingers, and I barely have time to take in a breath before I feel his hips against my ass, the hard heat of his cock at my entrance, and then he's shoving up inside me with one sharp thrust.

"Oh God!" I cry out, my palms flattening.

"I'm not your god." Brom seethes, his lips at my neck, biting, licking as his hips press me into the wall, his cock rammed inside me as far as it will go. I feel like I'm being torn in two, and I think I might faint, the world going fuzzy in a mix of pleasure and pain.

"I'm not your god," he says again. "I'm your devil."

He pulls out slowly, and I can feel his length drag over every nerve inside me before he shoves back inside me, to the hilt. His chest is pressed against my back, sweat dripping down onto my nightgown, the heat of him like an inferno.

He might be the devil, and so this might be hell.

But why does hell feel so good?

Because you're a witch, I remind myself. *A heathen with no god except sex.*

"Taste yourself," Brom says, letting go of my hair and reaching over my face, sliding his fingers into my mouth. "Suck them."

I obey him just as I've obeyed Crane. I suck the taste of me from his fingers as he continues to pump into me from behind. He keeps his fingers in my mouth, hooking them there like I'm a horse he's keeping in place, and I can't help but think of Crane in the stable, how he wanted to ride me like one. No wonder these two men found each other.

"You're thinking about him." Brom says between grunts, biting my earlobe. "What do I have to do to get you to stop? Do I need to make you come? Do I need to spill inside you until you're a sloppy mess? Shall I make you lick it all up, Daffodil?"

"Please," I say around his fingers, because I want that. I want everything this wild beast of a man has to give me.

"You like to beg," he says, spearing me with one hard thrust until my breasts are flat against the wall. "How often did you beg him for release?"

"Always."

He lets out a low roar, removing his hand that's wet from my mouth. He brings his hand behind me, and I hear him spit into it. Then I jolt as it makes its way down to my ass, running over the cleaved space between my cheeks.

"Has he touched you here?" he whispers, licking up my neck, taking grip of my hair again with his other hand. He yanks my strands, sending shards of pain that cascade over my body, making my hips buck.

"N-no," I tell him. I've wanted it but felt too devious to ask, even in front of someone like Crane.

He lets out a low noise of pleasure and then slides his fingers between the crack, finding the spot, his tips wet and pushing into where I'm tightest.

"Do you like that?" he asks, bringing my head back again so my neck is exposed and his mouth is at my ear. There's a tone to his question that reminds me of the old Brom, the desire to please. It's still there. He's still there.

I try to nod, swallow.

"Good," he says, pushing his finger inside my ass while he continues to drive his cock into me.

I suck in my breath, my body overwhelmed by too many sensations. He's inside me in two different places, his cock and finger working in tandem and working me hard, while his grip in my hair gives me pleasure and pain. I'm starting to ache so much between my legs, my blood hot, making my skin feel too tight. The need to climax is becoming painful, and I'm not sure how much more I can take.

"You need to come?" he asks me. "Come on my cock like the little slut you are? Leave me soaked and squeezed?"

"Yes," I tell him, breathless. "Please."

He bites the back of my shoulder in response, the sweat pooling between our bodies. I close my eyes to the pain, to the bliss.

"Only if you tell me that you're mine," he says, pulling his teeth away.

"I'm yours," I say.

"Only mine," he says.

I shake my head. "I can't."

A pause, his cock and finger squeezed inside me.

"Fuck," he growls. "I should come right here and walk away and let you beg for mercy. I should punish you."

My throat feels thick; I can barely swallow. He knows how desperate I am. The room smells of my desire, and I ache so badly I think I might die.

"Please, Brom," I whisper. "I need to come. I need you to come inside me. I need you. . . ."

He lets out a low moan. "You don't know what it feels like to hear that."

Then he lets go of my hair and slides his hand down over my breasts, squeezing them. His hand continues until it slips between my legs.

I come instantly.

I feel everything.

My back bows against him, the back of my head on his shoulder. A strangled cry comes from my mouth, and the world grows bright and effervescent. I feel like the bubbles in a glass of Champagne, bursting in light.

"Brom," I cry out through a ragged gasp.

It's good. It's heavenly. It's everything.

"Oh, fuck," Brom grunts, and I feel him swell inside me, his hips slowing, the push of his cock deeper, harder. "Kat, Kat," he whispers hoarsely, still sliding his fingers over my wetness until I'm too sensitive.

He comes with a shuddering moan, his broad chest trembling at my back as his orgasm works through him. I can feel his hot seed spurting inside me. He finishes with a couple of slow pumps, and I squeeze him hard, emptying him.

Eventually, he pulls out, his essence leaking out of me and running down my legs. He presses his chest against my back, pushing me against the wall, and leaves a trail of kisses down the back of my head, his breathing shallow and labored.

"Kat," he says, and there's a quiet desperation in his voice. "I . . ."

I try to catch my breath, waiting for what he's going to say.

He brings his mouth to my cheek, his facial hair rough against my skin, and kisses me there. Tender, so tender.

"I never stopped loving you," he says in barely a whisper.

I gulp, my heart blooming in my chest.

Dear God.

"Brom . . ."

I don't know what to say.

"I've loved you my whole life," he goes on softly, tenderly, resting his lips on my shoulder.

I turn my head toward him, unable to process his words.

He loves me?

He really loves me?

"Your whole life?" I ask, that Champagne feeling coming back.

"I knew I would marry you one day," he murmurs, his beard tickling my shoulder as he speaks. "It didn't matter what they said. It was never their decision. I fell in love with you from the very start because you're you. You're my daffodil. You're my Kat." His throat bobs against my skin as he swallows.

"I don't know who I am anymore," he goes on, his voice breaking. "But I know how I feel about you. And I'll do everything to do right by you. Whether you love me or want to marry me, it doesn't matter. I'll do everything in my power to stay . . . to . . ."

He trails off, his body going tense.

"What?" I whisper.

Silence.

Stillness.

Terror pricks at my spine.

He lifts off my back, his presence feeling heavy and ominous.

Carefully, I twist around enough to face him.

In the dim moonlight that's coming through the window, I can see his handsome face, the dark beard on his strong jaw, his perfect nose, those black arched brows.

But the eyes that are staring back at me don't belong to Brom.

They are black like tar.

Simmering with evil.

Oh God.

I open my mouth to say something, anything, but he reaches out and grabs my head and slams it into the wall.

I scream, my jaw slamming shut as my head makes contact, and the world starts to go black. But then Brom's grabbing me and flipping me over onto my back, pinning my hands above my head.

"Bitch," he growls at me, and his voice is inhuman, matching the soullessness of his eyes. "I'm going to make you pay for being a whore."

This isn't the same as it was before. This isn't Brom. This creature means it.

He moves above me, his body seeming both larger and harder to see, like shadows are taking over his skin. His hand goes to his cock. "I will give you pain."

"No!" I scream at him. "Brom, don't do this!"

But he reaches forward and grabs me by the throat. Unlike earlier, he now means to crush my windpipe between his fingers, and I can't get a breath in.

I'm going to die here. He's going to kill me.

He squeezes harder, leaning in until I see a malevolent spark in his glassy black eyes.

"If I can't have you to myself, then no one else can." He grinds out. "I will put you in the grave."

I struggle, panicked, trying to rip my hands free from his grip. But I'm helpless, just as I was with the horseman before.

Except . . . I wasn't.

I close my eyes and try to conjure that same energy inside me, bringing it out of me like I would to the flames of a fire.

Brom. Please. It's me, I think. *It's Kat. Let me go.*

I let that energy build until it explodes out of me. I feel fire flow, reaching for him.

I open my eyes to see Brom go still above me. His head tilts, mouth dropping open for a moment.

Then his eyes go wide with clarity.

Shock.

Horror.

It's Brom.

"Run," he whispers to me in anguish. A desperate plea. "Run!"

I don't hesitate.

He lets go of my wrists, and I scramble to my feet while he stays on the bed, his head in his hands. "Get away from me, get away from me!" he cries out, and I run to the door, expecting to fling it open. But the door won't open. It doesn't even have a lock on it, but it won't budge.

"Help me!" I scream, pounding on the door. "Mother! Famke!" They have to be home by now, don't they? Did they bar the door shut? Did they lock me in here?

"Go!" Brom yells. "I can't hold it off much longer!"

I whip around to see him getting to his feet, but it's like he's fighting a war with himself, part of him wanting to come toward me, the other part trying to hold him back.

I meet his eyes, see the pain in them, the battle, and then I run to the window and scramble out of it, dropping to the damp earth.

"Run," I hear him say again from inside my bedroom. "Please."

I run.

30

Brom

I can't breathe.

I'm on my knees, my head exploding with pain, and then I'm on the floor, my knees digging into Kat's thin rug.

There is so much darkness in me, a putrid tar that pulls me under, and I know if I don't fight it, I will submit again. Something evil has found my weak spot. It knows how good I am at letting someone else take over and control me, manipulating my urge to belong, except now there is no pleasure, and there is no reward. There is only death.

What am I doing here?

Where did Kat go?

One moment, I was deep inside her, fucking her hard against the wall until I thought the house would collapse, and the next, I'm . . . I'm . . .

I raise my head, stars behind my eyes.

Why did she run away?

Run.

I needed her, wanted her, craved her like a starving man.

She's the only bright spot in my life.

The star that guided me back home.

I can't remember the last four years, but I do remember wishing I could return to her.

What time is it?

When will the pain in my head go away?

I open my eyes, and they sting.

I burn.

Everything inside me burns.

My heart is on fire.

Kat. My daffodil. My love.

Why did she leave?

Where did she go?

Run. You told her to run.

She's running away from you.

I stagger to my feet.

I'm naked.

My dick sticks out half-hard. I remember coming inside her, wanting to bury my soul there so that she'd never be rid of me. She liked it. Loved it. I told her I loved her. She didn't tell me the same.

Did I do something wrong?

Did I say something wrong?

"Brom," Kat had gasped as I made her come, and it sounded like a prayer.

But I'm a devil, and I don't know if that prayer was for me.

I slip my trousers and shirt on. Pull on my boots.

Did I walk here from the school? Did I ride?

How late is it?

Who am I?

Who am I?

Who am I?

My head spins, and I stumble, having to lean against the wall for a moment. I try to catch my breath, but it feels like I'll never breathe again.

Beneath my skin, the darkness bubbles.

It wants to fuck again. It wants to kill.

No, I think. *No, you will not. You can't have me that easily, not anymore.*

Oh, but, God. To belong to someone. I want to belong to someone.

The door to Kat's door slowly creaks open.

I raise my head to see a woman's silhouette in the doorway, the living room behind her lit by candles.

"Brom," Sarah says softly. "My good soldier. How are you?"

She scares me. She always has.

I want to run, but I don't want to be a coward. I don't want to run again.

I try to speak but can only emit a noise. I sound like a wounded animal.

"It's okay," she says in a soothing voice. She walks into the room and stops in front of me. Puts her hand on my cheek. "You're almost there, Brom. Just a little bit further."

I flinch, try to move my face away, but she laughs. It's a mirthless laugh, one that tells me she comes from that same black space as the thing inside me.

"It can be so hard to be someone else's puppet, I know," she says, tapping at my cheek, harder and harder and harder. "But it must be done. It's our destiny, and it's just over the horizon. When it's all over, then you leave. Leave this place again. You'll be free for the first time in your life, Abraham Van Brunt. Doesn't that sound nice?"

She takes her hand off my cheek and presses the back of it against my lips.

"Give me a kiss. It's only polite."

I press my lips to her hand. It tastes like poison.

She smiles at me. Pure malice. "You should go and retrieve Katrina. She's run off. You know what you have to do, don't you, good soldier? You know what you've been bound to."

I feel myself nodding.

I have to get Kat.

The witch leans in to my ear. "You're a giver, Brom. I know you're so good at giving. But this time, you'll be taking. Taking what is owed to you, taking what you deserve. Go and get my daughter. Help us bring Goruun's wishes to life. Help us usher in a new age."

I will do no such thing! I scream, pushing her away. *I am not your puppet! I am not your soldier! I am a man who is in love with your daughter!*

Except the words don't leave my mouth, and I don't push her away.

Instead, my feet move on their own. I go past her into the living room, the candles lighting the way to the door.

God help me.

God forgive me.

God save me.

There is no God, the voice inside me whispers.

There is only me.

31

Kat

I'm barefoot, running through the cornfield behind my house, the stiff, dried-out stalks scratching at my skin, tearing at my nightgown.

My throat burns from his touch, my lungs are gasping for air, my legs ache, the soles of my feet bleeding from twigs and rocks, but I have to keep going, I have to.

Brom will be coming after me.

Brom who isn't Brom.

Brom who has turned into a monster.

Tears stream down my face, blurring my vision, and somehow, I keep going, pushing the stalks away as I run toward the road. I don't know where I'm going; I just know I have to get away from him.

Behind me, I hear a horse whinny, then hoofbeats.

He's going to hunt me down in the rows of corn, just as he did to Joshua Meeks.

The monster inside him will hunt me down and hold me down, and he'll rape me, and then he'll kill me.

Looking into Brom's eyes and watching them change from the man I know, the man who said he loved me still after all this time, into an evil force is something I'll never forget. I don't know if I can shake it. I don't know if I'll survive it.

But first, I have to survive tonight.

I'm running to Mary's, to ask for help. She'll understand—they're good people. They'll help me. I know if I run across the cornfields, I'll hit the road, and that will take me up to her farm.

I keep going, unable to see above the stalks of corn until the ground slopes up slightly, and I'm pushing through, stumbling onto the road, stones biting into my feet.

I whirl around, looking for a light, someone's lantern. There's nothing but darkness and the light of the half-moon, and I'm so disoriented I don't even know which way to go.

Brom's face flashes in my head. The sorrow in his eyes when he said he needed me.

The tenderness in his voice as he told me he missed me.

The way he shook slightly when he told me he loved me.

It twists and burns in my head, dissolving like paper in a fire, the smoke giving way to the emptiness in his eyes, the crush of his fingers on my throat, the sneer on his lips when he told me he was going to put me in the grave.

I feel deceived, so deceived that I think my heart might shatter if I give it more thought, but I can't, not now. I can only think about survival.

I run up the road until I see Mary's farm. In the distance, I still hear hoofbeats and the sound of rustling corn, and I know he's close.

The monster on my tail.

I scramble up the path to the front door of the farmhouse and start banging on it with my fists.

"Mary!" I scream. "Mary! Open up! Please, it's me, it's Kat!"

I try the door, but it won't open. They've never locked their doors before.

There hasn't been a murderer on the loose, I think. *One that's after you.*

I rattle it violently, but it won't give, so I start banging on the door again, smacking it with the heel of my palm, panic clawing up me like a wild beast.

Answer. Please answer.

"Help me!" I sob, tears of desperation running down my face.

The house remains quiet and dark, and even if they're slow to wake, I don't have time to wait and see.

There's only one person who can help me.

There's only ever been one person who can help me.

I run around the house to their stable, relieved to see Mathias's roan mare in the stall. I coax her out of the stall, and then use a stepping post to swing up onto her back.

"Take me north," I whisper to her frantically. "Take me to Crane."

The mare responds with a flattening of her ears and starts galloping out of the farm, careening out onto the road, dust and soil kicked up behind us.

I glance over my shoulder at the dark road. I don't see Brom behind me, but I swear I still hear him, hear his horse on our trail. As long as I get to the school before he does, I should be safe.

But will you be? the voice inside my head says. *Or are you going into the lion's den?*

All the more reason I need to get to Crane.

The mare picks up on my thoughts and goes as fast as her little pony legs will take her.

Up ahead, beyond the bend of withered sunflowers, the covered bridge comes into view.

It's then that I hear the hoofbeats more clearly.

I twist in my seat, looking over my shoulder, and I see dust rising in the distance like a ghost. I don't see Brom or his nightmare horse, but I know they're there now, coming for me and fast.

I'm not going to make it in time.

It's when I'm turning around as we approach the bridge that everything goes sideways.

There's another sound, another set of thunderous hooves that are getting louder and louder, and suddenly, a horse and rider come shooting out of the bridge. My horse rears up in surprise, and I reach forward to grab her mane, but then I'm falling off, landing in the ditch at the side of the road while she tears off.

The wind is knocked out of me as I roll over, and I hear Crane's voice. "Whoa!" he commands the horse, and Gunpowder comes to a stop beside me. "Kat!"

In seconds, his strong hands are under mine, pulling me to my feet, then embracing me.

My heart sobs with relief, and I collapse into him, just for a moment, just so I can have a taste of safety.

"Brom," I try to say to Crane, unable to get a breath in. "He's coming. He's the horseman."

"I know," Crane says, his voice grim. "I got a visit from him too."

He pulls back and peers at me, his expression anguished. "Did he hurt you?" he asks, brushing my hair off my face. Then his gaze goes from the corner of my forehead where Brom rammed my head into the wall and drops to my neck where he crushed my throat, and his jaw tightens, the cords of his neck becoming visible. "Did he do that to you?" he says in a voice so calm it frightens me.

"It's not him," I manage to say.

Crane's nostrils flare, rage burning in his eyes. "I'm going to kill him."

"No, you know it's not him," I say, grabbing hold of his coat, trying to keep him with me as he gets up. "Don't hurt him."

He ignores me, a vein rigid in his forehead.

"He's here," he says, looking off down the road, eyes narrowing.

I follow his gaze and see Brom and Daredevil galloping right for us, a force of darkness and evil rushing on the wind.

"Crane," I plead. "We need to get out of here."

"No," he says, pushing me back behind him. "You need to get out of here. Take Gunpowder. Cut through the fields and go into town. To the constable. I'll handle Brom."

"I'm not going anywhere without you."

"He's after *you*, Kat," he practically growls.

"And he'll kill you," I tell him. "He's just as possessive as you are. He doesn't want to share."

At that, he tilts his head, and for the first time, I see a real darkness in Crane's gray eyes. It makes my blood run cold. He opens his mouth to say something, and I know he's going to ask if I've just been intimate with Brom. But he presses his lips together and takes in a deep, shaking inhale as he looks over my night-gown.

But there's no time for Crane to recant on his own feelings about sharing me with Brom because he's almost at us now.

We both turn to face the galloping black horse.

Stop, I say inside my head, directing the command at Daredevil. *Stop now, stop!*

But though the horse lets out a whinny, Brom kicks him forward. And he obeys his master.

Meanwhile, Crane reaches into his coat pocket.

He pulls out a gun.

"Crane!" I cry out, shocked to see a weapon in his hand.

"Salt doesn't work much on him," he says as he points the gun at Brom as he approaches.

"But this is Brom, not the horseman now. You'll kill him if you shoot him!"

"God forgive me, then," Crane says solemnly.

Then he pulls the trigger.

I scream as the bullet fires in a blast of smoke. It grazes Daredevil's black ears, hitting Brom in the shoulder.

He yelps and lets go of the reins, flying off the stallion's back and tumbling onto the road in a heap. Daredevil gallops forward and then turns toward us, rearing on his hind legs.

"Down!" I command, throwing my arms out at the horse while Crane runs forward to Brom. "Easy now!"

Daredevil snorts wildly but listens, coming to a standstill, breathing hard with foam on its flanks, the reins hanging by his side.

Now that I know Brom's not going to try to kill us too, I run over to him on the ground.

"Brom!" I gasp, collapsing on my knees beside him, ignoring the rocks in my shins.

Brom is lying on his back, blood seeping through his white shirt at the shoulder, gasping in pain.

"Shh," Crane says, cradling Brom's head in his hand with disarming tenderness.

Brom's eyes pinch shut, and he cries out, back arching in agony.

"I didn't want to do it," Crane says to him. "But you left me no choice. I wasn't about to let you hurt her again."

At that, Brom's eyes go to mine, and I see that it's him, no trace of the horseman at the moment. He holds my gaze, bewildered and scared. Then another wave of pain rocks through him, and he grunts, his teeth gnashing together.

"Is he going to die?" I ask, pressing the hem of my nightgown on his wound, trying to keep pressure on it.

"Not if I have anything to do with it," Crane says. His gaze flicks up to mine. "Switch positions with me."

I do as he asks, holding Brom's head in my hands while Crane rips open his shirt, revealing the round ball of the bullet lodged in his shoulder, blood flowing out of it. Crane then reaches into his inner coat pocket and pulls out a ruler. "Put this in his mouth. Get him to bite down."

He places the ruler in my hand, and I can't help but give him an odd look. I've felt that same ruler striking my backside. I suppose he carries it with him at all times.

"What?" Crane asks, noticing my look.

I just shake my head and look down at Brom in my hands. "Open, please," I tell him, my voice trembling. Brom obeys, and I slip the ruler between his teeth.

"That's a good boy," Crane praises him, reaching into the wound with his finger. "I'm sorry. This is going to hurt like hell."

I look away from the gruesome sight, and Brom yelps, grunting and moaning, biting so hard on the ruler I hear it crack.

"You're doing so well," Crane croons to him. "You're taking it so well. Just a little more. I'm almost done."

I give Crane another look, but his focus is entirely on Brom. I suck in my breath, watching the devotion on Crane's face, the way he's gazing at Brom with such regard. There's tenderness in his words, the way he's handling Brom. It unwinds something inside my chest.

Finally, Crane pops the round bullet out with his finger, and it rolls to the ground. Brom cracks the ruler in half, the edges falling away from his mouth as he screams.

"Stay with me, sweet boy," Crane says, reaching into his other pocket and pulling out a small vial of liquid and crushed leaves. He pours out the contents onto his fingers. "Stay with me. Almost done. You're doing so good, Brom Bones."

Then he presses the poultice into the wound, and Brom screams again, gasping in agony, his body jerking against the ground in violent spasms.

Crane keeps his fingers there, closing his eyes, and starts reciting something that sounds like Latin but isn't. The words seem to float in the air around us, and Brom's eyes roll back in his head.

Crane is *healing* him.

I watch in awe as a warm glow appears on Crane's fingers and flows down to the wound like honey. Brom is still groaning, but his body has stopped writhing.

What a magnificent witch this man is. He may be my teacher, but I'm practically beaming with pride.

Finally, Crane pulls his hands away and sits back on his knees. He's breathing hard and looks drained, all the color gone from his already pale face, but there's a satisfied glint in his eyes, a small smile lifting the corner of his mouth.

"You didn't have to shoot me," Brom manages to say through a cough, and I nearly cry in relief at the sound of his voice.

Crane laughs softly. "I'm afraid I did," he says. "But I knew what to do to fix you."

I shift to the side so that I'm sitting on the road and Brom's head is in my lap. He glances up at me, his eyes exhausted and bloodshot, and even though the feeling of the monster he becomes is fresh in my mind, I can't help but want to keep him close, especially when he's wounded. I run my fingers through his hair.

He frowns and lifts his head, twisting it around, wincing in pain as he does so, trying to get a better look at me. "Who did that to you?" he asks, his voice hoarse as he looks from the marks on my throat to whatever damage he did to my head. Unlike the rage that came from Crane, Brom's expression crumbles in sorrow and shame.

"Did I do that to you?" he whispers.

I look up to meet Crane's eyes, wondering what to say.

Crane clears his throat. "Brom, I don't think I need to tell you this, nor do I think there's an easy way to tell you this, but you're possessed by a Hessian soldier."

Brom puts his head back down in my lap and closes his eyes, a tear escaping. "How could I do that to you?" he ekes out, the pain in his words breaking me.

"You weren't yourself," I try to soothe him.

"The soldier is a retrieval ghost," Crane goes on, getting to his feet. He wipes the dust off his trousers and starts to pace back and forth on the road. "Someone conjured him to bring you back, Brom. They used the spirit of the Hessian soldier, the headless horseman, to find you and possess you and physically bring you from wherever you were to Sleepy Hollow." He pauses, his hands behind his back as he glances at us. "We don't know who it was. Either your parents, perhaps Kat's mother, or the coven. But I'm starting to doubt the reasoning was pure."

I mull that over. Could my mother have conjured a spirit to bring Brom back? That does sound like something she'd do. But why not tell me?

Unless there's a reason why she didn't want me to know.

"And there's another complication," Crane adds, in teacher mode now. "The spirit should have left you. The Hessian decided to stay. He's both tied to you in his spirit form and in your physical form. He's just beneath the surface, Brom. I can see him there. It's like looking at a dark lake, ripples on the surface of something underneath."

"You need to get him out of me," Brom says in horror. "Please."

"That's exactly what we plan to do," Crane says, stopping in front of us and gazing down at Brom. "There are a few rituals that the three of us can try that might just free you from him."

"Well, we need to do them now," I cry out, flooded with impatience.

"They aren't that easy," Crane says slowly. "They might take some . . . convincing to get everyone on board."

"I'll do anything," I implore him.

He gives me a quick smile. "I have no doubt you will, sweet witch. But it's Brom who may need persuading."

Brom frowns. "I will do anything. I promise."

Crane gives him a rueful smile. "You say that now," he says. "But until you remember what I need you to remember, I'm not sure how easy this will be."

"What do you need me to remember?"

Crane exhales, tilts his head as he holds Brom's gaze. "I'm going to need you to remember me. And what I was to you. I need you to remember *us*, Abe."

32

Crane

Brom stares at me deeply, and I know he's trying to remember who I am, where we've met before. But every time it looks like he's on the cusp of something, he freezes. He's afraid. I know that fear. I know how debilitating it is. I'd seen that same fear in New York City before he'd submitted to me.

He swallows hard and looks up at Kat, who is still cradling his head in her lap. A moment passes between them, something instinctual, a product of two people who have known each other a long time, but instead of feeling jealous of their relationship, I just feel love for them instead.

God Almighty, am I in love with both of them? My pretty boy and my sweet witch?

The realization is terrifying.

But I don't run from it. I embrace the fear.

Because it's magic.

"Don't be afraid," I tell Brom. "Don't block it."

"I tried to tell you," Kat says softly, stroking the side of his face. "I tried to tell you that you knew each other in New York."

Brom's dark brows come together, and he swallows hard. "I don't remember."

"I think you don't want to remember," I tell him. "But I can help."

His jaw goes tight. That fear again.

"Maybe we should get off the road," Kat suggests. "Do you think you can stand, Brom?"

He nods, and I go behind him, putting my hands under his arms and pulling him to his feet. But I don't let go of him. I keep my arms around him, holding him from behind. He's a tall, muscular man, but I have half a foot on him, and I rest my chin on his good shoulder, my hands flat against his chest and pushing him against me. "Don't fight it," I urge him.

But he does try to fight it. He tries to move from my grasp, and he doesn't have the stupor of opium slowing him down and giving me the upper hand like had happened before.

I do my best to hold on. "Stay still, pretty boy. You don't want to reopen that wound."

He freezes at that. Just as the Hessian did in the library.

I can reach him.

I know I can.

"Brom," Kat says, coming in closer, her body against his, sandwiching him between us. "Don't fight it."

He lets out a snort of indignation.

I lean in and run the tip of my nose down the rim of his ear, and he rips his head away in disgust, but I'm nothing if not persistent.

"Do you remember how we first met?" I whisper to him, my breath on his neck. I pull back enough to notice the goose bumps on his flesh, and I smile in triumph.

"It was just like this," I continue. "We were in the opium joint in Chinatown. Manhattan. You were in the darkened corner of the room, smoking the pipe, and you were watching, always watching, a man who was being hunted. And, of course, I was watching you. I suppose I was the one doing the hunting."

"I don't remember," Brom protests, his voice raspy, his body stiff.

"I'll help you remember if you let me," I say, bringing my mouth to the soft spot behind his ear. I don't press my lips there, just let them hover like hummingbirds, and I know how much he loved it when I would do just that.

He swallows audibly, and I run a hand down over his chest, slowly, taking my time. "I went to you. I wanted you. You said your name was Abe. You were so very high and scared. So very scared. And I knew I would do anything to save you, protect you, help you." I bring my mouth to the crook of his neck and press my lips there, and he shudders. "I invited you to my place. I told you I had a private bath. I made it very clear what I intended to do with you."

My hands go down to his hips now, gripping him there and pulling him back against my erection, and he gasps. My gaze goes to Kat now, who is staring at me with her big blue eyes. She's in awe. She's in lust. She's mesmerized. I want to kiss her deeply, then have her kiss Brom, but I know that's not the plan for tonight. I have to be the one to reach him. It's the memories of me that are locked away in him.

It's his own desires that he's too afraid to face.

"You tried to fight me," I whisper to him. "You told me to fuck off. So I left, and I didn't think you'd come—I didn't think you would be into me. But you did. You came after me like a stray dog on the street, and I took you in. I bathed you. I gave you a home for weeks."

I fell in love with you, I think, but I don't dare say it. I'm already putting so much on the line, my soul laid bare with each sentence I speak.

"You're lying," he says gruffly, but I can hear the hesitation in his voice.

"Am I?" I ask, sliding my hands from his hips, down over the V of his sharp bones and over his cock. It's hard as a rock, stiff against his pants. I chuckle, feeling another stab of triumph. "Then that means your body is lying too."

His breath hitches, and the tiniest of moans escapes.

"Your body isn't lying, Brom," I tell him. "It remembers me when you don't."

I give his cock a squeeze.

"Oh God," he whispers, trembling in my arms now.

"That is what you'd call me," I say, kissing his neck, sucking in his sweet skin. He tastes like heaven. He melts back against me, and I grip him tighter. "Give in to me, pretty boy."

I reach up with my other hand and press my fingers at his jaw, pushing his head to the side, where I lean and capture his mouth with mine. My lips envelop his, my tongue parting his mouth for me.

He moans, the feeling vibrating through me, making me unbearably stiff, and I take advantage. With my lips never leaving his, I move around his body, Kat stepping out of the way, until

I'm right in front of him, my hands in his hair, on his face. I kiss him deeply, a year of wanting him, missing him, mourning him, all coming out in my tongue as it lashes the inside of his mouth, licking him.

He lets out another groan and kisses me back, his hands at my coat, making fists in the collar.

And it's in this moment that I decide to take my shot.

I gather the energy up inside of me, and I push it into Brom, feeling it travel through my mouth and into his head. I feel myself move through him, in the planes, and then I'm in the void, the black space between the veils, and while the door from earlier is there, still shut, still a war raging behind it, there's another one that's open a crack, light shining from the other side.

I go toward it, pushing open the door, and suddenly, I'm flooded with a million images.

I see Brom as a child, crying, his parents cold and indifferent to him.

I see him older, with Kat, sitting on a hay bale in a barn and giggling over something.

I see him as a teenager, mind drifting off in school as he notices the way the boy beside him swallows, how he likes the look of his neck, and how ashamed that makes him feel.

I see him older now, and he's in a church on his knees, and he's giving a pastor head. He feels excited, he feels dangerous. He's never felt so alive.

Then he's older again, and it's the same pastor from before, and he has Brom bent over at the altar, fucking him from behind. He's enjoying it, he's loving it, and then suddenly, the doors to the church swing open, and another man appears. He threatens

Brom. Tells him that he can't show his face around Sleepy Hollow again.

The next image that hits is of him outside Kat's window. Him desiring her but torn by a conflict inside. He knows he has to leave, but he doesn't want to leave without her. He can't bear the idea of life without her.

Then they're in the barn, and he's fucking her, and she's bleeding beneath him, and she's nervous and in pain, but she's submitting, and he loves it. He loves her.

He loves her and knows he has to leave.

Suddenly, Brom pulls back, puts his hands on my chest, and shoves me.

I come out of his head and back into my body, and I'm stumbling backward into Kat, her hands going to my arms to steady me.

I stare at Brom, eyes wide, panting hard, and he stares back at me, his expression like a wild animal. He blinks, chest heaving. His beard is wet from my kiss, his erection visible against his pants.

"You didn't run away because of Kat," I manage to say to Brom, and Kat's grip on my arms tightens. "You ran away because you had an affair with the pastor and you were caught."

"What?" Kat exclaims with a soft gasp.

Brom doesn't say anything, and he doesn't need to because I know all the memories I just unlocked are now raining down on him. His eyes blink as if they're processing each one, a lifetime flashing before his eyes.

"You were caught by someone," I go on. "The police chief, the mayor, someone like that, and they told you to leave, or you'd bring shame down on your family. They said you could never show your face here again. So you left. You had no choice."

"Pastor Ross?" Kat asks Brom. "He left the year you disappeared."

Brom presses his lips together, swallowing hard. "I . . . I didn't know what to do." He looks at Kat, pain radiating off him. "I thought I would ruin my family. I thought maybe, maybe I would come back one day, later, after the magistrate was gone. I was waiting to come back to you, Daffy. Biding my time until I could see you again."

She goes to him. "Why didn't you tell me? Why couldn't you tell me that night?"

"I tried to," he explains. "I tried, but I was scared. I was scared that you would think differently of me, that you wouldn't love me anymore, that you would think I didn't still want you, because I did, Kat. I did, and I do. I wanted to prove to you that I wanted you more than anything, and I . . . I . . ."

He puts his head in his hands, fingers in his hair. Oh, my poor sweet boy. So pretty and so broken. I want nothing more than to put him back together.

"I remember everything," he cries out, the sound muffled in his palms. He lifts up his head, his hands falling away, and his eyes meet mine in a thunderbolt of recognition.

His eyes are so dark, so wild, so beautiful.

And they finally see me again.

"Crane," he says softly, in the sweet, obedient voice that I heard so many times.

I grin at him. "Abe."

He grabs Kat's hand, giving it a squeeze before letting it go, and then he comes toward me and puts his arms around me, embracing me, his head on my chest.

I put my hand on the back of his head, my fingers in his thick strands, and hold him there. My gaze goes to Kat again, and she's crying, tears rolling down her cheeks, but she's smiling too. She looks so impossibly beautiful. I feel strangely full, like my heart never knew I could love two people at once, desire them both equally.

"Come here," I say to her.

She gives me a grateful yet shy smile and walks over. Both Brom and I part to let her in between us. Her skin is cold, perfumed with the night air, and it's only now that I'm noticing she's just in her nightgown and it's freezing outside. Some gentleman I am.

We envelop her between us, now the center of our attention.

"My sweet witch," I say to her, pressing a deep kiss on the top of her blond head. "We've been neglecting you. You're the most important part here. You're the glue that holds us together."

Brom's embracing her from behind and meets my eyes.

She's part of us, I say to him, using the voice. *And we're a part of her. We're going to do everything we can to protect her at all costs.*

He nods, his dark eyes gleaming before he kisses the back of her neck.

She sniffles, and I can feel the emotions radiating off her, overwhelming her. It's been a hell of a night, and it's not over yet. Despite Brom remembering everything, we still haven't fixed the fact that he's possessed. And we haven't even begun to figure out who called the headless horseman on him.

As if hearing my thoughts, Brom pulls back slightly. "What do we do now?" he asks, trepidation in his voice.

I step back and take off my coat, placing it on Kat's shoulders.

"We get Kat somewhere safe," I tell him. "And by that, I mean somewhere away from you."

His face falls. "All right. But I don't think she should go back home."

"Why not?" Kat asks.

He frowns at her, gives his head a shake. "I'm not sure. There are bits and pieces missing from the night, I guess where the horseman comes in and out. But I know your mother has something to do with it."

Kat stares at him for a moment, her brows up. "My mother called the horseman to get you. . . ."

"I think so," Brom says. "But it's not only that. I think she . . ."

"What?" she asks frantically. "She what?"

He clears his throat. "I think she wants me to bed you on behalf of something called Goruun."

"Goruun?" she repeats, and the word is so familiar to me, the memory of where I heard it just around the corner in my brain.

"I don't know what that is, but I stand by what I said the other day. I don't trust your mother, and you shouldn't either."

"I agree," I say. "We need to go back to the school. Kat, you can stay with me." I'm not trusting Brom around her alone, not until the horseman is gone.

She wrinkles her nose in thought. "Why would my mother want you to bed me?" she asks Brom.

He lifts his shoulders in a shrug and then winces. The wound looks much better, but it will hurt him for a few days. "I don't know."

"She wants you to be married. She wants you to have children," I point out. "We've never figured out why that is. But I feel once we find out who Goruun is, we will."

Kat worries her lip between her teeth. "Crane, how did you make that poultice tonight?"

"Just plucked some herbs from the garden," I tell her, leaving out the part where I yanked half the plants out of the ground in a frantic attempt to find something that would heal a wound. I didn't plan on shooting Brom, but I knew it could come to that.

"I might need to look up some tincture books in the library tomorrow," she says, looking concerned.

I wince. The library. Then I notice the same expression on Brom. He remembers what the horseman did there, leaving behind a chopped-up desk and someone's severed head.

"All right," I say. "We have two horses, three people. Kat, you're riding with me." I give Brom an apologetic look. "I'm sorry, but I can't trust you around her until the horseman has been exorcised."

He nods solemnly. "I understand."

"Good boy," I praise him, and watch as his face reddens.

We round up the horses, neither of which have gone very far and are standing obediently at the entrance of the covered bridge. In the darkness it looks like a mouth and I have to brush away the unsettling feeling that it wants to swallow us whole. As much as I don't want Kat to return to her home, I don't feel all that comfortable going to the school either. But it's still my residence for the time being, still a vaguely public place to keep Kat safe in, and has all the information and magic I need at our fingertips.

I place my hands around Kat's waist and lift her up onto

Gunpowder's back, then swing up behind her. Brom mounts Daredevil smoothly, seeming like a natural rider. When you're as tall as I am, horse riding doesn't come as naturally, and I feel a touch of envy at how at ease he is with his body.

A memory floods my mind. My palms sliding over the rippling muscles of his back, holding him in place. The fit of my hips against his ass, how tight he had taken me. Kat adjusts herself on the horse and I can tell she feels my cock harden against her, perhaps thinking it's all for her. And it is, because she's never not getting under my skin, and yet neither is Brom, and now I'm tangled in this web between them.

Suddenly I remember some of the last things that the teacher, Vivienne Henry, said:

We were all just flies in a web.

It was enough to drive her to death, enough for her to haunt me.

And I can't help but think this web was made for three.

And that Brom getting his memories back, realizing he's possessed by the headless horseman, is only just the beginning. That at some point, if we're not ready, the giant spider will come crawling out and finish us off one by one.

But we've got magic.

We've got rituals.

And we've got one another, for now.

Either way, I will be ready.

I will protect the both of them.

Even if I have to die to do so.

To be continued . . .

Acknowledgments

s I sit in my hotel room in Venice, I struggle to think of who to thank because there are so many people who helped with this. And also, I'm currently in Valtu's house (if you've read *Blood Orange* then you know) and it's a little nuts to be in a place where I feel one book so deeply while finishing another. It's magic, I tell you.

But I digress.

This book wasn't originally supposed to be a duet, but there was so much to unravel with not only the plot but also Brom, Kat, and Crane's relationship that it needed another book. I know. I'm a mess.

And thus I need to thank Laura Helseth for tolerating the fact that I turned our trip to Italy into a writing and editing vacation; Kathleen Tucker and Spicy P for distracting me when I needed it with meaty goods and Moscow mules on Florentine rooftop bars; the bartenders at said bars, Alessio and Carlo, for catering to our every whim and allowing me to write there all day and night; Sandy Dee for her editing on the fly; E. F. Watson for her proofing and encouraging comments; and every reader and author who has expressed love and excitement for this book. Please stick around for *Legend*—it will be worth it. Of course, Michelle Moras for all her hard work and help! Can't do it without you!

Last but not least, Scott for being my number one cheerleader and letting me put on scary movies when I needed some vibes. We're going harder for *Legend*, so I'm warning you now!

KEEP READING FOR A SNEAK PEEK OF

LEGEND

The deliciously dark conclusion to Hollow.

And remember, readers, watch your head . . .

Brom

One year ago

The creature stalks toward me.

Darkness coming out from darkness.

He's inside my head, inside my nightmare.

He's stepping out of my mind and into the hall.

The hall outside the room.

Malevolence pours under the doorway, flowing toward me like oil.

The creature forms here.

Tall, broad-shouldered, cloaked in night.

Missing a head.

He's holding something in his hand behind his back.

Something that drips onto the floor.

I see a hint of long blond hair hanging.

The color of cornsilk.

I know what it is.

I open my mouth to scream.

The headless man brings the object forward.

It's Kat's severed head, her blue eyes frozen in terror.

"Let me inside," the man says in a deeply inhuman voice that sinks into the marrow of my bones. "Let me inside and I'll put her head back on."

I sit straight up and scream. It echoes in the room and for a moment I don't remember where I am.

Then someone sits up next to me. A man.

He puts his arm around me, his skin cool against my burning body, and gives me a squeeze.

"It's a nightmare, Abe," he says in his low, rich voice. "You're all right."

I try to breathe, my lungs aching, and he runs his palm up and down my arm, soothing me.

"It's all right," he says again, resting his chin on my shoulder. "There's nothing to fear."

But there's so much to fear.

All I feel is fear.

I can't stop running from it, and it can't stop coming for me.

I turn my head to glance at him from the corner of my eye.

Crane. His name is Ichabod Crane.

The mystery man at the opium den.

He had been watching me, and I had been watching him.

Wondering what he wanted with me. His mannerisms were so refined despite the smoke going into his lungs. He seemed worldly.

And it seemed he wanted me.

I hated that I wanted him.

Then tonight he got up and approached me and offered me a bath and a place to stay. Anywhere was better than the slums I had been sleeping in, even though the idea of being with him both terrified and thrilled me.

So I went with him here.

I took a much-needed bath.

And then I sucked him off and reveled in his praise.

Feeling like I was good.

Worthy.

I was wanted.

I was safe.

It had been such a long time since I felt any of those things.

I've been running for *so* long.

"What haunts you, Abe?" he asks, brushing the hair off my head. I close my eyes to his touch but then stop myself, pulling away and putting distance between us.

"Everything," I tell him, though I know this man won't leave it at that.

"That much I know," he muses.

I lean forward, and he puts his hand on my back, fingers gently brushing my spine. I hate how good it feels, hate how badly I want this man to use me again like he did earlier. That feeling of being wanted and desired so much, that urge I have inside to please.

I want to please him and keep pleasing him.

His praise makes me shine.

"This isn't the first time for you," he says. "Or is it?"

I shake my head no. "I don't do this often," I say, my voice raw.

There was only Pastor Ross. That man had started off as a father figure for me, someone who I turned to because my own father acted like I didn't exist. I trusted Pastor Ross. And I wanted him too. We only succumbed to our desires twice, knowing how dangerous and forbidden it was.

The first time we were together was the first time I had a man's cock in my mouth.

The second time he took my virginity.

And shortly after that, I took Kat's.

My heart squeezes at the thought of her. I left Sleepy Hollow for her. I was so afraid that the magistrate would make an example of me to the entire town, not only telling my parents that I was a product of the devil but that Kat would find out too. I truly didn't care what my parents thought of me; they already treated me like I was something they had to tolerate, as if I was thrown in their laps like a stray kitten they felt obliged to take care of.

But Kat . . . Kat was my everything. She still is. I didn't know if she'd accept me if she learned I'd been with another man. It didn't matter that Pastor Ross was twenty years older than me and I was only eighteen, I would be made the example of along with him. There was no sparing me for being younger. I would be shamed.

Leaving her was the hardest thing I had ever done. I wanted to tell her the truth. I wanted to ask her to come with me. I should have. Sometimes I think about her alone in that house with her mother and it fills me with dread. The minute I know that the magistrate is dead, I'll head back to Sleepy Hollow and I'll rescue her, take her with me to some place far across the country where her mother can't get her.

But for now, I'm here. I'm here and I'm hiding.

Because there's something out there that wants to bring me back.

Something dark and dangerous and evil. It wants to possess me, drag me back to Sleepy Hollow and hold me there so that I can never leave. It's hunting me down in my dreams; I see the shadows on the street; I see the eyes in every painting I pass following me, tracking my every move.

But how do I explain that to this man?

"You carry too much guilt with you," Crane says, running his fingers up and over my shoulder blades. Soft as a breeze but carried with precision.

I swallow thickly, feeling anger flare inside me. "What do you know about guilt?" I grumble.

"More than one man should, perhaps," he says gently. "I grew up with six sisters in a tiny house in Kansas, my father was the town pastor."

So maybe he does know.

"I grew up hearing that sodomy was a sin," he muses, his fingers tracing shapes on my skin. "The problem is, I'm so good at sinning."

I can hear him smile.

"It took time to dissect what it all meant. My attraction to men being on the same level as my attraction to women. It can be terrifying living in a world that is primed to not accept who you truly are. Can't it?"

I find myself nodding. I want to tell him what happened with the pastor, but I want to leave Sleepy Hollow behind me for now. I want to be Abe, not Brom. I want to hide. Disappear. Become someone else entirely.

His hand trails up to my neck and wraps around it, holding me gently.

"I want you to sin with me," he whispers, his voice raw with desire.

My cock immediately hardens.

Yes. Yes, I will sin with you, sir.

His grip on my neck tightens, and he pulls me back down into the bed.

AUTHOR PHOTO COPYRIGHT © SCOTT MACKENZIE

Karina Halle is a screenwriter, a former music and travel journalist, and the *New York Times* bestselling author of *Realm of Thieves*, *River of Shadows*, and *The Royals Next Door* as well as eighty other romances across all subgenres, ranging from spicy rom-coms to gothic horror and dark fantasy. Needless to say, whatever you're into, she's probably written an HEA for it. When she's not traveling, she, her husband, and their pup, Perry, split their time between a possibly haunted 120-year-old house in Victoria, British Columbia, and their not-haunted condo in Los Angeles.

Visit Karina Halle Online

AuthorKarinaHalle.com

 AuthorKarinaHalle

 AuthorHalle

 AuthorHalle

 AuthorKarinaHalle.Bsky.Social